God's Man

God's Man

A Novel on the Life of John Calvin

Duncan Norton-Taylor

BAKER BOOK HOUSE
GRAND RAPIDS, MICHIGAN

In memory of
our grandson,
Scott Duncan May
October, 1960–April, 1968

CONTENTS

PART FOUR
Maigret the Magnificent

PART FIVE
John Calvin, Accuser

PART SIX
John Calvin, Citizen of Geneva

PART ONE

The Lord said to Jeremiah,
"Before I formed you in the belly
I knew you.
Before you came out of the womb
I ordained you a prophet."

"But Lord God, I am such a child,
I cannot speak,"
said Jeremiah.

"Don't say you are a child,"
the Lord commanded,
"Go wherever I send you
and speak what I say."

I, baptized Jean,
the second son
of Gérard Cauvin,
was born in Noyon in 1509.

1

I HOLD THE OLD MAN'S HAND. He shouldn't have come; it is a hundred miles through the Juras from Neuchâtel to Geneva. "I would be with you, John," he says.

My voice is not very good, and Guillaume puts his head closer to mine, saying he does not quite hear me. "Best and truest brother," I repeat.

Guillaume Farel smiles through his wild beard. The fragrance of the locust tree comes in the window. Do I imagine that the blossoms always smell sweeter at night? No, God conspires with the flowers and the springtime night and has the nightingale sing until daybreak, all to make us grateful to him. And he brings to me a beloved friend. My lamp is the only light showing along the rue des Chanoines, perhaps in the whole once wicked city where in a time gone by I risked being murdered in the street at this hour. Guillaume tells me happily about his scandalous marriage—a girl who could be his granddaughter, the foolish old man—and about turmoil in France, and about Rome's latest attacks on our church.

We fall into silence, we two lions of the Reformation who shouted at each other in our arguments and roared from our pulpits—Farel stumbling on to his eightieth year and I unable

to finish the April communion so that I had to be carried
home, racked by coughing. And as if God would remind me,
the cough seizes hold of me now, and I clutch a towel to my
mouth to receive the blood. The commotion brings my sister
running from the next room. She spoons out some potion
Aubert has mixed up and puts it on my tongue. The potion
burns but quiets my cough. "Our union was of some use to
God, Guillaume. I somewhere found courage to do what he
wanted. You must pray that those who follow me, Beza,
Knox, and all the others, be given courage."

"You talk as if you were about to leave us, John. You are a
young man yet." But his eyes cannot hide what he knows, the
knowledge that brought him all the way from Neuchâtel.

He must go and get some sleep. Yes, yes, I will be all
right—he sees how Marie comes rushing in at the smallest
noise I make. We will go on talking in the morning.

The bulk of him almost fills the doorway. My sister asks if
she shouldn't blow out the lamp. No, I am not ready to go to
sleep. I would have the lamp hold off the darkness for a little
while yet, and I lie there, my eyes drifting about, coming to
rest on a picture I had found in Chatelet's shop and hung over
my bed, the only picture in my room—*Vue de la Ville et du lac
de Geneve*. It is done in a way that is to my taste. Trees, rocks,
and the crags of the Juras are rendered meticulously, and yet
quite fancifully, inviting one's imagination and giving the
feeling of something fabled. The lake loses itself among nature's snow-covered battlements; the walls and towers of the
town rise mysteriously in the center of the illusion, a center
towards which a man rides on horseback. It is at this point my
heart always stops, for I see myself riding one evening
through the same pass, tired of fleeing, wanting only a night's
rest before going on to Strasbourg where I would settle down
in peace. That was twenty-eight years ago, at which juncture
of my life God seized hold of me and never let me escape. O
Lord, what would you have now of your servant John Calvin?

My writing pad and pen are on the table beside me, and I
take them up in order to make some notes for the sermon,

God willing, I will preach next Sunday. It will have to do with
the fragility of our existence—a topic somewhat difficult to
write about. *His house constantly threatened by fire, his fields
laid waste by floods and droughts: can a man be anything but
miserable? Only half alive, whirled about: where can he find
comfort? He has only to commit himself to God. His comfort
will come in knowing nothing can happen that God has not
ordained. The ultimate misery—rejecting Providence. The highest
blessedness—knowing that God is always at work. I am in trouble, David cried. I am like a broken vessel, but I trust in thee, O
Lord; my times are in your hands.* My thoughts wander. My
own times have not been very long. On an impulse I write,
Jean Cauvin, son of Gérard, 1509–. There I am almost, if not
yet finally, contained in the lamp's circumference—fifty-five
years later, is it?—a creature who walks with a cane in the rue
des Chanoines, a goat's beard hanging from his long face, a
fellow without much flesh on his bones and a little stooped.
Numerous afflictions have done this to him; for years he has
had gout, chronic headaches, and indigestion. And now he
has this devil in his lungs. He is a trial to his friends, being
easily wounded and weeping when he thinks he has been
deserted, and possessed of a temper that sets him to howling
like a dog when he is crossed, but he is a coward who trem-
bles before crowds, and he quakes at physical violence. Now
this bearded creature, dressed in a cap and nightgown (he is
usually attired with some elegance, although on the somber
side, according to his sister), turns over and over in a disheveled bed, an atom in a divine mystery. What is going to happen to him next? Fearful of the world though he is, he re-
members that his soul is in God's hand. He has no fear then.
God knows what is next, because with him all things have
already happened—the mother putting her breast to her
infant's mouth, and the contract made and broken, and the
thrust of an assassin's knife, and the command to charge at
Pavia. . . . Every mortal act happens as he has destined it to
happen. While we are born hardly aware of ourselves, exist
half-blind with fading memories that are like the petals of

plucked flowers, and know nothing of our future, everything from beginning to end is marvelously in his sight.

I N A CATHEDRAL NEAR THE PLACE au Blès in Noyon, a detritus of objects; a woman resembling paintings of the Virgin Mary lifts me up so that I can kiss a piece of the skull of St. Anne. I must be three because the woman, my mother, is with child, and my brother, Antoine, is born about then. She shows me other relics, so numerous in Noyon it is called a holy city. "See, Jean, it is the hair of John the Baptist; the stain on the cloth is our Savior's blood." She has me make the sign of the cross, which I do over and over again, delighting in the gesture, and has me march in church processions. I can hear my older brother Charles laughing at me because I am dressed in a white robe made out of one of my mother's petticoats. A portrait of me dressed in it, commissioned by Grandfather Le Franc, showing me with wings and distended eyeballs, would later on be destroyed when my father, in one of his rages, accidentally pushed a chair through it.

Lives circle around the cathedral. It looms at every turn of memory, as it towers through Picardy's history. Charlemagne and Hugh Capet were crowned there, fire gutted it, the Spaniards sacked it. But burned, ravaged, desecrated, time after time rebuilt, it stands on its hill in Noyon, magnificent and grotesque.

My friends, Joachim and Ives and I stand swallowed up in the cathedral's nave. High above us under a carved wooden canopy is a priest waving his arms like a windmill. On top of the canopy is a chocolate-colored angel, and under the vaulted rafters the Savior hangs suspended on a cross. Joachim whispers to me, "What if you're really Jesus back on earth?" We run around back of the canons' quarters. "Jesus was a good student like you. He didn't realize who he really was until God told him. Hey, Jean, maybe we should wash your feet."

How can I be Jesus doing some of the things I do?

"Like what?"

Like peeing in the bushes behind the canons' quarters and losing my temper and having a brother like Charles. Instead I will be a hawk flying over the walls of Noyon and the fields that are owned by Joachim and Ives's father, the lord of Montmor, and fly along the River Verse to Pont de l'Évêque where my father was born. My father is a clerk of the cathedral chapter. He speaks respectfully of the lord of Montmor, Louis de Hangest, who is also bishop of Noyon and one of the seven peers of France by hereditary rights. But he denounces the chapter's fifty-seven canons in a loud voice and rushes about colliding with the furniture that came from the inn that Grandfather Le Franc owned before he retired and became a town official. My mother tries to calm him, but his patience is exhausted. "Now they want to see my accounts—the bloodsuckers, the wineswizzlers!" he steams. And mother runs weeping from the room.

One of the ghosts that circle around the cathedral vanishes. I am conducted into my parents' bedroom to view my mother lying as motionless as the Virgin's statue, and it is my father who is weeping.

He was an emotional man as most Picards are, a practical man, too, who was thinking about how it was going to be for him now, having to rear three boys. He married again soon afterwards, but he had to pay a penalty for this expediency—everything has its price—because his new wife bore him a daughter they named Marie, whose wailing every night drowned out his own complaints.

I SEE A SCHOOLYARD FILLED with little heads in grey caps. Rain comes sweeping up the River Verse and the heads dis-

appear into the worn stone building of the School of Capettes
where teachers for a hundred years have been stuffing Latin
conjugations inside the caps. It is true, I am a good student,
as Joachim says. I study subjects beyond my years, even delv-
ing into astrology, unaware of the sacrilege of thinking that
the stars, not God, govern men's lives. My birth date indi-
cates I will have beauty of mind. But the moon with the eye
of the bull—my conceit collapses—shows that I will have a
tendency to viciousness and sacrilege! I don't tell Joachim
and Ives about this; I just pray for help in conquering my
baser nature. But Satan is on the watch for me. He has
Joachim and Ives, with God's permission, wrestle me to the
ground and take away the medal I won for declamation. I get
up and draw the knife my Grandfather Cauvin gave me one
day. He had flipped it into a barrel head at his cooperage in
Pont de l'Évêque.

"It is not allowed," I had told him.

"Who doesn't allow it, your father?"

"The master at school."

"Who is he to say? Every boy should have a knife to cut
string or clean fish; you never know what," and he put it in a
sheath he had made for it and showed me how to hide it
under my belt.

I try to stab one of them, Joachim or Ives; I don't know
which, but the other one catches me from behind and throws
me down. They wrest the knife away, and I lie there sobbing.

"Here's your knife back, Jean."

"I don't want to see it again," I tell them.

"But your grandfather gave it to you."

They can throw it in the Verse. They tell me they are my
best friends and would even die for me. I would die for them.

God has many ways of trying us, sometimes using Satan.
There are many instances of this in the Bible, which it would
be blasphemous to inquire into—what he does or why he
does it, or the instruments he uses to do his work. I see my
father's face, his long nose and shrewd eyes. The nose,

Grandfather Le Franc says, I have inherited. "Your eyes and
mouth are your mother's, a saintlike woman." He thinks my
father is a schemer, coming from a family of rivermen, without much education, wooing and marrying his daughter (he, a
town councilman), and talking the bishop into giving him the
titles of notary apostolic, episcopal secretary, and fiscal pro-
curator of the cathedral chapter when he is really only a clerk.
"He doesn't have much faith in God and none at all in the
saints. He only loves himself." This is not true; he loves his
three sons and is ambitious for us, and I can hear the triumph
in his voice one afternoon when he announces to me, "I have
arranged for you to have the chaplaincy of the cathedral's
altar of Gésine." It means I am going to have a scholarship
out of the grain taxes from two country hamlets. Such things
are among the corrupt practices of the church, but I do not
think then of its being wicked. "I didn't take it up with the
chapter; I went directly to the bishop and showed him your
marks at Capettes. You should have heard him, 'Halloo, halloo; look at this.' The chaplaincy will see you through the
University of Paris. His sons are also going there this fall."
We embrace with tears in our eyes. He composes himself.
"You will live at your Uncle Richard's and get your degree in
the arts, then in divinity. You will become a cardinal, Jean.
Why not, with your talents? One day you will kick the asses
off the canons in Noyon, those frauds who cast canards on a
notary apostolic."

   It was a glorious autumn. We rode our mules south from
Noyon under the willow trees along the Oise, Joachim and
Ives and I. Coming along behind us was the Montmors' tutor,
who could not dampen our spirits if he tried. We came after
several days to the windmills surrounding Paris and rode in
by the north gate along the cobbled streets through the
crowds imprisoned between the buildings, across the bridge
over the Seine, and up the hill to the university. The sons of

Montmor signed the registry with names that evoked the history of Picardy, and the son of the cathedral clerk signed *Johannes Calvinus,* as befitting a scholar of Latin.

Marie comes in saying that I must go to sleep, she is going to put out the lamp. "The oil is almost gone," and she kisses me on the forehead. The darkness is not utter because there is some light from the moon.

2

UNCLE RICHARD'S LOCKSMITH SHOP was on the east bank of the Seine. My quarters were an attic room that seemed to open to the very sky. Indeed, when the rain came from a certain direction it entered my room near the foot of my bed. If Uncle Richard could only find the treachery in the tiles he would fix it, he said; meanwhile the chamber pot was at hand. *Tink, tink* would go the leak, changing after a while to a sound like small fish rising in the evening in the River Verse, until it was time for me to run with the overflowing pot to the window.

I didn't mind it, I didn't mind anything—even having to be up long before the sun to attend mass around the corner at St-Germain-l'Auxerrois. I didn't mind meeting the wind sweeping the bridge over the Seine, or passing the docks where the farmers were unloading barges and the grey morning creaked with the noise of barrows and smelled sweetly of vegetables, making me homesick. And I didn't mind slipping on the slithery cobblestones, climbing the hill to arrive out of breath at the rundown buildings of the Collège de la Marche, where classes began at five o'clock when the roosters were crowing. If I dozed off in the afternoon, to be brought to by the crack of a cane on my desk, it was because I had been up

so long, not because I was drowsy from lunch. The refectory
was foul, the bad eggs and sour wine made my stomach revolt. If I minded anything at all it was the walk back home to
Uncle Richard's. Classes ended at eight, and the dingy streets
around the college that were all but empty in the morning
became filled with jostling and yelling students and uncouth
young women who came from I don't know where. It was
worth your life to get past them. There were students who
were ready to revolt at a moment's notice at the food in the
refectory or at being caned or what not, who would run wild
around the streets and throw stones at the masters trying to
round them up. They did not take school very seriously.
Others I would come upon sleeping in the hallways of the
Collège de la Marche, and when I ventured to ask them why
they did so they said it was because they didn't have money
for lodgings. They stole food from the shops and begged
from people promenading along the river, which was inex-
cusable, of course, but at least they were trying to get edu-
cated.

As for me, I couldn't get enough of my studies. I let nothing I read or heard at lectures escape me. Master Mathurin
Cordier, the university's greatest Latinist, told me I was insa-
tiable. "Was that wrong?" I asked.

"No, no," he said. "It is God working in you. The pursuit
of truth—it is marvelous, wonderful, true humanism, my
pet."

I connected *humanism* with *humanity* as I had observed it
in the streets in the degrading behavior of my fellow students. "That is not what is meant, Johannes," Master Cordier
said. "Humanism is the turning of our thoughts inward to
man's true being. It is reverencing grammar, as the Greeks
did, because it is the structure on which men build their
thoughts, and it is poetry that exalts, because it expresses
men's souls." I grew to worship Master Cordier, and I wondered if I should not become a humanist.

"Why surely, you may even become another Jacques Le
Fèvre; he also came from Picardy." He told me then about

Master Le Fèvre, who, he said, was France's greatest humanist teacher, loved above all others at the university when he had lectured there. Among other things he had translated the Latin Bible into French so that it could be read by everyone. He was now in his eighties and had recently fled to Strasbourg. Fled? I could not understand. Why, and at such an age?

I could see that it was difficult for Master Cordier to give me an answer.

"If everyone can read the Bible," he said, "the Sorbonne thinks there is danger of interpretations contradictory to those of the church." I could certainly see that. "In fact, in some of his writings Le Fèvre asserted the right to interpret the Bible privately. They had his translation burned." He stared at me in a rather frightening way. "They suspected him of Lutheran leanings, and if it had not been for his great prestige as a scholar, they would have put him to the stake."

I asked if it were true that Le Fèvre had Lutheran leanings.

"The opposite is true. The leaning was the other way. Some of what Luther is teaching he got from Le Fèvre. Oh, forget these matters, Johannes, and just stick to your Latin grammar."

But I could not forget them. How could Master Cordier admire a man from whom Martin Luther had taken his ideas? I had read pamphlets written by Luther secretly passed around the classrooms and had thrown them aside they were so terrible, referring to the pope as the Antichrist. I did not discuss Le Fèvre any more with Master Cordier, but I did with a fellow student, Pierre Robert, who was a distant cousin of mine and came from near Noyon. For some reason, perhaps because he was small and fat, he was known as Olivétan. Did he know of Jacques Le Fèvre?

"Of course, everyone knows of the great Le Fèvre." Olivétan was a year older than I and inclined to be superior. "What do you want to know about him?"

"Is he a heretic?"

"Do you know what heresy is?"

I knew it was the worst crime you could be guilty of. It was certainly heresy to call a pope the Antichrist.

"But that was Luther talking, not Le Fèvre," Olivétan reminded me. "Le Fèvre is not a heretic unless you want to say that anything is heresy if the Sorbonne says it is."

It is what I would say. No body of men was better able to make the judgment, I told him.

"You have some things to learn, little cousin," he said to me, who was a head taller than he. "The Sorbonne smells heresy in Le Fèvre, claiming as he does that salvation is a free gift of God and cannot be acquired through good works or bought with payments to the church. Le Fèvre wants to correct doctrine. He wants to reform the church, not destroy it. That's Luther who thinks it should be knocked down and put up all over again. I see by your look, you don't think the church needs reforming. Try reading something else besides Latin classics." I was reading lots of other things, but I let him go on. "Have you read anything by this Dutchman Erasmus? No? Read his *Praise of Folly*. I'll lend you my copy."

I read it, thinking at first how ridiculous it was to praise folly until I saw that Erasmus was being satirical, and although I was forced to laugh uproariously at some of his quips, I saw that he was attacking everything right and left, including priests, bishops, even popes, in fact, the whole Roman Catholic church, which I had been taught by my mother to reverence. I wondered at Olivétan possessing such a book and felt some apprehension at my own exposure to these ideas; it was almost as if the fire used to punish heretics was licking at my feet. In any case, I began to sense that the pursuit of truth as between such thinkers as Le Fèvre, Master Cordier, and Erasmus on the one hand, and the faculty of the Sorbonne on the other, was not easy, even with God working in me.

I had to say goodbye to Master Cordier after only one year. The Montmors' tutor decided that the scholastic standing of the Collège de la Marche was not very high and transferred us all to the Collège de Montaigu. Its head was Pierre Tempête, nicknamed "Horrida Tempestas," and one of its lecturers was the famous theologian Noël Béda. I missed Master Cordier, and I saw less and less of Joachim and Ives, who were thinking of taking up military careers. But I acquired a new friend.

One winter's evening Olivétan took me to meet a professor of philosophy at the Collège Ste-Barbe where Olivétan was enrolled. He was Nicholas Cop, the youngest son of the king's physician. I disliked him at first. He broke into laughter when the two of us appeared at the door of his room. "The vertical and the oval!" he exclaimed. "I know Olivétan gets his shape from stuffing himself. But do you ever eat anything at all, Johannes Calvinus. How old are you, my son?"

I told him I was fifteen.

"Olivétan says you are an outstanding student." He brought out a bottle of wine, and after a while said: "So what shall we discuss? Let us take up intercession, using Latin, of course." He had a little pointed beard. He went on in a grand way: "I pose the question—do we not dishonor Christ when we ask the saints to intercede for us?"

I gave him the answer I thought the question deserved, that anyone who says we do does not know what he is talking about.

He laughed. "Did John of the Gospels not know what he was talking about? He said, if anyone sins he has an advocate with the Father, Jesus Christ. He didn't say anything about the saints."

That was because there weren't any saints when he wrote it, I reminded him. They came later, suffering and dying like Christ. "That is why they can intercede for us. Besides, the church says they can."

"Dogma doesn't necessarily make a good argument. Let me ask you, where does it say in Holy Scripture that the church can tell us anything about anything?"

I pointed out to him that the church has the right to interpret the Bible, never mind what Jacques Le Fèvre said.

"Christ made Peter his rock and the popes are his successors." My Latin stumbled from time to time, but I rushed on. "If everyone interprets the Bible the way he wants you have the end of the church. That's why Martin Luther is so bad."

"So you have read Luther."

"I've read enough to know that he is wicked."

"Is it wicked to tear out what is rotten in the church? Isn't it more wicked to leave it there to spread corruption?"

"Nicholas," Olivétan interjected at this point, "walls have ears. Is it a good time to discuss such matters?"

I knew what he meant. In the year I had spent at the university I had learned something of what went on outside my classrooms. I had heard about the king's sister, Marguerite, who was much admired by some students, and about soirées she held where rather advanced ideas about church doctrine were discussed. So long as Princess Marguerite was in Paris, people like Nicholas Cop felt fairly safe going around raising questions in private about the church. But now she had gone to Spain to be with the king, who had met defeat in a battle at Pavia with the forces of the emperor, and was actually being held a prisoner in the tower of Alcazar in Madrid. His Queen Claude had died only a few days after he left for the wars, and it was now said that he himself was dying of his wounds. This seemed to me to be a very serious turn of events, although the country was being run all right by the king's mother. But what affected some people most was the fact that with Marguerite away they were unprotected; they had no one to intercede for them with the Sorbonne faculty and the Parlement. Nicholas looked at me suspiciously, and I put on an expression meant to reassure him that I was not going to tattle on him, but he did change the subject.

"Tell us, Johannes Calvinus, what have you been doing in Montaigu?"

"Philosophy and dialectics. Dialectics under Béda."

"You could not have a more conscientious teacher."

"John is good at dialectics," Olivétan put in.

"I can imagine. Let's hear what they have you doing in dialectics, John."

"All sorts of silly things," I said, pleased at being called by my first name. "Is a hog led to market by a rope or by the man who holds the rope? Things like that."

"What are your conclusions?"

"It never matters. Béda just wants you to be able to take any position in an argument."

"He's a savage man with a cane. Has he caned you yet?"

"Not yet."

"You must be very well behaved. Not many escape him."

I did not tell Nicholas—I would call him "Nicholas"—about my horoscope and how I always tried to show that I was not inclined in any way to wickedness and sacrilege.

"What are you reading?"

"Everything—even Aristotle, even though he was a pagan. Isn't it mysterious, his describing God as First Cause Uncaused?"

"And the scholastics?"

"Of course. Rimini and Anselm and Duns Scotus and Ockham." I reeled them off, feeling a little giddy from the wine. "John Major lectures on them. I'm not sure about Ockham saying you can't prove Christianity by reason. Do you think that is true?"

"He says you have to build faith on faith."

"Yes, I know. But I am sometimes confused. I do know that what they are all looking for is God's purpose, isn't that it?"

"Philosophers have been looking for God's purpose forever," Nicholas said loftily. "Have you read Thomas à Kempis? He says that all philosophy is vanity, you know, that God has only one purpose for us—that we should love him."

"I have read him," I claimed, although I felt a little uncertain about it.

"And where do you come down?"

"I guess I have not come down," I admitted, and I sat trying to think it out, while Nicholas opened another bottle of wine. Master Cordier had told me that the way I pursued knowledge was good. But was it good just to have things in your head without "coming down"? Nicholas had quoted something to me that I remembered having read without any feeling because I only half believed it—that God had just one purpose for men. I began to think now that there was something awesome about that, if you could understand it. I felt guilty, thinking that my life had been wasted because I did not realize what God's purpose was for me.

But back home in bed I thought less of this than of the clever things I had said, which must have made an impression on Nicholas Cop. I felt giddy from too much wine, and I don't know whether I ever did get to sleep, because the next thing I knew Uncle Richard was banging on my door to get me up to go to mass before my classes.

I stumbled into the dark church. My throat was dry and everything was blurred and quivery, the candles, the rood screen, the painted faces of the saints, the figure of our Savior on the cross, and the priests changing bread and wine into his body and consuming it. Outside fog filled the street. I took a few steps and felt someone beside me. For some reason I dared not look around. Something touched me; it could not be the wind. It was as though someone put a hand on my arm. I saw nothing, only felt a presence. I knew it was Jesus Christ whom Cop said I might have dishonored, who just a moment before I had seen transubstantiated. Mother Mary, Mary, should I fall on my knees? A woman coming out of church turned to stare at me. I broke into a run. The bridge floated over the Seine and vanished into the fog. Over all was a silence until a gull lighted, shrieking, in front of me and still shrieking flapped off. I reached the other side where I heard the sounds of the men at the docks unloading vegetables, and made my way on up the hill and into my classroom just before Béda arrived to begin droning through his morning lecture. I closed my eyes—they were so heavy—oh, just for a moment, I thought. But when I opened them, Béda had stopped talking and the class was still. I looked up and thought I saw Jesus standing in front of me, his arms upraised as on the cross. Instead it was Béda, holding up his cane, which he brought down on my shoulder.

"This time I've caught you, Johannes Calvinus," he said. "Stand up, let down your trousers while I make up for the times I didn't catch you, and teach you some Latin on the side."

I had watched others take a caning without uttering a sound. At every stroke, as he counted, "Unus, duo, tres—" I cried out. But on my lips, unheard above those cowardly cries, was the name of Jesus. "Decem, undecim, duocem," at which he let me pull my trousers over my skinny legs. "The twelve apostles witnesseth," he said. Unable to sit down, I half lay across my desk, my head on my arms. Béda thought, no doubt, that I was weeping, but I was talking to our Lord: "You took me by the arm, and you made me suffer as you suffered in order that I should know you want me to serve you. I will. I will, if you will show me how, O Lord. Amen."

3

U NCLE RICHARD, WITH NO WIFE TO PROD HIM, never did get around to fixing the roof, and I continued to run to the window with the pot overflowing for the rest of the four years that I was at the university. The pot was filling up on an afternoon in the winter of 1528 while I read a letter I had just received from my father.

He expressed his satisfaction that I had acquired my master's degree in the arts, and then he wrote: "Forget being a priest. I have made this decision after much thought. You are to go to Orléans and study law. Orléans is the best in France for Law. Paris is nothing. You will have the income from the curacy of Pont l'Évêque, no less. The rascally canons at the cathedral have done this much—they gave us this additional benefice. I have written your Uncle Richard to make you a loan to get you started." I sat there a long, long time thinking, while the rain dripped through the roof.

My father's decision affected me in a way I could not immediately explain. The vow I had made to Jesus Christ was never out of my mind. In order to serve him I must first, of course, become a priest, and I had certainly put all the effort I could into preparing myself for the Sorbonne. But I had been haunted by an increasing feeling of guilt. My faith, during my last years at college, had become—I could not deny it although I tried—faint. Not my faith in God and Christ but in the church. I had begun to doubt whether I was worthy of holy orders. Conversations with Nicholas and Olivétan confused me. Olivétan had become even more critical and outspoken than Nicholas, especially about our Christian king. It was true, François's conduct upset me. He had not died in Alcazar after all. He had obtained his release by cynically promising to marry the emperor's homely sister and by sending his two little sons as hostages to be confined in the vile dungeon in Madrid. "Weeping as he sent them off," Olivétan said savagely. "Oh, anything to get back to his whoring and building palaces and squandering the country's money on Italian art. What kind of an example does he set his people? An example of selfindulgence and wickedness. And the whole hierarchy, archbishop, cardinal, and bishops, are condoning him. You know what I think, John? God created Paris so that one day he could make his own example by destroying it like Sodom and Gommorah."

Olivétan had finally made *his* decision. He would not study any longer for orders. He himself had departed a year ago for the University of Orléans. Well, we would be together again, and this pleased me. How I was to serve our Lord would be made known to me; or I supposed it would. Clutching the letter that changed the whole direction of my life, as God again used my father as his instrument, I went down the steep steps to Uncle Richard's workshop.

Brass and iron key blanks hung on the walls; a layer of metal dust, vises, files, pliers, emery wheels, and trays of old locks and tagged keys covered the workbench. Uncle Richard could open all the doors of Paris. I showed him the letter. How did he explain my father's change of mind about my future?

"Your brother Charles has gone into the church, and one is enough," he said. "There's no future in it except for rogues. Law is the road to the king's doorstep. He himself never got a law degree. That's Gérard's thinking. Besides, he has been excommunicated."

My poor father! "What for?" I cried.

My uncle had the Cauvins' long, intense face, but it reflected no concern. "He probably found a new way to roil the canons. He has always fought with them. You know the bishop, his great protector, died." I had learned about it when the Montmor boys told me they were going to Noyon to their father's funeral. "De Hangest's nephew Jean succeeded him and has his own troubles with the canons. Your father always made it a point to stand in with the Montmors. It looks as if he made a miscalculation."

But I pointed out that the canons had given me another benefice.

"Partly on the basis of your scholastic record, I'm sure. And your Grandfather Le Franc, no doubt, had a lot to do with it. He's a respectable man. You had better be grateful for the respectable side of your family."

"But I am to study law."

"The canons evidently don't know you're not going to study for the church."

I was conscience stricken. I would go to Noyon immediately, I told him, and resign the chaplaincies.

"No, no, John, that's foolish," he insisted. "You'd have to give up your studies. Waste no time in foolish scruples. Waste no time at all. You do what you're told. I'll get you a mule and you can be off in the morning."

I emptied the chamber pot for the last time, delayed only long enough to say goodbye to Nicholas, and rode my mule fearfully along the highway to Orléans.

The road turned out to be not as dangerous as it had been when the king's troops had marched south to Italy, followed, I had been told, by thieves and prostitutes. The greatest hazard now was from the carts moving up from the south, no doubt carrying Italian statuary and paintings for François's palaces. Nicholas had told me that Princess Marguerite had returned to Paris after the king's release, and since she divided her time between the capital and Nérac she might well have occupied one of the closed carriages, as wide as the carts, that kept crowding me into the ditches. But I arrived without any mishaps.

I TEND (MY FRIENDS SAY that it is more than just a tendency) to hurl myself into whatever I have to do. I was in Orléans at my father's orders, with no enthusiasm for the study of law and certainly no idea of what I was going to do in the future. But once I had found a room, with Olivétan's help, and got adjusted, I plunged into Orléans's disciplines. Time rushed past. I immersed myself in secular and canonical literature—Justinian's *Corpus Juris Civilis* weighted with ten centuries of revisions, Gratian's *Decretum* and 400 years of papal supplements and amendments, the laws of cities and feudal societies, and laws covering all the relationships people got into with one another, contract, debt, theft, and trespass. Men had to make their own laws, I thought, to replace the intractable bargain of forgiveness in the Lord's Prayer. I acquired skill in forensics and was chosen the representative of one of the ten "nations" of students, (mine being the Picardy "nation" of course) in legal matters affecting our relations with the administration. I was flattered to have my instructors ask me to take their classes on afternoons when they wanted to be doing something else. The Italian jurist Alciati had joined the faculty of the University at Bourges and was blowing some of the dust off the law books into the faces of conservative French jurists. He attracted me, and I joined some of my friends in transferring for a while to Bourges; but in the end I found Alciati to be too self-opinionated and coarse for my taste.

But all this absorbed only part of my waking hours, hours

that I could stretch by forfeiting to sleep the most meager intervals of the night. I studied Hebrew and Greek on the side. I read classical literature, particularly Seneca, whose Stoic morality interested me; and the early fathers, Origen and Anasthasias; especially I read and speculated over Augustine. And when I remembered, I ate.

Olivétan was always at me for this. "How you survived the refectory at Montaigu I will never know, and now you give yourself dyspepsia eating anything that comes to hand, if you eat at all. It is absolute craziness."

We all know what is best for the other fellow. Olivétan was a little crazy himself, as I saw it, and in a way more dangerous to him than not eating. I had found him, that day I arrived in Orléans, to be consorting with a group of very liberal people. He had drawn me into their circle, in fact. He was now frankly avowing Luther, and he urged me to read translations of the German made by Louis de Berquin, a nobleman and a scholar who, like us, was from Picardy. I read them, but I still recoiled from this ex-monk; whether he came clothed in German or French, he was an enemy of the church. Olivétan burned with the Reformist flame, but one day he came to me trembling with fear, or rage—both, I quickly found out. "Do you know what has happened? The Parlement condemned him—Berquin, who was on the royal council and a favorite of Marguerite! They did it quickly when both François and Marguerite were out of Paris, but they did it; they burned Berquin at the stake!"

"This should be a warning to you," I said. "You are attracting attention even here in Orléans." And I pleaded: "You must be more temperate."

"How can you go on not seeing the monstrous thing the church has become?" he demanded. "For all your reading you are still in your childhood." He mimicked my admonitory tone: "'You must be more temperate.' You mean, accept the corruption of Jesus Christ's church. Maybe you can, but I can't." When he saw how angry I was at this, he seized my hand, "Forgive me, John. We shall always love each other.

Well, I have no desire to be put to the stake. I'm leaving; I'm going to Strasbourg."

He was so dogmatic and hotheaded, storming off rather than staying where he would have to restrain himself. What would he do in Strasbourg? Maybe he would write; he thought of doing a translation of the Vulgate—to have it burned, no doubt. But he left, and it was only after he had gone that I was angry at myself for being so impatient with him and for not telling him of my true affection for him.

I easily finished my law courses, even while immersed in Seneca and Augustine, and received high honors at my graduation. And thereupon I asked myself what *I* would do. I did not want to make law my career. Would I go into a monastery? I had read enough of a book by an ex-friar named François Rabelais, which had been circulating around the University, to be discouraged at the absence of any intellectuality in the monasteries, and the lechery and so on that were apparently habitual with a large number of monks. Here I was, quite erudite—and aimless. "O Christ," I prayed, "have you forgotten me?"

I MPORTANT NEWS WOULD FLY ACROSS FRANCE; foam-flecked horses would be changed for fresh ones and gates would be flung open. "The king's messenger . . . word from Amboise. . . ." And so on. But a message that the notary of the cathedral chapter in Noyon was ill moved slowly in the packet of a merchant who had happened to be going to Orléans. My mule took almost as long retracing the route of the message, which had been sent me by my father's second wife. By the time I reached the house off the place au Blès my father was dead.

Excommunicated, readmitted, excommunicated again, and dying that way, he was about to be buried under the town gallows. He had repeatedly refused to show the canons of the cathedral his accounts. They admitted that since his death they had found no irregularities, still they could not countenance his obstinacy and defiance. "But he was guilty only of a venial sin," I argued, and I reminded them that I held a *licencié ès lois.* "Obstinacy before God is one thing, but obstinacy before men should not incur anathema." If it did, I thought, then the canons, who continued stubbornly to revile my father should themselves all be condemned.

It was the new bishop, Joachim's and Ives's cousin, Jean, who interceded, lifting the anathema so that my father could be laid to rest beside the cathedral. A thought that was almost heretical came to me while my brothers, our stepmother and our halfsister, Marie, and I stood around the grave—that my father was right in having me abandon a career in the church. He had loved us all, as we had loved him and forgiven him his faults, but all that the canons of the church could find in their hearts was hate.

I returned with the others to the house where I was born. Marie, who had wept at the grave, now cheered us up with her tinkling laughter. She was a plump little girl with dancing round eyes. I might have stayed with them for a while; I had no definite plans. But I felt impelled after a few days to get out of Noyon. I felt uneasy in the midst of memories of my boyhood, repelled by the town's selfconscious holiness, its shrines and relics and intoning bells. Paris beckoned me. I must say goodbye; I had friends awaiting me. Marie gave me a kiss, then I was off again, riding along the River Oise as I had eight years ago.

A CTUALLY I WAS GOING TO PARIS because I didn't know where else to go, and as for friends, I didn't know whether or not I had any. But I would look up Nicholas Cop, and I did with some hesitancy which I need not have felt. He was overjoyed to see me, and made it immediately clear that he would take charge of my life. "You must write; you must get published. I can see it—a new Erasmus." He was teasing me. "No. I heard about you from Orléans and your tremendous ability," he insisted. I had gained some reputation as a student, I said. Mathurin Cordier once predicted I might become a humanist scholar. He clapped me on the back. "You've returned to Paris at just the right time. The changeling François is smiling on our little liberal band. It's the face he now wears for the benefit of the German Protestant princes—anything to discomfit the Emperor Charles. He gives a cold eye to the Sorbonne faculty because they've been objecting to his sister's activities. He even persuaded Jacques Le Fèvre to come back from Strasbourg and tutor his sons, two half-starved waifs who couldn't speak French, only Spanish, when they were finally let out of the dungeon in Madrid. You will see how things are. This very night I will take you to one of the Princess Marguerite's soirées."

It was a June evening with the moon shining on the Seine as we crossed the river to the princess's apartment in the Louvre. I could only feel morose, who should have been quivering with anticipation. The apartment was crowded with writers and doctors of philosophy, among whom Marguerite floated, clasping everyone's hand. I could see that she was adored by all, and indeed when she took my hand I felt a surge of emotion even while I knew that she was over forty. She had her brother's prominent nose, but her face was made beautiful by suffering, the causes of which were well known. The scar on her cheek was the result of her trying to disfigure herself once in order to discourage a nobleman who wanted to make her his mistress, when she was already married, although unhappily, to the duke of Alençon. the duke died, and her brother had her marry Henry, the king of Navarre, a king in name only, for Henry had never dared set foot in Navarre, lying between France and Spain, because the Emperor Charles claimed it. Henry had set up his court safely in

France, in Nérac, where he pursued frivolous ladies who were closer to his own age, Marguerite being ten years older than he. She consoled herself for being married to a scoundrel by turning her brilliant mind to literature.

I was a little troubled by the knowledge that she was collecting risque stories for a *Heptameron* which she intended to write in the faddish style of Boccacio. But I knew she also wrote beautiful poetry and essays dealing with heaven and platonic love.

Her friends had gathered around her that night with special eagerness. She had written a play and she had promised to tell us about it and read us a small portion. I was given to understand by Nicholas that it was inspired by the Lenten lectures of Gerard Roussel, the humanist preacher, and that it was going to be very daring. She herself had invited Roussel to deliver the lectures in the Louvre, to the indignation of, among others, Noël Béda, who had protested to the king. But François, instead of reprimanding his sister, had banished Béda to a distance twenty leagues from Paris until he could cool off. I learned this as we were arranging ourselves on small gold chairs in a half-circle.

"I have called my play *The Mirror of a Sinful Soul,*" she announced. "It is an imaginary conversation I have with my niece Charlotte, who died at eight. Being now in heaven, Charlotte has learned the answers to a great many things vexing us poor mortals here on earth." I appreciated the ingenuity of the device that put Charlotte out of reach of any rebuttal. "I will take both parts," the princess explained.

"Are there saints who will intercede for me in Paradise, dear Charlotte?" Marguerite read in her natural voice, raised a little as in plays.

"Who says so has put your heart in error, dear Aunt Marguerite"—spoken in a childlike treble. "He speaks in error who says someone else than Christ can be your advocate in Paradise."

"Can one win justification through good works?"

"No!" Marguerite's treble rang out. "For the good you do

will often hide sin, Aunt Marguerite. You may observe the
fasting days and the feasts, say orisons, and do such good
works as giving alms and buying indulgences. But you are still
the old Adam, Aunt Marguerite."

She was interrupted by handclapping, and she gave several
appreciative nods before continuing: "Must I not prepare my
soul to receive the grace of God, Charlotte?" She paused
dramatically while we awaited Charlotte's answer. "If we
were able to acquire this grace by ourselves then it would be
not a gift but a reward. And then you could say that you
yourself had accomplished it."

She put down her manuscript, whereupon there was a final
burst of handclapping. I was pressed into a corner as
everyone rushed up to her, each trying to be heard above
the other: "Superb"—"So beautifully rendered"—"Beyond
words"—and so on. I heard someone ask, "Will you have it
published?"

"Yes, of course," she said, which brought forth more cries
of delight.

I myself felt that the niece had spoken a little out of character for a child of eight, despite her being in heaven. I also
wondered how the theologians of the Sorbonne would react.
I thought it a rather frivolous treatment of an important
subject—a feeling I carried with me to my lodging, after
gaining the princess's ear long enough to congratulate her
and have her earnestly invite me to come again.

I had taken a room at the Collège Fortet, which was across
the street from my old college of Montaigu. There I started
my writing. I had decided what I wanted to do. It was to be a
commentary on Lucius Anneas Seneca's essay on clemency.

"But Erasmus has done it," Nicholas objected.

"Erasmus admitted in his book there might be more to
say."

"I doubt he meant that someone else beside himself could
say it."

I told him confidently that I had found a great deal more to
say. I was not to have him tell me *what* to write.

It was not a long book, but I was determined to make it worthy of me, and I cited seventy-eight Greek and Latin writers and included thirty-three quotations from Cicero's orations and more from Terrence's plays; there were additional citations from seven of the early church fathers. I found the Bible to be relevant only once or twice and then just in passing.

I approved of much of *de Clementia.*

I agreed that kings are divinely appointed but that their rule is legitimate only so long as it is not despotic. I shared Seneca's and the Stoics' idea of the glory of man, and also Seneca's deep distrust of men in a crowd. But Stoicism failed on one score: it held pity to be a vice. I deemed pity to be the supreme virtue. It is the very nature of men to suffer pain and their very nature to yearn for consolation. As a matter of fact, can a man be called good if he does not show pity and try to console those who suffer?

I paid to have the book printed and carried copies around to the bookstalls, saving out a few to present to several of the more important persons who attended Marguerite's salon. One I gave to the great scholar Guillaume Budé, confessing to him that I had used his *Annotations on the Pandects of Justinian* as a model for my small work. It was a measure of his greatness that he said he was flattered. I also gave a copy to Nicholas's father, Guillaume Cop, who was the king's first physician and a member of the faculty of medicine, and of course I presented one to Marguerite. They all commended me for my scholarship, lucid reasoning, and fine Latin style.

But as I peered into the bookstalls in the weeks that followed, I saw my book sitting there. "I am sure it will simply be devoured some day," Marguerite tried to reassure me. But while her play, only recently published, was being sold so fast the dealers could not keep it on their shelves, my book remained unwanted.

I was very depressed. Who wouldn't be? I continued to frequent Marguerite's soirées, although I never derived anything like the thrill I expected. I did make a few new friends

there, one of whom was Louis du Tillet, who showed great
interest in what I was doing. (What was I doing? I asked
myself). He came from the prominent family of that name in
Angoulême; his father had been a vice president of the royal
chamber of accounts and his brother, Abel, was the chief
registrar of the Parlement; Louis was a canon at the Angoulême Cathedral. He was a hesitant person who stood on
the edge of our gatherings quoting Erasmus. "Have you read
what Folly says of begetting children?" he ventured to ask me
one evening. I probably had, but it was a long time now since
Olivétan had thrust *The Praise of Folly* at me, and Louis's
reference was to one of the inconsequential things which I
hadn't bothered to remember. Louis, with his small voice,
must have my attention.

"Erasmus says that even Jove is obliged to lay aside his
thunder and Titanic look and act the fool when he does what
he likes most to do, which is beget children. Likewise your
Stoic, John, lays aside his gravity and stops thinking for a time
while he toys and talks nonsense. Oh, that Erasmus! He has
Folly ask whether honorable members of our body, such as
ears, hands, our face, generate gods and men. Of course not.
It is that foolish, silly part of us that cannot be named without
laughter that propagates the human race."

Louis gave me a nudge. He was a rather silly young man,
and yet I became quite fond of him, perhaps because he
seemed to be fond of me. I think he found in Erasmus's
cynical comments on procreation a reinforcement for his vow
of celibacy, to which he remained true, I am sure, even in the
midst of the worldliness of Marguerite's court. I should have
taken him as an example, so should Michel Cop, Nicholas's
younger brother, and another of my new friends. Having
taken courses in virtually everything at the university, he had
no idea what he wanted to do next, so that we found ourselves drawn to each other by our frustrations. Sometimes
after one of Marguerite's soirées when we were both bored
with the sometimes silly talk, we would make our way up to
the dark streets around the university to a lodging house

Michel had found out about that was inhabited by lewd
women. We would go up the steps supporting each other
with bravado, and come out shortly thereafter in silence, I for
one vowing I would not go back. To my shame I did. But my
debauchery only made me feel worse. My career was at a
dead end. What could I write about next when so worthy an
effort as my analysis of Seneca went unnoticed? How I en-
vied Marguerite, whose writing was not as good as mine, but
who had a name and who had produced something that
caused discussion.

I was in a particularly black mood one evening when
Nicholas came to my room and sat down, gazing at me fixedly
as if he were taking my measure. He had come from a meeting of all the faculties of the university, who had discussed
The Mirror of a Sinful Soul. "See," I moaned, "how her book
gets attention."

"Yes it's been getting attention. The Sorbonne faculty demanded that Parlement condemn her and have her burned at
the stake as a heretic."

I could not believe it—the king's own sister!

Béda and the Sorbonne have had enough of the king's
tolerance, Nicholas told me, and have screwed themselves up
to challenge him. "You can understand their feelings at this
latest thing. Marguerite's Charlotte not only scorns their discipline but would undermine the church's economy. Take
away the collecting of alms, the endowments, sales of
indulgences—besides it's Lutheranism. Were they wrought
up! I defended her. I was virtually the only one who had the
courage to step forward. Fortunately she had a better defender than I. François had got word of what was up and informed the faculties that his sister loved him so much that she
would believe only what he believes. Did the Sorbonne mean
to condemn their king as a heretic? As you might imagine,
that was conclusive.

I felt Nicholas's eyes on me. He seemed strangely exalted.
He had recently had an honor bestowed on him. With the
support of the faculties of medicine and art he had been

elected to the one-year term of rector of the university and was shortly to deliver the customary rectorial address at the Church of the Mathurins. He announced to me now that he intended to seize this opportunity to defend Marguerite's ideas. "The time has come to draw the line between the sophistry and tyranny of the Sorbonne and the true spirituality of Christianity." He rushed on: "We must save the church from her prelates, John. All my thinking has prepared me for this. We must turn the church back to the Holy Gospel, which promises salvation not through obedience to pope and tradition but through forgiveness and love. John, you must help me compose my sermon." So this was what he had come for.

In the midst of my discouragement he affected me by his intensity. His words confronted me with my ambiguities— studying a pagan philosopher, professing a Christian faith. But such a pallid faith. No certainties, a life so far wasted. Helping him might help me to find out where I stood, where I came down. Was it Christ's summons at last—to help Nicholas turn the church back to the Holy Gospel? I had some reservations about the appropriateness of criticizing the Sorbonne in a rectorial sermon, but I agreed to go along with it.

We worked for several days on it. We turned to Erasmus's proposing in his *Enchiridion* that we return to the Scriptures, and, at Nicholas's insistence, we used some of the less contentious points in some of Luther's sermons without mentioning his name. When it was finished I was not too sure as to its entire validity, and I realized that it was less a dialectic than an exhortation, and I was privately glad that it was Nicholas who was going to deliver it, not I.

The evening arrived. I sat in a back pew of the Church of the Mathurins as Nicholas in his rector's robe arranged himself at the lectern. I knew he was shaking inside, but his voice came out strongly: Erasmus's Christian philosophy shows that all men are sons of God; the Holy Spirit is promised to everyone. "Blessed are the poor in spirit," he quoted from

the service of the day, then read our passages chiding the
faculty of theology in the Sorbonne for rejecting the doctrine
of Christ, who was man's *only* intercessor with the Father.
And "Twice blessed are they who endure persecution for
righteousness' sake," Nicholas added. It had been his idea to
put that in, and to close with a prayer that God would open
all their minds to Holy Scripture.

I found myself in the midst of robed masters making their
way out of the church in what seemed to be more of a cavalry
charge than an academic procession. They were all talking at
once. "Heresy" ran through their ranks like a hiss. Waving
their arms, they all hurried off in the same direction. I saw
Nicholas emerge looking pleased with himself and accompanied by a handful of masters. I tried to catch his eye, but he
did not notice me, and he and his friends went off in another
direction. I followed them until they turned into a tavern.

I went back to my room. I wished that I had not let myself
become involved in this business. I could not believe that it
was heresy to say that salvation came from God's love, but I
knew now, as I had felt from the beginning, that the speech
was imprudent. Several hours went by. I thought Nicholas
would come to my room; he would want to hear from me
more than anyone how he had sounded. When he did not
appear I walked down the hill to the tavern. It was closed, so
I retraced my steps to his room in the Collège Ste-Barbe. It
was past midnight and the corridors were deserted.
Nicholas's door was ajar and I tapped on it, pushed it open
and found the room empty. I returned home and went to
bed. It was close to daybreak when I finally fell asleep, and
then when I woke up I saw it was almost noon, and got up
and rushed off again to Nicholas's room. It was still empty,
the bed unslept in.

I remembered the swift exodus of the masters from the
church. Had they learned before the service what Nicholas
was going to say? What had transpired among them? Charges
and condemnation proceedings might already be under way
before the judges of the Parlement. Nicholas could even be

under arrest. If that was so, how soon would it be before they came looking for me? Should I flee—but where? I returned to my room and lay down. My stomach was in knots. I felt a terrible torpor. Around suppertime, unable to endure any longer not knowing what had happened, I got up and went down to the refectory, thinking I might hear something. There was the usual clatter of students and professors trying to down the terrible food and depart as fast as they could. Were some of them staring at me? No, this was my imagination. I did not hear Nicholas's name in any of the conversations around the tables. I went back to my room and tried to read St. Augustine's *The City of God.*

The building was quiet. This was the time when the students took to the streets. I thought, would I own up to helping Nicholas with his sermon? Should I let them accuse me of heresy because of the views that Nicholas put forth? I chewed the question over in agony, knowing that I had, in fact, reached the answer while I was listening to Nicholas. I had said to myself then: "These are my views, too. I cannot confess to anything else."

I heard steps on the stairs, and clutched *The City of God.* If this was the summons they would find me reading the saint who taught that salvation depends wholly on God's grace. There was a knock and a whisper: "I have a message from Nicholas Cop."

It was a student who was vaguely familiar to me. I might have seen him at one of Nicholas's lectures. "You're Johannes Calvinus, aren't you?" He had a Flemish accent. "I was not sure where your room was."

"What is the message?"

"Master Cop said to tell you he has left the city."

"Is that all?"

"No. The rest is you must also leave at once. He said, go to your friend the Erasmian. That's his exact words. Do you know who he meant?"

"Yes, I know."

The youth assumed a look of concern. "When will you go? You can't just leave like that, can you?"

"No." I gave him some money, pushed him out and bolted the door. Nicholas had fled, abandoning me and his professorship and his rectorship, which he only would have done to save his life. And he had left me to fend for myself. I was stricken. I saw my mother's virgin-like face replaced by the chilling countenance of Noël Béda's church. We all must die, and the impious must die by the torch; heresy must be consumed by fire. All this I had always known, never thinking that I, a regular communicant, would ever be overtaken by a fate that was only meant for the wicked. But I thought then of de Berquin, condemned for translating Luther, in whom I had found some truth in spite of myself, and of Marguerite's true grace, and of Nicholas and me, whose culpability was exalting the supremacy of Jesus Christ. For that mother church was hunting me, who had always followed her. Hers was the wickedness, not mine. I saw the ghastly image of Béda before he struck me for nodding at my desk. I must have lived in blindness not to have discerned before this the evil in the church's face. This would not be punishment for heresy, not under heaven; it would be murder.

I suddenly recalled the Flemish voice: "I was not sure where your room was. . . . When will you go?" The youth had earned a reward for delivering Nicholas's message, and he could undoubtedly earn a little more by informing the police as to where I could be found.

I roused myself. I put a copy of my *Commentary on Seneca* in a bag with some undershirts, opened my door, and stepped out on the landing. As I did so I heard the street door at the bottom of the stairs open and someone start up. It could not be a student, not with those careful steps, which stopped, resumed, and set down again so as not to cause too much creaking. I ducked back in my room and bolted the door. It was a sickening height from my second floor room to the courtyard between two wings of the building. Nevertheless I dropped my bag out the window, climbed out, and hung for a second by the sill. Even in my panic I thought of how ludicrous it was for a scholar such as I to be dangling out a window thus over a courtyard filled with cats—but no persons, thank heaven. I let myself go and landed heavily. An alleyway led into the rue Valette, where the students had congregated in their nightly bedlam. I lost myself among them and half ran down the hill until I was safely out of the vicinity of the university. I had a momentary idea of going to my Uncle Richard's but rejected it and made my legs carry me across the city and out through the south gate. I walked until I was exhausted and spent the rest of the night sleeping fitfully beside the road. In the morning at the next town I obtained a mule and continued along the road that would take me to Louis du Tillet's in Angoulême.

4

I GAVE MY NAME AS MONSIEUR DESPEVILLE and to inquisitive persons I answered, as I helped myself shudderingly from the common pots in the inns where I stopped, that I was on my way to Le Mans, or Tours, or Poitiers, whatever came into my head. I let questioners see by my expression that I was not used to discussing my business with everyone. Impertinent fellows asked, "Lawyer, eh? Four kinds of robbers there are—free-booting knights, priests, merchants, and lawyers." They were filled with wine, gabbling about their strange world. They were merchants mostly: the smell of greed was as heavy as the odor of their bodies as they stood around the fire. Some were on their way to the bourse in Antwerp to trade anything that could be turned to a profit—wine, pepper, English cloth, Italian silk, and wool from Spain. And yet, I thought, commerce has its place in God's world, as did money, of which I myself had none at all. Neither did the French government, I learned, for the king was now using up his country's treasure buying artillery. "Artillery! It will kill more Frenchmen than Spaniards. No wonder he needs a standing army of a hundred thousand. That's what they tell me."

"Where's the money coming from?"

"From the bankers at 18 percent."

"Not from the Fuggers. They're the emperor's usurers."

"From taxes of course; that's what we work for." I learned from this talk that it was as inconvenient to have money as to be without it.

I crept on my mule along the road to Angoulême past fields where dim figures before daybreak crouched over the soil, appointed by God to perform this necessary labor. I passed their thatched mud cottages, and one whole hamlet as empty as death, ransacked and gutted—by brigands perhaps, or by the king's unpaid soldiers making their way home from their defeat at Pavia. I rode past vineyards hanging with grapes about ready to harvest. Outside of Poitiers I came on a large oak bearing another kind of fruit, four bodies covered by a virtual canopy of vultures. I could make out that they were women, hanged for witchcraft, no doubt, a horrid spectacle, but no more horrid than the thought, which I expressed aloud, for the benefit of my mule, I guess, of Satan inhabiting human bodies.

Mule, you have to listen to me, there's no one else. Who is this creature you are carrying? I am an orphan. I am homeless, uprooted, and upended. What do I do? I flee for my life, deserted by my best friend, hunted by my church, and so far as I can see, abandoned by God.

I mused on that. Had not God given me a good mind? He gave some men this grace so that they could carry out his purpose. I thought immediately of Augustine. But to what divine purpose had I been put? I had arrived at a conviction one night only to be driven into the countryside to find my way among fields of cabbages—at which point in my musing I gave my mule an angry kick. Forgive me, Mule, that was meant for myself. You are so superior to the creature sitting on your back, letting himself be devoured by self-pity. Self-pity would make you as useless as I, wouldn't it? Oh, you are so fortunate in your certainty.

One evening at last I reached Angoulême and saw Louis come flying down a rose-bordered path to the cathedral to meet me, to lead me up the road to the du Tillets' mansion and there to sit me down with some wine and a decent repast, telling me all the while how he had been watching for me for days, terrified that something had happened to me. "What did happen?" But I knew nothing beyond the message Nicholas had sent me. He must tell me.

"I will, I will, John, but it is terribly secret. That very night after Nicholas's sermon the Sorbonne faculty met and decided he was heretical. In the morning they went before the judges of the Parlement, who condemned Nicholas without debate, and before the day was over they had persuaded the king that he had to make an example of his physician's son, the heresy was so vicious. But by that time Nicholas had fled. He packed off the very night of his sermon, headed for Basel. This is the secret: my brother Abel warned him. Abel plays a risky game, I think, serving as registrar of the Parlement and passing on information about it. He's a liberal—too liberal for his own good. Anyhow, Abel also told Nicholas that someone at the convening had connected your name with the writing of the sermon, and they would probably arrest you after disposing of him. Nicholas said he would get word to you before he left."

Why the Flemish student was so long delivering his message we would never know, but I felt a soreness of heart towards Nicholas, whose first concern had been for himself.

Louis engulfed me with his affection. "You shall stay here until this blows over. Here, where nobody knows you, you will be safe. John," he went on eagerly, "stay here forever. We will read, you will see what there is to read, we will talk all day and night."

What wasn't there to read, what a refuge God had brought me to! Books filled the shelves from the floor to the ceiling of the du Tillet library, a veritable wall of vellum broken only by arched windows letting in the light of the countryside. Louis's father was touring the book fairs now and would return in a few months with a cartful of the new works coming off the printing presses of Germany and Switzerland. In this mansion in Angoulême surely must be all the world's knowledge.

Every morning two monks from a Benedictine monastery arrived, a Brother Thomas to catalogue, a Brother Titus to dust and make repairs. However, to find the book I wanted I learned to appeal not to Thomas, the cataloguer, who thought a book's proper place was on its shelf, but to Titus, who over the months would have taken down each volume to wipe it off and fondle it. Working by the church calendar, Titus knew where each one had been filed by Thomas while Thomas was still grudgingly looking it up. "Cicero—laws? Here in the first week of Advent," Titus would whisper in the churchly hush of the room, and I would have in my hand forthwith such matters as tyranny, democracy, slavery, freedom. But chiefly I immersed myself, for the first time in my life, in Holy Scripture, poring over Jerome's Vulgate and banned translations, including an early one of Jacques LeFèvre's, which Louis's father had picked up, avid collector that he was. Hour after hour I read until Louis would come to me ordering me to quit before I grew onto the desk.

A servant brought a letter to me one day which I opened with a shout of delight. It was from Olivétan. He too had done a translation of the Bible. He had been living with the Waldenses in a town in Piedmont, he wrote. "They are such brave, splendid people. Think of it, John, they have been preaching the teaching of Jesus Christ out of the Bible for four centuries while Rome has tried to exterminate them, but it never will. Cut them down, and they grow back. They flower here like the edelweiss, pure and white. I have been dwelling in the mountains with them as close to God as one can get." But the purpose of his letter was to ask if I would write a preface to his translation. Would I write it and send it to Basel, where he was going with his manuscript?

I agreed to. I first thought that I would draw on the enlightenment that had come to me in my reading. My preface would declare that the Bible is all the evidence we need of the presence of God on earth, no other witness is necessary. No council of men in their conceit can take one sentence from, or add one sentence to, divine revelation. But instead, inspired by the Psalms, I wrote:

"How can men open their eyes and not see God? He has engraved his glory in all parts of the world, in heaven and earth. He has witnesses on every hand. The little birds that sing, sing of him. The mountains echo him. The fountains and flowing waters cast their glances at him and the grass and flowers laugh before him."

I read it to Louis, explaining that there was something yet to add—that we do not need to make a search for God; he is right here inside us. In each of us is his sustaining power. If we look, we can find him in ourselves. "This is not new," I admitted, "but it will always come as something new. I think it is one of God's purposes for people, Louis, that they should make this discovery."

It was my first declaration of the faith towards which, in my long hours in the library, I had been groping. Louis thought it was very moving. He did not realize that what I was saying swept aside all priestly intercession in our salvation.

I finished it and sent it off by one of the du Tillets' servants to Basel. I did not tell Louis of the new mood that had come upon me, but the library was now like a prison; it held me entombed when God wanted me elsewhere. And one day when Louis came to me with the news that Jacques Le Fèvre had left Paris again—"He has come down south here to Marguerite's estate in Nérac. He is there now, saying he has come to die there,"—I said with sudden decision: "I must see him, Louis. Why? I will tell you something I have never told anyone. One morning after I had been to mass and was walking along the street, Christ came to me."

"How do you know? Can you be sure? Wouldn't it be an awful thing to think so if you were not sure of it?"

"I know. He spoke no word. I didn't know what he wanted. Now I do know."

I could not tell him any more. When would I return? His
face was filled with consternation. I could not say when I
would be back. I borrowed some money from him, unable to
make any promise when I would be able to repay it, and left
the next day.

H E WAS IN HIS HUNDREDTH YEAR, sitting huddled beside
a window in the book-filled cottage Marguerite had provided
him, with the sun falling across his bearded face. I had the
startled impression I was looking on the face of Jehovah, or
was it rather the face of Job, with whom Jehovah contended
and who pleaded with God not to condemn him? "I have
failed to confess to the truth," he murmured. "I was not
afraid of death but of the indignities. Did you know de Berquin? He was a pupil of mine. I did not know what the king
might decide next. What was I doing in Paris anyhow? Tutor-
ing two boys, just released from prison. Almost a century
between us. François was using me. He whirls like a weather-
cock. But he always ends up pointing at Rome. I am old. A
nervous old man, who still has not confessed to the truth."
His voice trailed away.

"What is the truth?" I asked, trying to keep a conversation
moving that I had come so many miles to hold.

The clouded eyes focused on me. "I have heard of you,
Calvin. I come from Picardy too. I read your book on Seneca.
You and Erasmus. The Dutchman isn't one to stir things up. I
haven't been either. Truth? You won't attain to it being
agreeable to the bishops of the church." He became quite
animated. "I was agreeable because I reverenced the church.
I reverenced it because it civilized Europe. Because it preserved the Word of Jesus Christ."

"I also reverenced it," I urged him on.

"It is in ruins. It is infamous. It is rotten with simony, concubinage, worse."

"What could be worse?"

"That it denies the Word to God's sheep. Rome only teaches terror and obedience. I translated the Bible so it would be read. They burnt my book. The sheep must be fenced in by superstition. They must not be freed to feed on the truth." He closed his eyes, while I crossed and recrossed my feet, thinking Master Le Fèvre had gone to sleep, until suddenly he roused himself and muttered, "What did you come for?"

"To hear you say what you have said, and make my confession. I have sinned. Indifference is a sin, is it not?"

"The acceptance of wickedness is a sin. All of us are sinners."

"I am ready to witness to the truth. It has come to me in a way I cannot escape; I must go out and preach the gospel."

"How old are you? Twenty-five? We Picards are very ardent, aren't we? Where are you going?"

"To Noyon first. I have been living on chaplaincies. I must resign them. Then to Paris."

"You will be in danger."

"I am prepared for it."

"How prepared?"

"By the Gospel," I said bravely.

"Your enchiridion. That's one of Erasmus's words that he got from Augustine. Both pretty good at words." I waited through another long silence, until he tremblingly took a pen from a writing table beside him and said, "There's a man in Paris named Estienne de la Forge. He lives somewhere near the market place and St-Eustache Church. He will know how God can use you." He scratched some words on a piece of paper and handed it to me. I read, "I believe in this man— LeF."

And apparently having nothing more to say, with what I must agree is the wisdom of old age, he retired into his valley of sleep. I had gained what I had come for; I had been touched by the great Le Fèvre's grace. The note he wrote was his benediction. So I rose and left him.

I WALKED AROUND AND AROUND THE MARKETPLACE and St-Eustache Square staring at the buildings. I did not ask anyone if they could direct me to the residence of Estienne de la Forge because I half-hoped that I might not be able to find it. I even hoped that he might have left the city. I had arrived in Paris with my resolutions turned to water.

My courage at the start had been a fine thing. Knowing the risk I ran with Parlement probably still looking for me, I had nevertheless gone to Noyon determined to placate my conscience by resigning my chaplaincies, but more than that, by this act to formalize the vow I had made to myself—not freely but under God's compulsion—to break with the church. I would complete this business quickly and get out of the place. I had found Charles and little Marie and my step-mother in our old house off the place au Blès; Antoine was attending the university in Paris. Charles went with me immediately to the office of the cathedral chapter and there before the notary who had succeeded my father, I signed the papers of resignation. We hurried back to the house where they had some refreshment for me. When I opened the door to depart, there were the police, who announced that they had been sent by the canons of the cathedral.

Charles, grown remarkably in the mold of our father, made a scene, and both of us were led off to the stone building that I used to hurry by anxiously as a boy. We were locked up, and days went by while Charles wrote letters to the bishop, reminding him that he was one of his curates. Finally the door opened one morning, and we were escorted almost deferentially to the bishop's mansion.

Bishop Jean de Hangest was the age of his cousins Joachim

and Ives, my dear friends. He had been away and had just returned that morning to hear what had happened. "When the notary realized whose signature was on your resignation, John, he immediately notified the canons." He had had his own troubles with them, as I remember my uncle telling me. "They were going to have me excommunicated once because my beard is an uncanonical length." It was in fact quite long, lustrous from much brushing. "When I learned you and Charles were in jail I told the fools they were courting trouble, that Princess Marguerite, on whom I call whenever I am in Paris, is a great admirer of John Calvin. While they went off to think this over I ordered your release. However, I would lose no time in getting out of town, John. Where will you go? No, don't tell me."

I had ridden all that day and through the next day before finally stopping at an inn to rest. But I couldn't sleep alongside a lout who smelled of the barns and kept thrashing about, so in despair I got up before dawn and took to the road again. The morning was cold and black. I wondered if I wanted to go on. My experience in Noyon had given me a taste of what I faced. Imprisonment? Certainly a life of hiding and impoverishment. I still could make a compromise. I could admit to my complicity in Nicholas's sermon, ask to be forgiven and remain within the church, return to the study of philosophy, possibly even supported in a priestly office, and try cautiously, like my humanist friends, to reform the church from within—a sensible course in keeping with my scholarly inclination. To become an evangelist, preaching the Gospel in defiance of the church—wasn't this more than I should demand of myself? So why did I go on? But one foot automatically followed the other along the road. I had one of those foolish thoughts that will suddenly intrude on one's effort to concentrate: Béda posing the question, is a hog led to market by the rope or by the man who holds the rope? I meditated on this ridiculous sophism as the sun came up, and God drew me on, and my legs carried me to Paris.

The shopkeepers around the marketplace were beginning

to close their stalls. Desperately I asked one of them if he knew where Estienne de la Forge lived. "Where are your eyes, simpleton?" said the man and pointed across the street to a building I had passed several times whose ground floor windows displayed bolts of colored cloth. Across its front, just under the roof was a sign in large brass letters: "Tissus de la Forge."

As I entered the shop he came towards me jerkily, and I saw that he had a club foot. He was a very small man, looking at me with the pleading eyes one often sees in crippled persons, as though asking for forebearance. "We are about to close," he said in a soft voice. "What do you want?"

"I have a note from Master Le Fèvre."

We stood in an aisle between counters piled with fabrics. In the back of the shop a giantess of a woman was rearranging piles of material on shelves that would be out of reach for Monsieur de la Forge. "Who are you?" he asked.

"John Calvin."

"I know about you," he said after a moment. "I know Nicholas Cop. What do you want, Calvin?"

All at once, in the presence of this afflicted man, I felt shame at the cowardice I had so recently admitted to myself. And in a resurgence of my spirit I said, "I want to preach the Word of God." Did it sound foolish and brazen?

"Are you in hiding? Where are you staying?"

"I have nowhere to go."

He called, "Charlotte," and the woman stopped what she was doing and came down the aisle to us. "This is my wife," he said. "This is John Calvin, Charlotte. He is going to stay with us." She gazed down on me, shrugged noncommittally and lit a candle and led me upstairs.

C HARLOTTE DE LA FORGE, I FOUND, accepted anything that happened to her, including the incidence of her seven children, with no visible emotion. The children served now as a way for her to explain my presence in her household; she told people that I had come to teach them Latin, although actually I had little to do with them. Thank heaven! I was sleeping once more on the roof of Paris, in a top floor room of a building that was like a warehouse. My windows looked out between the brass letters of "Tissus," which proclaimed to the city Monsieur de la Forge's innocence while he was down in his cellar rending the fabric of the Roman Catholic church, for people gathered there to hear him put forth what the papists called heresy. "We call it Protestantism," he said. It was a new word to me. It had been given to German princes who had signed a *protest* against the emperor's decree that they permit Roman services in their Lutheran states, he explained. "It is a good word," he said. "We are protestants of the Antichrist in Rome." In the basement that smelled of sewage, by the light of a few candles, Estienne read passages from Le Fèvre's Bible and Luther's sermons. "I am no preacher myself," he said. This was to be my church.

I had spent little time in preparation before I faced my first congregation, fifteen people. It was the evening of the day of Pentecost, and all that Sunday in Paris's churches the priests had been celebrating the mass that blasphemes Christ by denying that we are redeemed by his one sacrifice and can only obtain forgiveness by the mummery of sacrificing the Savior over and over again. I took my text from Second Acts: "I shall pour out my spirit upon my servants. It will happen that whosoever will call upon the name of the Lord will be saved." I cried out against the papists who thought that with such trash as "Ave Maria" and "Our Father who art in heaven," muttered three or four times, the whole business was arranged; against the doctrine that said no one can presume to call upon God because he cannot know whether he is in a state of grace so that he must pray in doubt, committing himself to the Roman church, answering everything by saying, "I believe what holy mother church believes." We have the Gospel not to put us in doubt but to assure us of our

salvation, I said, and I, who had had so little instruction myself nevertheless exhorted them to receive instruction that
they might lead others into the knowledge of God. "Let each
one take the hand of his neighbor to help him ascend into the
holy mountain," I quoted Isaiah. "Be confident that
whosoever will call upon the name of God will be saved."
Could salvation be so simple, I wondered myself, as they left
cautiously by two's and three's and Estienne limped about
snuffing out the candles. "It was God's hand that brought you
to us," he said.

From then on I preached two or three times a week. My
congregations grew as word of my preaching was discreetly
spread. How could I not be brave when I was confronted by
such courage, such exaltation? They were all kinds, of the
middle class, shopkeepers, artisans, and working men of various sorts. A few brought their wives. They carried no names.
It was imprudent to have a name in that cellar, where a
door behind some empty wine casks led into a sewer they
could hide in if the police appeared. We would hear Madame
de la Forge's heavy steps in the closed shop where she kept
watch.

During the day I pored over the Bible in my attic room,
teaching myself so that I could truly teach. But I found myself distracted by a growing awareness of the conflicts Martin
Luther had let loose, learning, as I did, of what had taken
place in Germany and especially in Switzerland while I had
had my nose in a book. I could not accept peace under
Rome's tyranny, but it did seem that half of Europe was now
raging fratricidally over God.

I heard about this at night when merchants from other
cities would appear at the de la Forges' for supper. They were
persons who were informed about everything—including, I
saw, the amplitude of Madame de la Forge's table, where
meat was served every day of the week. "I stand with Huldreich Zwingli," Estienne would proclaim. "Since Christ did
not command otherwise, we eat what we want when we want
it. Whatever my wife serves is blessed by her love for me, as

marriage is blessed by love and is right for all men, including the clergy."

"On that point," said a merchant from Zurich, "do you know there is a bishop in Switzerland who permits his priests to keep all the concubines they like provided they pay him four guilders for every bastard they sire?"

"And how prospereth our bishop in this commerce?"

"Prosper! With the original investment solely the priests' and the labor the ladie's, the bishop has only to sit by and collect on their production. It is a better business, I tell you, than peddling cloth."

Angry laughter filled the room. But such depressing news of the Reformation circulated around the table. Luther, whom I once detested until my conversion brought me to revere him, had grown obese and irascible. "His temper gets shorter," a merchant from Wittenberg said, "as his belly expands." The father of the Reformation damned the humanists, once his allies, having been heard to cry out, "I hate Erasmus, I hate Erasmus," because Erasmus believed the Church of Rome could be reformed from within and entertained the idea, which Luther rejected (and I was beginning to question), that men are perfectible. He denounced outgrowths of his Reformation, which in some cases was not to be wondered at, taking the Anabaptists, for example, who baptized a second time, in adulthood, refused to take oaths, did away with private property, and lapsed sometimes into madness.

"A Jan Bockelson from Leiden and his followers have seized the city of Münster," the Wittenberg merchant told us one night. "He calls it the kingdom of God and himself the king of Israel. Since the kingdom needs repopulating he ordered all the men to fill their households with maidens. He set the pace by taking in sixteen virgins, I'm told. And he claims his license comes from the Old Testament. Bockelson is a great embarrassment to Germany's Protestant princes, as you might imagine."

I could have wept. Was this the world that had been conquered for Christ? The turmoil in Germany swept over Switzerland. Freiberg, Lucerne, and other cantons that still clung to the superstitions of the Roman church, warred against the cantons converted to Protestantism, Basel, Bern, Zurich, and most recently Geneva, which I was told, had been wrested away from its Savoy bishop by a pupil of Le Fèvre, one Guillaume Farel. Good men had died prematurely in God's work. Huldreich Zwingli himself was slain leading an army out of Zurich against the Catholic cantons. A scholar and gifted musician, his body was savagely quartered and burned. Johannes Hauschein, of Bern, Herr *Houselamp,* the great scholar whom I knew as Oecolampadius, a master of Hebrew and a man not meant for violence who named his three daughters Peace, Piety, and Truth, was dead of grief over Zwingli's fate, and worn out furthermore by his failure to reconcile Luther and certain Swiss Reformists who had ventured to amend some of Master Martin's doctrine. That there should be these conflicts within our movement was what distressed me the most. I heard how Luther and his companion Melanchthon had sat around a table with Zwingli and Oecolampadius to settle, if they could, whether Christ was physically present at the serving of the communion bread and wine, as Luther, surprisingly like the papists, maintained he was, and Zwingli maintained he wasn't. Was the Reformation to come asunder over interpretations of Christ's words at the Last Supper? Luther had drawn a knife, pointed, unbending steel, and scratched across the table top, *This is my body.* Then he stamped out, dragging Melanchthon with him. And even after Zwingli had been slain Luther continued to berate him, calling him "that assassin."

I said one night, "How can I deny that it is a scandal for priests to keep concubines? But isn't it a greater scandal that we who preach from Holy Scripture fight among ourselves like pit dogs?"

"So what is to be done, Master Calvin?" the Wittenberger asked me. I had been pondering over it. "Our faith," I said, "is without form. Lutheranism is an exhortation, not a true

church. It is to the political advantage of the princes to protect it against the emperor. It is a worship tolerated and even
administered by secular power."

"In Zurich, thanks to Zwingli," Monsieur de la Forge put
in, "the Reform church *is* the secular power. Zurich is a
church state."

"I think neither can be the true church of Christ," I said.

"So what is Master Calvin going to do?" the Wittenberger
persisted.

"One day I will design an edifice that is Protestant and
universal."

"A new tyranny like Rome's?"

"No, no. It will come from the Bible not from concordats.
And I will write a guide to which men can turn and say, 'This
is the way in,' and they will advance into the new edifice
without stumbling." The guide would be something of the
nature of the preface I had in mind for Olivétan's Bible which
I had put aside for a paean to God.

Except for Estienne, who looked at me kindly, the faces
around the table were mocking. "So how soon will you produce this tablet for us?" one of them asked.

"I cannot promise." But I thought how much better suited
I was to this kind of work than to warfare. I had a sickening
vision of Zwingli quartered and burned.

"We cannot know, any of us, what God's purpose is for
us," Estienne spoke up. "But I can conceive of John doing
what he says."

I began in fact to draft such a work, although I did put it
aside temporarily in order to deal with a minor metaphysical
point raised by the Anabaptists' belief that the soul sleeps
without consciousness from death until the day of judgment,
not such a minor point, since it denied everlasting life. The
notion had to be demolished, and I wrote a book, *Psychopan-
nychia,* putting the manuscript aside until I could have it
published safely under my name.

I was living in a kind of void, within the cognizance of
heaven, yet creeping about namelessly on earth. I communi-

cated with none of my old friends in Paris—whom could I trust?—so no one outside of Estienne and his wife knew that I was there, that is, no one but my brother Antoine, whom I visited one night at the Collège de Montaigu. My appearance had somewhat changed: I had grown a beard which subdued the lines of my rather sharp chin, and wearing a long cloak, I ventured up the hill to the university. I did not linger in Antoine's room. We agreed to meet once a week near the produce wharf in the evening when the area was all but deserted. My idea, it was; I craved one link to my former life, and I would not let Antoine risk coming to Estienne's. We met thus like two thieves, or clandestine lovers. I let him think at first that I was doing some writing of a radical sort, that it was prudent for me to keep out of sight, but I finally had to confess what I was chiefly engaged in.

He was deeply distressed. "You are still being sought for your part in Cop's speech. They will find you. The police have agents everywhere." One evening when I was late at our meeting place he was almost beside himself, turning and turning about on the river bank. "Where have you been? What nightmares I've been seeing." He told me then that our brother Charles had been excommunicated for striking a mace-bearer—why he had done so Antoine did not know— some insane gesture against authority. "What a pair of brothers I have, John!" He pleaded, "You must leave Paris and take me with you. I cannot study while I'm sick with fear for you."

It was impossible. He must get his degree. "God will protect me." I kissed him on the cheek, noticing its softness, which made me think of our mother.

Then one day Estienne said to me unexpectedly, "You must go."

Go, where? What had happened?

"Get out of Paris. There are men in the movement I can't control. They are going to do a foolish thing. It is better that you don't know any more. Father Strappado knows how to win confessions."

What about him, I asked; wasn't he in as great danger as I?

"I'm a respectable cloth merchant. I am seen going to mass regularly at St-Eustache. I'll hold no more services in the cellar for a while." I was to go to Poitiers, he said. There was a group there who had heard of me and would hide me while I preached to them.

I would go wherever I was sent. I did what God through his servant Monsieur de la Forge showed me he wanted me to do. I only wondered how much longer I, bearing God's true Word, must live in these shadows.

There was one thing Estienne requested of me. Before I left I was to talk to a man named Servetus.

"I can tell you this about him. Michael Servetus comes from Villeneuve in Spain. This information was on an order put out by the Spanish Inquisition for his arrest. He studied law at Toulouse. He was employed for a while by Quintana, Confessor to Charles V. I laughed over that. He turned up then in Strasbourg. There Oecolampadius and Bucer were taken in by his brilliance, even though he danced around raising an idiot's questions about the divinity of Christ. They were less tolerant when he had his book published; some German, a mischief maker, printed it. You've heard of it, *On the Errors of the Trinity*. The archbishop of Saragossa got hold of a copy of it. Some say Servetus brazenly sent it to him. When the hounds of the Inquisition started on his trail he disappeared. Even Strasbourg was too hot for him after it read the book. I know where he is. He's here in Paris."

"Why should I talk to him?"

"Because you are of the same cast of mind. Both of you are lawyers. You're a heretic in the eyes of the Roman church. You've rejected its dogma like Servetus, only he rejected dogma that belongs to all of Christianity. He went too far. Try to draw him back. We could make use of him."

"Why do we want him?"

"Maybe he will become as dedicated to truth as he is to error. Try to save him, John. He is living in a house in the rue St-Antoine under the name of Villeneuve."

The house was barely wide enough to accommodate a dilapidated doorway. I knocked and knocked and had turned away when a voice said, "Who are you looking for?"

"Monsieur Villeneuve," I said at the crack in the door. "He has ordered some cloth from Monsieur de la Forge, the draper."

"Is that the cloth you have there?"

"It's a sample to see if Monsieur Villeneuve approves of it."

The door opened. In a dark and frightening little hallway I made out a man of about my age with a black curly beard, handsome in a Spanish way, dressed almost foppishly.

"I know who you are, John Calvin," he said accusingly. "You preach in cellars against the teachings of the church."

"I know who you are. You are Michael Servetus of Villeneuve who has written a book denouncing the doctrine of the Holy Trinity."

"And if I am, what do you want of me?"

"I would straighten you out on your errors."

He became very excited.

"There is nothing to substantiate it in Scripture. There is nothing about it except Nicaea, nothing from fine thinkers but logic-chopping. Ockham knew it could not be proved."

"Ockham thought very little could be proved, but he had his armor against logic—his great faith."

"I could show you the logic that wrests faith from this foolishness." His voice was passionate.

"That's why I am here—to argue."

"Go away immediately. Where would I be if they caught me entertaining a heretic of your stripe?" We both laughed in spite of ourselves, but he pushed me towards the door. "You could have been followed. I'll tell you, I'll come to de la Forge's and look for some cloth. We can duel in his basement. I'll make an anti-trinitarian of you."

"When will you come? I'm about to leave the city."

"Tomorrow."

I thought he would appear. But several days went by, and

Estienne finally said, "You can't wait any longer." I said goodbye to Antoine that night and left in the morning, bearing three disconnected images: of Antoine weeping and walking along the Seine, of Estienne seizing my purse and insistently filling it with coins, and of Servetus in his fashionable clothes in a dark little hallway saying, "It cannot be proved. I can show you the logic that wrests faith from this foolishness."

The ignorant say that things happen by chance, that people's paths cross by chance, that it is only by accident that two souls whirling around in the void meet and fall in love, perhaps one soul to be left to mourn the other some day, or to destroy the other. They say all things, all encounters are accidental. It is not true; all things are preordained by God.

I PREACHED IN POITIERS IN A GROTTO, quite conscious of the appearance I presented when I arrived—burned by the sun, my beard unkempt and long enough, in truth, to swear by. My clothes were threadbare and hanging on a frame that was thinner than ever, for La Forge's heavy table had never been any favor to my stomach, nor had the awful fare in the inns. I looked like St. Anthony, the father of prophets, no denying it. In the grotto one day I served holy communion, an ultimate defiance of the Roman Catholic church but a wholly acceptable act in the sight of the Lord, I was sure.

They would have had me stay there forever. But after a few weeks I came to a decision, praying that I was doing right. I said goodbye to my congregation and set out for Angoulême. I would withdraw to the world I loved, my books, my study. I would resume work on the thing I had talked about.

Recalling Erasmus's *Institutio Principis Christiani,* to wit, instruction of a Christian prince, I decided to entitle my book *Institutio Christianae Religionis,* for that is what it would be,

instruction in the true faith of Christianity. I could appreciate
the irony in my composing this work in the very shadow of
the Roman cathedral at Angoulême, and while living with
Louis du Tillet, who served Rome as a canon. But he was so
overjoyed at seeing me again, nothing I told him of my inten-
tions mattered. I derived some satisfaction at being able to
repay the loan he had made me. Once again Brother Titus
hauled down books for me while I sat and wrote in complete
peace, until one day I heard hoofbeats in the courtyard and
looked out to see Louis's brother, Abel, registrar of the
Parlement, who was so well informed about that body's business, vaulting from his horse. In a matter of moments, Louis
and he were facing me in the library. He said he had only
stopped between Paris and Angoulême to change horses.
"You have to get out of the country, Louis, too. Haven't you
heard anything of what has happened?"

I had heard everything—that is, God's voice guiding me in
my writing.

"They are burning heretics everywhere. As I left Paris I
saw them drag a man into a fire in the marketplace outside
St-Eustache." My heart turned to stone. "It started three
nights ago with the placards being nailed up."

"What placards?" Louis asked. "We are in total darkness."

"The work of fools. What else could they expect?" He
would tell us about it beginning with the beginning while he
had something to eat, for he was famished. Sight of the food
and wine sickened me. I could only think of the man burned
to death in the marketplace. "Placards were found one morning nailed up in the public squares of Orléans, Tours, many
places, Paris itself, and even on the king's bedroom door. The
king had gone to his palace at Amboise, taking for company
the queen's lady-in-waiting, the Duchess d'Etampes, and got
up early to go hunting and there it was. How did it get there?
A young man carrying a lute had told the king's guard that he
had been instructed to play a serenade outside the royal bedchamber and the guard, knowing François's fondness for
music, especially during his amours, had let the man by unat-

tended. The guard has since been decapitated. Lizet immediately convened the Parlement which did not have to be told the extent of the king's rage."

"But what did the placards say?" Louis asked.

"They said the pope and his whole venomous rabble of bishops, priests, and monks are all liars and blasphemers; that's what they said. There were references to caterwaulings of priests and their comical costumes. Oh, the composers knew how to evoke rage. And all were written in the same crude style, ending with something about the truth attacking the papist church and destroying it."

Abel wiped his mouth. He had finished eating so his hands were free to gesticulate. "President Lizet's large nose was more than usually enflamed. With him at the Parlement stood our cardinal, de Tournon, and the Inquisitor of Moral Pravity, Ory. 'As I told his majesty, who has shown some tolerance of heretics,' said Lizet, 'heresy is the *summa* of all crimes.'" Counting on his fingers, Abel went over Lizet's words. "'One, it is worse than matricide; it would destroy mother church. Two, it is worse than murder, which only does away with a body that is mortal anyhow. Three, it is worse than counterfeiting, because it debases God's truth. Four, it is more heinous than treason, since it destroys the unity of God's kingdom.'"

This was a dialectic I had heard before and knew not how to refute. And yet I thought of the devotion to Christ of the crippled merchant, who was guilty of all these crimes, as was I.

"'Impalement, beheading, burning in oil are all accredited ways of dealing with these various crimes,' Lizet reminded us, as he had reminded the king, he said. 'The worst of crimes should be punished, therefore, with no less severity.' He called attention to the Acts, nineteen, verse nineteen, wherein many who had come to confess Jesus Christ brought their books and burned them. 'If dead books may be committed to flames, how much more live books—that is to say, men.'

"Ory told us then that for his part he had pointed out to the king that heresy is a putrefaction that must be cut out before it devours the whole body of the state. 'Cut it out then,' the king had roared. Gone in a trice was any tolerance he had ever shown towards criticism of the church. Spare no one, was the order. The king would tell the princes of the Schmalkidic League we are only killing Anabaptists. Mere suspicion of Reformist activities is now enough to bring people to the stake. They've even executed the man who printed Marguerite's *Mirror of a Sinful Soul,* which has so frightened the princess that nothing has been heard from her. Don't think, John, that the Parlement has forgotten your part in Nicholas Cop's speech."

How much more did the police know about me? I saw Estienne de la Forge being dragged to the stake in St-Eustache Square. I did not know that it was he, but I could not not know it. I remembered him saying, "Father Strappado knows how to win confession." How little more pain would an already crippled man be able to endure?

"Don't waste any time. I myself am in danger, warning you, and Louis for harboring you."

We left France behind us—our land, whose public squares were odorous with burning flesh.

5

W E GALLOPED ACROSS THE BORDER into the humane city
of Basel. Except for Louis's servant absconding with a
saddlebag, our flight, by a miracle, was without incident. We
had no idea what our future would be, but we were safe now.

Basel, converted some years ago to the Reformation by
Oecolampadius, was a refuge for all kinds of persons—
evangelists, writers, students. Erasmus was there, old and
very feeble, I was told, working with his printer Froben on
his latest book, his *Ecclesiastes,* arguing, I was also told, that
mankind was hastening on to a perfect state. I was overjoyed
to find Olivétan, who had delivered his Bible to a printer in
Neuchâtel, waiting in Basel until François's slayings ceased.
And Nicholas was teaching at the university. Had I been
unfair to him? How sick of heart I was at the way he abandoned me in Paris. He had to flee, he said. He could not
delay a moment when Abel du Tillet brought him word that
he had been condemned. "If I had gone to your room that
day they would have caught us both. The student I sent to
you I thought I could trust. He should have gone to you
immediately with my message. If you only knew how I suffered until I heard you had reached Angoulême." My faith in
him was restored. It was good once more to be with him and

Olivétan. But I thought constantly of Estienne de la Forge.
What hope of him I still clung to ended one day when I met
the Zurich merchant who had sometimes stopped at the de la
Forges'. He had been a witness to my friend's awful death.
The following day he had gone around to the "Tissus de la
Forge," where he found the police stripping it of all its merchandise; Madame de la Forge and her children were nowhere about. I was in anguish also at the reports that kept
coming of burnings all over France. François was ridding the
world of Anabaptists, he proclaimed, which no doubt engaged the sympathy of the German princes, who had finally
captured Münster from the insane Bockelson, slain him, and
hung his and the remains of two of his companions from the
cathedral belfry, there to rot. How many of François's victims
had been people who had listened to my sermons? I could
not sleep for the visions I had. Screams filled my ears.

"There is nothing you can do about it," Louis said.

I had one weapon, even if it was a poor one, I said. The
writing of my *Institutes* became a pressing matter. I saw how
the book must begin—myself in the role of advocate, defend-
ing our Reform church against its accusers. It would be a
reasoned case to which the king must listen.

Louis and I had found quarters at a widow's house, a Mrs.
Klein, and there I started in. "Mighty and Illustrious François, Christian King of the French," I began, not unmindful
of this irony, but I, acting as barrister, was addressing François as a judge.

I pointed out that the fury of certain persons had so prevailed that no room had been left in his realm for sound
Christian doctrine, and it would be worthwhile if I presented
a description of our poor little church, which was being so
assaulted, and the nature of our faith. I begged him to give
full inquiry to the case which so far had been handled—
"tossed about," I put it—with no order of law. We were not
in conflict with the church that Christ established, and I
called his attention to the fact that a true king is a minister of
God, and that a king who does not serve God's glory exer-

cises not kingly rule but brigandage—a point from Augustine.

Let the king examine us. We claimed nothing of virtue in ourselves. We were naked of virtue so that we might be clothed by God. We were empty of all good in order that we might be filled by him. We were blind so that we could be illumined, lame in order to be made straight. We stood stripped of all vainglory so that we might earn glory in the Lord.

I turned then to our adversaries. Who were they? They were those who thought that it did not matter what anyone believed of God so long as he did not raise a finger against the primacy of the holy see and accepted such trifles as saying mass and believing in purgatory as true godliness.

They called our doctrine "new," contrary to what the holy fathers agreed upon, and to ancient custom. I wrote: "If we might speak in our turn, this bitterness which they spew at us with impunity from swollen cheeks might subside." Our doctrine was new to them because they had kept Christ and his Gospel hidden so long under impiety. Custom is what is popular. Vice, when widely practiced, becomes generally acceptable; people become accustomed to it. "The affairs of men," I wrote, "are seldom so well regulated that the majority of people are pleased by the better things. As "custom,' how many plagues invade the earth. But men do not perish any the less because they fall with the multitude."

They cited the early fathers. But the pronouncements of these great teachers—I could quote them, Jerome, Epiphanius, Augustine; I could go on and on—had been superseded and cut to fit Rome's calculated dogma, as I was prepared to show. One of the fathers was my own witness against the extravagances accompanying sacred rites; another was my witness against the decoration of churches with painted images of Christ; another had testified against the belief that our Lord's body could be transubstantiated by a few words into body and blood at the eucharist. A legion of holy men testified against Rome's writing canons and making doctrinal decisions without reference to Scripture. As for

subtleties of sophists and the squabbles of dialecticians—"If
the Fathers could hear their discussions they would never
know that these people were disputing about God."

Louis looked unhappy. "I don't think it will incline François in your favor," he said.

But by this time I was so warmed up, I thought little more
of persuading François, who stood over us not as a judge—
God was our judge—but as one of the accusers whom I accused.

Our adversaries claimed the pope could not err and that
whatever anathema he pronounced on us had the approval of
heaven. But was not Paul III one of a succession that had
come forth from Eugenius IV, who in 1439 was deposed as a
heretic and schismatic in favor of Amadeus, the duke of
Savoy, then later reinstated while Amadeus was appeased
with a cardinal's hat as a barking dog by a morsel? How can
one imagine true apostolic succession and infallibility issuing
out of such events? I would pass over the notorious morality
and misdeeds of popes since then.

So much for this.

What, in the end, was the cause of all the tumult in France?
Not our little church, certainly. Satan was at the bottom of
the business. I reviewed how, in the centuries before Christ,
Satan could lie around in darkness and make sport of mortal
men, but when the Divine Word shattered his cover he had
sprung forth, stirring men to take action, and making use of
their violent hands to uproot the truth. He had many strategies,
one being to cause confusion through such monstrous rascals
as the Anabaptists, who had enflamed people, including the
king, against us, even though between us and the Anabaptists
there was no resemblance.

This was my case, and in conclusion I begged François not
to connive any longer at imprisonings, scourgings, rackings,
maimings, and burnings that will make us as sheep all destined for slaughter—which Nicholas agreed I might as well
add, although we knew that this was what François meant to
do anyhow.

My address to him, to be sure, was like a half-drawn sword, which shone nakedly in my last sentence: "We will await the hand of the Lord, which will surely appear in due season, coming forth armed to deliver the poor from their affliction and punish their despisers."

I settled down then to my next task. The address to François would be the preface to the instruction that could constitute the body of my work, and I wrote the title: *The Institutes of the Christian Religion, Containing the Whole Sum of Piety and Whatever is Necessary to Know in the Doctrine of Salvation.* At Nicholas's urging I showed the preface and title to Johann Oporin, the publisher, who said he would undertake to publish my book, making only one suggestion, that I amend the title to read "Almost *the Whole Sum of Piety*," to which I agreed.

I had all the privacy I wanted at Mrs. Klein's but very little calm of spirit. She remonstrated with me one day. "Don't you ever sleep? I heard you up all night. Not that I care, but for your own good." She could not know what I was struggling with.

It was God with whom I had to do.

I wrote at the very start: "Nearly all the true wisdom we possess consists of the knowledge of him and of ourselves." What is God? It can only be speculation. The better question is, what is God's nature? We can know his nature by our imperfections. And by his perfections, we can know ourselves. It is our nature to aspire to what our nature resists, which is not the paradox it seems; we come closest to a knowledge of ourselves when we are aware of our disgrace in his eyes. For man is abominable to God; every woman's womb carries the seed of Adam's sin, so we are infected with blindness, vanity, and impurity. Ever since Adam chose to sin we have been lost in it. No matter how terrible this is to think about, it is true.

It is not true. Voices of Greek philosophers invade my room to contend with me. *Virtue and vice are of our choosing,* they say. *We can do this or that. We have free will. . . .* and I hear Erasmus arguing, *Our Lord's promise of forgiveness has no meaning if we have no freedom to choose.*

I sometimes walked past his house when, in order not to add to poor Mrs. Klein's unease, with Louis at my side I paced the streets instead of my room. I would not go in to argue with Erasmus, a dying man, but I would say to him: "Christ did not promise to forgive us as a reward for choosing good rather than evil. He promised forgiveness solely because of his ineffable love."

Other voices assailed me. *If man has no choice, if you say God orders all things, then you say it is he who is the cause of all evil—the very beginning of all evil, for he might have forestalled Adam's fall. Why did he not? Is it God who imposes evil and disaster on the world; is that what you say?* But to ask such questions was to try to investigate God and penetrate him. It is enough to know that he loves us despite our sins because he created us and continues to preserve us. All we need to know is that everything God does is done and we must glorify his name. "God himself," I wrote, "is the sole and proper witness of himself."

I wrote about this matter at great length, until I recalled that the purpose of my *Institutes* was also to instruct readers in the laws of Christ's church as they are set forth in Scripture. The whole law is in the two tables of the Ten Commandments, the first having to do with the honor, fear, and love of him; the second table pertains to love toward other men. I had no trouble with the first. I knelt and prayed for understanding of the second, which Christ was to summarize: we must love our neighbor as ourselves—the very ultimate of love, for we love ourselves so much. But how can I love the slayers of Estienne de lar Forge? Or corrupt and hypocritical prelates, or thieves, murderers, fornicators who may be my neighbors? I had to confess, the very sight of some people turned my heart to hatred. I cried out to myself, I must look on God who created me in his own image, and I must love all people because I love him. There, I have written that down. It is easy to write things down. I must believe. I must aspire to a good of which I am empty, abandoning all thought that I can do good through my own will.

Holy Scripture was my resource. There was nothing original in what I wrote except my striving to pierce through words to their message. It would be wrong to expect complete inerrancy in words put down by men, however inspired. One sought out the spirit of the words, guided by the Holy Spirit within oneself.

So we can learn from the Bible true worthiness. Are people to be judged worthy who simply refrain from sinful acts? No. Christ made it clear that God's law must be obeyed in the most secret recesses of the heart. Fantasies and raving desires are wicked in our Lord's eyes: a man who looks at a woman unchastely is an adulterer, and a man who hates his neighbor is a murderer.

I TURNED TO CIVIL AFFAIRS. The ancient Greeks, pagans that they were, believed nevertheless that a supreme being directed all events. What had happened to that belief? Kings and princes had been persuaded that reality lay in the cleverness and self-interest with which they exercised power, and pursued their aims through intrigue, wars, and unholy alliances. Looking at Europe, one despaired of there ever being an end to conflict. There never would be until Christ's teachings informed all governments.

I saw how people lived in their communities in immorality and disorder, like rats in straw.

Do we give up then to our misery? No, God would not have us do that. He has given us certain means to achieve a life here on earth that holds some hope for our condition. He has given us, in addition to a spiritual government which resides in the soul and pertains to eternal life, civil government which has as its appointed end to cherish and protect the outward worship of God, to defend sound doctrine of piety and the position of the church, to reconcile us with one another in order to promote general peace and tranquility. This is not the government of greed and cynicism but the one whose leaders are God's vicars and under the admonishment of Jehoshaphat: "Consider what you do for you exercise judgment not for man but for the Lord."

God gives magistrates a sword that they can use against murderers. Governments may wage war in self-defense. Governments may levy taxes in order to support magistrates in their office—although they must remember that such revenues are the very blood of the people and should not be imposed without cause.

People should not rebel against their kings and magistrates. God would have us obey them and, if necessary, suffer under them. Despotism is his to avenge, not ours; how many times he has put conquerors on earth to punish people for their wickedness—taming the pride of Tyre by the Egyptians, and the insolence of the Egyptians by the Assyrians. I write this down. Yet I am troubled, because I recognize that despotism can go so far that it is against God. I myself had fled from it. It is true that Christ tells us to obey, but it is also true that we have not been redeemed by our Savior at so great a price that we should enslave ourselves forever to wickedness. "Let the princes hear and be afraid," I warned at the end.

I was at the end—not of everything I had to say, for every word seemed to open into further thoughts—but at the end of my strength for the moment. I had written my book in less than eight months—a treatise, I estimated, about two-thirds the length of the New Testament.

My friends picked up scattered pages and arranged them in proper order. Louis, that wandering and uncertain canon of Angoulême, could not hide his distress over passages attacking the mass, and my rejection of all sacraments save that of baptism and the eucharist. Nicholas commended me for the "elegance" of my Latin, but would have had me launch into predestination, which we had discussed a number of times. And I had studied Augustine on this dreadful subject. But I

did not go into it now, although I referred to Augustine
frequently on other matters. "No, Nicholas," I told him, "I
am not yet ready for it." Dear, ardent Olivétan had no reservations. "It cannot be surpassed," he said. "It is new in this
age. . . ."

"There is nothing new in it, and it is only a beginning, a
kind of little handbook of Christ's church."

"The injunction to love God comes as something new to
every age. But that is not what I meant."

"Love does not come first." I saw that this surprised him.
"Faith and hope come first, for it is they that engender love.
Faith, the seeing of things not seen. And hope, faith's companion. Take hope away and we can have no faith. Faith is
what we believe God promises. Hope is expectation." I had
written a dialogue between Faith and Hope that I would
incorporate somewhere and I read it to them as they sat
around me in my paper-littered room at Mrs. Klein's.

"Faith speaks first," I said. " 'We groan, we are sick of our
lot. We sigh for lost worthiness.' "

"And Hope responds, 'That is because sin and death crept
in with Adam. But Christ abolished both. Adam destroyed us
all when he destroyed himself. But Christ restores us to salvation.' "

"Faith says uncertainly, 'I believe God to be true.' "

"Hope promises, 'In time it will become manifest.' "

" 'I believe he is our Father.' "

" 'He will show himself.' "

"Faith says desperately, 'I believe that eternal life has been
given us.' "

" 'In time it will be revealed.' "

"Faith groans, 'But I am weak, I fail, I faint.' "

" 'Wait in silence,' Hope says."

My friends were silent. "What I started to say," Olivétan
spoke at last, "is that it will be read all over Europe. It is the
first statement of the Protestant faith, complete."

"Not complete. There is more, much more elaboration and
development of its points."

"I see generations of people witnessing by it," Olivétan

insisted, "it is so filled with the certainty and rapture of being in God. Until it will have acquired a name, we will call it Calvinism."

I was flattered, and amused. I, only twenty-six years old, lifting my head amidst Catholicism, Lutheranism, humanism, classicism, and all the other isms shaking the earth, to become an ism myself!

I made a few revisions, put the letter to François in its proper place at the beginning, and tied it up, then carried "Calvinism" to Oporin. I walked back to Mrs. Klein's with a small advance from my publisher in my pocket, wondering, now what?

6

W E HAD BEEN TRAVELING all morning through a snow-laden pass in the Alps that would bring us in time to the Rhone. The day had begun weighed down under clouds, but suddenly the sun burst through and I looked up to see great ragged banners streaming from the peaks. I pulled in my mule and commanded Louis also to stop and see how the snow now glistened beside the blackness of the brook that followed our road. "We think that is the way it is," I said. But then I told Louis to look up at the sun and then look down again. He was temporarily blinded. It was the same as looking up at God, I explained. "We are certain about our virtues until we look up at his glory, then all we see around us is a greyness."

He looked up, then down, but was too weary, perhaps, to make any comment. I could still be moved by this wonderful thought, weary as I was too.

We had been riding for days. We had come from Ferarra to Milan, north along the endless shore of Lake Maggiore, then plunged into the mountain pass, which was particularly tiring for us because we had taken the journey in the opposite direction only a few weeks before. It had been my idea to go to Ferrara. After I had delivered my book to Oporin I wanted nothing so much as to get away from Basel; the printers, Thomas Platter and Balthazar Lasius showed no inclination to hurry, and the *Institutes* was going to miss this year's Frankfort fair. I could not stay in the city raging over their indolence. Olivétan had returned to Piedmont and the Waldenses, despite reports of terrible persecutions there. He was braver than I. I had no wish to venture back into François's jurisdiction. Nicholas's friends brought him news of France and the latest was of the king carrying a candle and leading a procession to Notre Dame in atonement for having once been so easy on Protestants. This took place after a pontifical mass ordering the execution of six of his countrymen for heresy. Some of the intellectuals in Princess Marguerite's court had taken wing. Even Clément Marot, the king's favorite poet, who had made the mistake of pricking the clergy with his wit, had deemed it best to flee to Italy. "He's gone to the duchess of Ferrara, Marguerite's cousin Renée," Nicholas said. "They're of a like liberal mind. Renée, they say, is saddened beyond words over events in France." My decision was born. I would carry the hope and inspiration of the Holy Gospel to the duchess.

We had arrived at her court to find that Marot and the other refugees had left. Renée's husband, she told me tearfully, had thrown them out. I had several hurried talks with her in her chambers, and we discussed how God was constantly present. But the felt presence of the duke and the clanking armor of his Swiss mercenaries in the corridors of his palace discouraged any meaningful meditation. I assured her I would pray for her, and she told me how much she had been helped by my coming.

And Louis and I had ridden off, not any too soon, I guessed.

We made it at last to the Rhone Valley. Tired as I was I felt quite joyful, rid of a melancholy that kept overtaking me when I wondered if I had only written another book that no one would read, now filled with ideas for a second edition. And as our mules plodded along I told Louis what I had to do, my remarks punctuated by my mule's gait. I must go into creation. What is its origin? What have we fallen from? What is the end of creation? What have we been estranged from? I must go into predestination. I must ponder Augustine's saying that only those who have been elected will be saved, and consider what follows logically from that: are all others destined to perish?

"Many things I find hard to understand," poor Louis said tiredly from his own joggling seat.

We would go to Strasbourg because Strasbourg had become a center of Reformist education. I had learned this in Basel; we should have gone there in the first place. There were great scholars and theologians there, including Martin Bucer whose *Evangelienkommentar* I had been reading on divine election. Louis would see. On to Strasbourg!

But first, here was Geneva, walled and forbidding, standing at the far end of Lake Leman. It was late in the day and we would have to stop. Its people were known to be crude and not too amiable, but the evangelist Guillaume Farel had established Protestant worship in all the churches, its government was anti-papist, and it was as safe a place as any along our route. We entered at the south gate and pulled up at the first inn.

I felt strangely fatigued. I was overcome by the odors in the common room, and I left Louis there and had the innkeeper take me upstairs. A single candle in an incongruous ecclesiastical candelabrum lighted the room he showed me, which contained a large bed with an obscene mattress on it, and two lumpy pads thrown without charity on the floor. I chose one of the pads—I might have to share the bed—and lay down, and shivering convulsively I wrapped my cloak tightly around me. I did not know how long I had lain there or whether I had gone to sleep, when I heard the door creak and raised my head, expecting to see Louis. Instead, two men staggered in, their voices loud in argument.

"Three things, that's all." The voice had a German accent. "Finding a hole to crawl into—look at that wretch on the floor—and eating and fornicating." Monstrous birds in the flickering candlelight, the one who had spoken depositing himself on the edge of the bed to unlace his boots, his neck stretched out like a fishing crane, the other in a black cape and black hat, who flapped to rest on the other side of the bed. A crow, a crane—my poor head was now fevered—two fowls in foul conversation.

"What you leave out is man's fear of God."

"Ach, some people say there is no God."

"They're the ones who fear him most, afraid to face the God-awful chance that there is a God. Besides, your theory that men are only animals cohabiting in holes leaves out mankind's progress over the centuries."

I tried but could not close my ears to this drunken cackling.

"What did you say your name is?"

"Hans Hoch." The crane's voice rose to a wail: "I lived in Zurich and my wife became a Zwinglian. She left me to marry an ex-monk."

"What's your business, Hoch?"

"Bookbinding."

"They're not much on books here."

"I could not live any longer in Zurich. What's your name?"

The crow lifted his black hat and replied, "Maigret the Magnificent."

The crane laughed loudly, and I was constrained to laugh myself. "What's your business?"

"I perform various services for people like the king of France."

"I should be a donkey to believe that."

"You should be a donkey not to believe it. Who was here in the thick of things when Geneva gave the pig-headed duke of Savoy the boot?"

"Doing what?"

"Observing for François. Do I have your attention?" Maigret the Magnificent lurched to his feet and strode around the room, nearly stepping on me, making several sweeps with his cape, and exclaiming: "The duke has been routed. The bishop has decamped. Protestant preachers are arriving from Bern. But priests are still holding onto the churches. An uproar!" He flung himself about, almost falling across the bed.

"Go on, go on," the man called Hoch screeched.

"I was walking my dog in the cathedral square when this fellow appeared, priests and canons swarming after him. They said, 'We know you, Guillaume Farel. Who sent you?' He said, 'God sent me.' 'The devil sent you.'"

He had moved out of my range of vision, but I could see his shadow on the ceiling miming the event. In truth, he had my attention. Was I hearing from Thucydides, drunk as he was, how Geneva had been captured by our little church? "Farel says coolly, 'I come to preach the Word of God.' And they yelled, 'Throw the Reformist bastard in the lake; kill the dog.' A monk from Fribourg named Werli swung at him with an arquebus, and they would have murdered him, no doubt, if the town's syndics hadn't rowed him up the lake."

The recital had exhausted him. He lay down on the bed, and there was silence. It seemed that he had gone to sleep. "Come on," his companion urged, "that's not the end of it."

"Nowhere near," Maigret the Magnificent muttered. He sat up and resumed his story but in a monotone that I had to strain my ears to follow. I was able to make out that after Farel a youth named Froment had come who advertised to teach people to write in French. "A lot of even high-born ladies in Geneva are illiterate, Hoch. When they came to him he used passages from the Bible in his lessons. The sly dog was showing them how they could be saved without reference to the Roman Catholic church."

I must have gone to sleep then from the fever that had invaded me, when his voice came like a thunderclap: "Too much success! Went to his head!" Maigret the Magnificent was sitting up, swinging his arms around. "He tried preaching to a crowd in the place du Molard, calling on God to deliver them from the false prophets of the papist church. Priests came charging down the hill from one direction and the bailiffs came after Froment from the other. I yelled at him—

I'm accustomed to taking risks: 'Follow me,' and I rushed him off to the house of my friend Ami Perrin, a merchant of repute—not a Protestant particularly but a heroic contender against Savoy and his bishop, who told the town's syndics he would give Froment work making ribbons—at least keep him from being a threat to the public weal."

"The public weal! What's that, who's to say?" the bookbinder cried. "That's what everybody fights over. My weal comes from God; your weal comes from the devil."

"We will get to that, Hoch." Maigret the Magnificent was on his feet and in full career again. "A few weeks have gone by. The *bise,* the cruel north wind, is blowing on Sunday morning, but the streets are crowded with free-minded bourgeois heading up Cathedral Hill. They want to take over the cathedral and hear some Protestant preaching. A lot of them are merchants who have acquired Protestant ideas doing business with Bern. The canons ring the Clemence bell on St-Pierre and priests come running with knives and hatchets, singing the *Salve Regina.* And women in their black hats, even children, everyone in Geneva is ready to settle whether the world is going to be Protestant or Catholic—two mobs like two animals. It is the *guets* who save things. They are indispensable men who act only in the interest of maintaining order, standing watch at night, sweeping life's debris from the streets, blowing horns when the sun comes up—worthy men—the city's policemen who, when called upon, dressed in coats of mail, also issue forth as bailiffs." His voice rose to a crescendo. There was a knocking on the wall, but he paid no attention to it. "They take up a stand between the mobs, and the syndics appear to proclaim everyone can worship the way he wants; 'just, for the love of God, go home.' But now, this is the point you yourself have just made, Hoch."

"What point is that?"

"About how men will fight over whether a thing comes from God or the devil. That's right, and it refutes your theory of man's main concerns according to which everyone would go home to eat, fornicate, and sleep. Then how do you account for subsequent events? Or, for that matter, numerous incidents in history when men have been at each other's throats over what's righteous."

"What happened?"

The knocking on the wall became louder, and I heard a voice pleading, "For the love of God, let people go to sleep."

"See, Hoch? All people want is to go to sleep. But not these Reformists. They never sleep. Farel returned, and this time he had with him one of the lords of Bern who demanded that Geneva let him preach. It put the council in a quandary. It counted on Bern for help if the duke of Savoy tried to recapture them. He was ravaging the farmland around the town trying to starve it out. But the council also needed help from Fribourg, and it's more Catholic than Rome. Fribourg demanded that Reformist preaching be suppressed. What do you do? The council was like a man trying to piss down two holes at once."

His shadow on the ceiling moved frenziedly, seeming about to swoop down on me and swallow me up while I was being reduced by a thunderous voice: "Reformists and Catholics pursuing one another around the streets. Werli, the monk, was stabbed to death. Would you believe it? The syndics seized the assassin and cut off his head. A cook tried to poison Farel with arsenic in his soup. Would you believe that? All in the name of God. He puked it up and the syndics decapitated the cook. But now here comes the climax, Hoch. A mob of Protestants led by little boys, little boys, mind you, stormed into the cathedral and stripped it—statues, paintings, candlesticks—that's one of them in the corner shedding light on our luxurious quarters. They even disgorged the receptacles of the holy elements. I was walking my dog at the time, and someone threw me some wafers and said to give them to my dog. They said if they're holy she will choke to death. She swallowed them at one gulp." He stopped. I raised my head to see him take off his hat and hang it on one of the bedposts.

"Is that the end?"

"It was the end of the Church of Rome in Geneva." In a matter-of-fact voice he evoked scenes of priests and nuns fleeing for their lives, of Bernese soldiers falling on the forces of Savoy, of the duke riding off with a look of rage, and of the people of Geneva assembling in the cathedral and voting for reform. "Farel now holds the churches. They turned the bishop's palace into the town jail and threw the gamblers, whores, and brawlers into it. It wasn't big enough for all of them. Farel holds the churches but not the city—nobody can hold Geneva very long."

"See, that's the way it is," Hoch said.

"But look at the way they were fighting over God, Hoch."

"But now they're back at their real interests."

"I'm too tired; I'll deal with it in the morning. Move over, Hoch. Wouldn't you be more comfortable on that mattress on the floor? You'll be down on the level of your philosophy."

"I'm all right where I am." There was the sound of a sigh, then of muttering and bodies moving about on straw. The candle guttered out. A fevered sleep must have overcome me, for how long I could not tell, when I heard Louis's voice calling, "John, John, where are you?"

By the light of a candle being held aloft in the doorway I saw two figures and heard a voice proclaiming, "It's a miracle, a miracle."

I asked weakly, "Who are you?"

I heard the voice of Maigret the Magnificent: "It's the prophet, Farel."

Farel, that madman!

"God has brought you to me," he was bellowing. "Get up, John Calvin."

"I am sick," I groaned. "Leave me alone."

I made out a bearded man bending over me, surely a conjuration of this dreadful night. He was trumpeting: "You are to help me contend with wickedness. Do you think it was chance that brought you to Geneva? How I have been praying for someone! In the name of poor martyred Estienne de la Forge, I call on you. In the name of our crucified Lord; God has sent you."

"Leave me in peace."

"How can you talk about peace? Do the papists talk about peace? The priests of the Antichrist are still in the villages round about, and people go to them to be blessed. Peace! Was the psalmist thanking God for peace when he sang, 'Thou hast given me the necks of mine enemies that I might destroy them that hate me'?"

"The psalmist said to seek peace and pursue it." I could muster up the Scriptures as well as he could. "Peter said, 'He that will love life and see good days, let him seek peace and ensue it.'"

"What makes for peace except war against the wicked?"

"Save your breath, Farel."

"Not Farel but God commands it."

How could he say that? I must pray. I lifted myself up on my knees. "Dear Lord, hear me. I beg like David, give ear to my supplication, Lord, the terrors of death are fallen on me."

Incredibly, the fellow called down a curse on me. "God will reject you. He will say you found an excuse to look out for yourself instead of Christ."

"Is this man's hand truly your hand on me, O Lord?"

"How can anyone know?" It was the voice of Maigret again.

"He will curse you and reject you. Come now, we're going to my house. Take his other arm, Louis. How he is shaking! But our love for him will warm him."

I was helpless in their hands. "Don't forget his sack," I heard Hoch say. I had a glimpse of him sitting on the bed as I was half carried from the room.

I WAS AFFLICTED BY THE FEVER and the racking cough for several weeks while Louis applied fomentations to my chest until the fever left me, and I lay there listening to a voice that spoke of peace, which was my own, and another, which was God's. Louis said to me one day, "You are so much better. In a little while will you not feel like going on to Strasbourg?"

I told him then, "I am not going."

Why should he be so distraught at this? He had brought Farel to my room; he had got me into this. "I could not help it," he said. "When he appeared in the common room we recognized each other from Paris. He wanted to know what I was doing there. I had to tell him. He knew all about you. He began talking then about a miracle and insisted I take him to you. Do you know what he was doing at the inn? Seeing that an ordinance against drinking overmuch was being enforced. Do you want to be impressed into that kind of loathsome work?"

Did he not think that God had put out his hand to stop me in my journey, and that it was he speaking to me in Farel's fearful adjuration?

"No, I don't think so. If God wanted you for such work he would have given you the strength for it. Your body is hardly able to drag your soul behind it. You are not listening to me."

I was thinking how God had never given me any rest. He had pursued me all my life. I told Louis how he had drawn me out of the superstition of my boyhood and had made me see that doctrines sprung from the human mind can be sacrilege, and had put in my hands the truth that lies only in Scripture. He had drawn me from my books and set me to preaching. I ran away from that because I was always fearful before the public. I fled from France afraid for my life. I yearned for nothing so much as a place where I could hide from the world. "But God would not grant it," I said. "Now he has brought me here."

"Geneva will destroy you."

"Perhaps it will. I am mortally afraid and ashamed of such lack of faith."

"It does not have to be lack of faith to choose what you are best suited for. Your mission is to teach. The *Institutes* is your life's work. That will be your monument forever."

"For me to make the choice—that would be to have no faith," I told him. "It is God's choosing. He has thrust me onto the stage again. I must stay."

PART TWO

The Lord said to Jeremiah:
I have put my words in your mouth.
I have set you to root out,
and pull down,
and destroy—
and to build and plant."

I sometimes think of myself,
Louis du Tillet,
as a man of too many affections.

7

My BROTHER WROTE ME from Angoulême: "The king's
rage has cooled. I can assure you that it is quite safe for you to
return now." It made me grievously homesick, thinking of
Angoulême. "But this does not go for your friend," Abel
added. Then it did not go for me, because I would not leave
John Calvin, whom I loved.

I rented a house in the rue des Chanoines, Farel's quarters
being too small for all of us. A room on the second floor
became John's bedroom and study, and he set about preparing to take on a job for which, I thought, he was tempera-
mentally not suited. He made notes for sermons, poring over
Paul's Letter to the Romans. "How terribly he accuses," John
said to me, "when he writes of those who changed the truth
of God into an image resembling corruptible man." But often, scarcely recovered from his illness, he would bury his
head in his arms, too weak to continue. The notes lay scattered about while Farel kept inquiring when he was going to
start preaching.

I could see how his sense of being God-ridden increased
his desperation. As he got his strength back, the spirit nevertheless lagging behind the flesh, we began taking short walks
around the neighborhood, and one evening, having ventured

a little ways into the lower city, we were brought up short by a woman's voice coming out of the darkness. "What are you two gentlemen looking for?"

"We are looking to be left in peace," I said.

"Well, my lords, I'll give you all the peace any man needs, and it won't cost you much either."

"We'll find it elsewhere, you slut."

"I thought you were a gentleman. How about your friend here?" And she lunged out from the doorway where she stood and grasped John's arm, causing him to turn around so that the light from a window fell across his face, which, etched in light and shadow, looked so wrought up she fell back, whispering, "Who are you?"

"Sister, I'm your brother!" he said hoarsely.

She ran down the street, sure, I suppose, that she had encountered a madman, and John walked so rapidly in the other direction that I had to stretch my legs to catch him, and when I did I heard him say almost inaudibly, "I am trembling at the touch of a depraved woman. Am I so weak? O God, are you trying me?"

"She's the devil's agent," I told him.

"I am as corruptible as anyone," he whispered. "How can I preach to others? I'm not worthy."

His unworthiness, to which he referred several times, was not all that troubled him. I could see how the city affected him, and how he shrank from its strangeness, as did I.

We walked about the wretched place. It had been nothing but a tribal camp before it was swallowed up by imperial Rome. Northern barbarians had overrun it; it had produced nothing of any consequence; traders had used it as a place to stop on their way somewhere else. Often torn down by invaders, it had been piled up again on the inclines around the lake. It was a poor city nowadays because Savoy had choked off its trade for so long. What wealth there was belonged to a handful of bourgeoisie and owners of vineyards beyond the city's limits, Bertheliers, Philippes, Chapeaurouges, Perrins, whose houses with narrow eyes and stony fronts manifested their owners' authority. They were the city's rulers, many of them patriots who had led the revolt against Savoy's duke.

In the poorer sections women worked their miserable backyard gardens. Butchers in the Bourg-de-Four racked up horsemeat. On the bridge that joined the lower city with the district of St-Gervais across the Rhone, cutlers, tailors, hatters, and shoemakers opened their mean little shops at sunup and worked until sundown. But at nightfall all common sense seemed to leave the city. Prostitutes were not the only danger to two men out walking; the streets would suddenly be filled with bands of masked youths making catlike noises. Lights danced on the lake from hundreds of boats, making a pretty effect, and the boaters were harmless enough except for an occasional drowning. At night, I was told, matrons had their servants sleep with their daughters to protect their innocence. As John and I walked past taverns we would hear the sounds of dicing and singing, and worse, of mocking applause for intoxicated men who, John and I made out, were parodying the sermons of Guillaume Farel.

"The city has plenty of fine laws," Farel told us, "passed by the revolutionists after they got rid of Savoy. And some of the laws they enforce. They put iron collars on thieves and vagabonds, if they don't banish them or cut off their heads. But when it comes to cursing, dancing, or playing games at church time—and these things are all against their laws—the very people who made these laws are often the worst offenders. Prostitution—God help us. I got the council to clean the whores out of their nests in the rue des Belles Femmes— they actually named the street that!—and they flocked off to the Turkish baths. So I got the council to forbid men to go to baths run by women and women to go to baths run by men. Then I see councilmen themselves slipping into these dens, and not always slipping, sometimes quite brazenly."

I felt sorry for Farel. He preached as often as five times a week with no one to assist him in the city's three churches but a blind ex-priest from France, one Eli Corauld. The young French scholar Pierre Viret, who had been with him for a while, had had to transfer to Lausanne, which had no preacher at all. A few Genevans that Farel had recruited had proved to be not worth their salt, he said. "I haven't been able to organize the churches; I'm no organizer. Thanks be that God sent you, John!" Whereupon he would embrace my poor trembling friend.

On the whole Guillaume Farel was distasteful to me. His clothes were disheveled, his hair and beard were uncombed, and his eyes were nearly popping. I knew all about him. He was a loud-mouthed radical who had caused disturbances across France and Switzerland. He had grown up in a wealthy family in Gap and might have reposed comfortably on his portion forever if he had not listened to lectures by Jacques Le Fèvre, whereupon he had rushed off like a man possessed, preaching a straight Lutheran doctrine, which had distressed Le Fèvre and upset the people of the provinces. He had been chased from one town to another and finally out of France. In Basel they tried to get him to lower his voice and finally ordered him to go somewhere else. He went to Montbeliard, the Pays de Vaud, preaching and writing books, and was one of a hundred preachers whom Zwingli had gathered and who met the scholars of the Roman church in a disputation at Bern that decided that city to become Reformist. He had stayed there just long enough to single out Geneva for his next enterprise. He was a violent and incendiary man who had drawn my dear friend into a situation from which he had every reason to recoil.

One day we went up to the Cathedral of St-Pierre atop the highest hill in the city. A man whose cap hid a tonsure, I suspected, came to us and began talking. "Good Christians hauled stones one by one up the hill to erect this building. There is an account in our chronicles of how it took a hundred men and women to pull one cart while children waved holy banners over them. Well, it all came to naught. If you have been inside you have seen that the cathedral has been ravaged of every symbol pertaining to the eternal Church of Rome."

"It now stands to the eternal glory of God," John said.

The man eyed him somberly and walked off. Aye, to the eternal glory of God, I thought to myself, but a stripped building would have to be invested with some kind of glory, as Geneva itself, stripped of a holy, organized religion, would have to be invested with a faith it was willing now to live in. It had rejected Rome but so far as I could see was a long way from bowing its neck to Reform.

The cathedral gave an appearance outside of a fortress. But inside, we saw, it presented a vast scene of arches and curved pillars that were surmounted with biblical scenes, crudely chiseled but with an innocence that could not but appeal to one. We stood inside the door gazing down the long nave, which was indeed bereft of any paintings or statues. Our footsteps echoed on the stone floor. When we reached the towering pulpit John suggested that I climb its steps, which I did. "Mother, father, sister, brother," I counted as in a childhood game. Twelve steps, representing the disciples, perhaps? I looked out dizzily into a great void, and gave a little wave of my hand to John, watching me from below with what emotions I could imagine, thinking of himself standing where I was. He did not wave back, only stared up at me.

"You are ready to begin God's work, are you not?" Farel said one day. "You will take the service this Sunday at St-Pierre. I won't ask you to go all the way to St-Gervais. The service is quite simple. A prayer of your own making, the Lord's Prayer, a hymn or two, and the sermon, which comprises most of the service. And a benediction. God will uphold you."

I watched him as he managed the twelve steps up to the pulpit. His congregation numbered perhaps a hundred, mostly women, scattered about on benches in the vast nave. He was a little out of breath at first, after negotiating the steps. But his voice grew louder. I sat behind one pair of women who whispered during the prayers, "Who is he?" "Another Frenchman like Farel." "He's young." But they fell silent when John began his sermon on the Letter to the Romans. He became suddenly transported, and they listened attentively throughout. Several women waited for him at the door, and I saw one of them try to kiss his hand, much to his embarrassment. "What is your name?" they asked him. He told them, and they said he spoke very well about our Lord.

"I try to speak as God directs me," he said.

What a miraculous change took place in him then! Miraculously, yet gradually, he began to walk at his old rapid gait. He preached almost as frequently as Farel, climbing purposefully into the pulpit, and facing growing congregations, although they were still predominantly made up of women. His sermons on Paul's epistles began to contain references to Geneva's backsliding and general unrighteousness. "Why must we live like rats in straw?" he cried out. Ah, yes, from his *Institutes*. I remembered how Olivétan had thought he perceived in the *Institutes* something new—"Calvinism"—although I myself while not saying so, had felt at the time that Olivétan was being carried away. But Calvinism, or Lutheranism or whatever, it came forth from the pulpit in St-Pierre— the faith that only by learning to live by the Word of God can we exist in order and tranquility. He was cutting the clothing for a naked city.

O NE SUNDAY MORNING, the quiet that his appearance now induced in his congregation was shattered by the sounds of a game being played in the courtyard outside. A ball rolled through the open door, and a boy darted in after it. There were cheers from the courtyard, men's voices mingling with boys', and the noise of the game continued, almost matched now by a chorus of indignant voices inside the church. Calvin was on the last chapter of Romans, at which he had arrived in due course. He raised his own voice in order to be heard: "We then that are strong ought to bear the infirmities of the weak." He finished without visible emotion and spoke the blessing. The crowd outside had dispersed, and he said nothing to me on our way home, but when Farel dropped by, returning from his service at St-Gervais, Calvin turned on him angrily and demanded: "Didn't they vote in general assembly to live under Reformist worship?"

"Yes, they did."

"Then they must be shown what it is. Choosing between good and evil is not merely raising your hand in meeting. It means respect. It means not acting like swine. It means obedience to God's law and civil law as well." When he had calmed down a little he went on: "Their civil laws must be laid down in terms of biblical injunction. This has not been done. I intend to write out the articles of this mutuality. These people must be shown what is required of them by a government under God. The articles will contain a confession of faith and a catechism for the instruction of the young. These children learn nothing from their parents but irreverency. And finally, there must be measures for the enforcement of moral conduct. I am going to demand this of the council."

I went along with the two of them to the town hall, to the Little Council that was supposed to enforce the laws. A handful of men regarded him coldly when Farel introduced him. Most of them would not have known who he was unless their wives had told them of his appearance at the cathedral.

He adopted a respectful attitude, addressing them as "honorable lords," and spoke of the responsibilities of their great office. They knew how the city's laws were being winked at on all sides. This was not their fault but rose from the lack of formal guidance by the clergy. From their humble and subordinate position the clergy must now suggest to them what it was God would have them do. He and Master Farel would prepare the articles of a moral order in a Christian state. Being men who had vowed their allegiance to the Reformist-Protestant faith, the councilmen could hardly reject this proposal. Besides, I thought to myself, the accep-

tance of such an instrument would be up to the other, larger
council, which passed the laws. And there might have been
among the Little Council itself some who were distressed at
the undisciplined, not to say disruptive, spirit that prevailed
in the city. I thought they might have resented his presump-
tuousness—after all, he was not even a citizen—but they were
impressed both by his air of humility and his reference to God,
and they told him to go ahead.

He set to work immediately, at his elbow a copy of his
Institutes, which had recently appeared in the bookstalls. He
interrupted himself only for his sermons, which by this time
had carried him into the letters to the Corinthians.

One other interruption he allowed himself, and that was to
make a trip to Lausanne. Bern had summoned a disputation
there to decide whether the Pays de Vaud, all the land
around Geneva that Bern had seized from Savoy, should
worship in the Reformist or Catholic faith. Bern preferred
not to expel the Roman clergy without first going through
the formality of a debate, not wishing to provoke the
Catholic states in the Swiss Confederation and shake that
uncertain alliance any more than it already was. Calvin had no
business in the affair—it was Farel who was officially
invited—but he went. I went too, and sat with John in the
back of the hall in Lausanne where, I observed, believers all
in the one true God gathered on opposite sides to denounce
each other as ignorant of the real truth.

Through much of the debate John sat in silence. But when
a monk from Fribourg tried to sustain the doctrine of the
corporeal presence at the eucharist by quoting the early
fathers, John leaped to his feet. I could have wept for the
poor monk. "Why don't you papists really read the fathers?"
John demanded. He demolished the unfortunate monk with
quotations from Tertullian. And from Chrysostom, "about
the middle of his eleventh homily." And from Augustine,
"towards the end of his twenty-third epistle." He quoted
from memory to the amazement of everyone, including
monks, vicars, curates, some of whom admitted afterwards

that they had almost been persuaded of the worthiness of Protestantism. Bern decided—of course there had been little doubt that it would—that the Pays de Vaud would be Reformist.

"Who is this man?" a number of church leaders asked me.

"He's a young scholar from Paris," I told them. "He has become the leader of the Reformist movement in Geneva."

"We thought it was Guillaume Farel."

"He has taken over from Farel."

He worked on his articles all that autumn and into the early winter in order to have them ready to present to the Council of Two Hundred at its January meeting.

I wandered around the city, oppressed by everything surrounding me, by the ugliness of the town squatting inside its walls, by a lake with no visible conclusion, by the great drifts of clouds that hung down amidst the awful mountains, and I dreamed of Angoulême and its sunny fields and my father's library. I had written my father begging him to tell the bishop that I was visiting our relatives in the Pays de Vaud. He had replied to this prevarication affectionately—a rambling letter absorbed with book collecting. He, in fact, recounted how he had acquired an edition of a banned book by the young Spanish heretic Michael Servetus—"a terrible thing, I have put it under lock and key." And he sent me some money and asked me to convey his regards to our cousins.

I felt the pull of my lifelong faith. I saw myself going about on two legs as an ostensible Reformist, but on my knees, before I went to bed, I had one foot in Roman Catholicism, praying to the Virgin along with the Father and Son. If I returned to Angoulême, John would think I no longer loved him.

I listened to his and Farel's discussions of the articles, which were now all but finished. One day I ventured to ask, "What if the council rejects them?"

"They cannot," he said.

"Still, they might. What will you do then?"

"Do you know the words of the Lord in Jeremiah, Louis? 'I

will bring upon Jerusalem all evil, because they have hardened their necks so they might not hear my words.'"

"But these articles are your words," I murmured, and when it seemed that John was not listening to me, I persisted: "Will you quote Jeremiah to the Council of Two Hundred?"

"It will not be necessary."

"They will accept them," Farel said confidently.

I WANDERED ALONG THE LAKE FRONT. It was warm for January, and I came on two fishermen sitting in a spot of captured sunlight, one in a long, fur-lined cape, the other with a shawl thrown across his shoulders, both holding their poles with an effect of hopelessness.

"No luck at all," said the man in the cape. "Sit down and commiserate with us. I've seen you around, Monsieur du Tillet. My own home is near Paris. I'm known to my friends and others as Maigret the Magnificent. It takes some living up to. This is Hans Hoch here. He's a bookbinder, a neighbor of yours who has just opened a shop in the rue des Chanoines in a stable where the bishop used to keep his horse. Well, Master Calvin has turned out to be someone to conjure with, has he not?"

"You've got a bite," said the person in the shawl, stirring slightly. "Why are you always the one?"

"It's the clever way I wiggle my line. Whoops, got away from me. From my observation Farel has not had too much luck reforming Geneva, but with Calvin he may get somewhere. I understand the articles Calvin is going to present for the council's approval are based on a book he has written. I took a peek at it in the bookstalls."

"Yes. His *Institutes of the Christian Religion.*"

"A worthwhile book. We would all be better off if everyone would read it. Well, you can't read everything. Hoch, open our basket of tasty viands. Perhaps our friend will join us."

"Look, you've got another bite," said Hoch. "Now you've lost it. Why don't I ever get at least a bite?"

"Because you're a person of no faith."

Hoch, of no faith and no luck, dispiritedly spread the contents of the basket on a rock, picked out a chop and indicated to me to help myself.

"I will have a little of the wine."

"I've been trying to get Hoch to read the book so he can find out what he needs to know for his salvation."

"Why do I need to go into such matters?"

"Do you want your soul to be utterly blotted out?"

"So what do I need to know to be saved?"

"You mustn't look at a woman covetously, because that's the same as committing fornication."

"Just thinking about it?"

"Some of Calvin's rules are discouraging," sighed the man who was getting all the bites but so far no fish.

I might have reminded him that the law against coveting was not original with Calvin. "You must have read quite a little of the *Institutes,*" I suggested.

"I suppose I spent an hour or so at the bookstall."

"He has been parsing this Reformist's grammar to me ever since," said his companion, who, since I was sharing their wine, was ready to embrace me in their intimacy. "He quotes me whole sentences, and they are all negatives. Maigret has been sentenced—heh, heh."

"I admit it makes it hard for me to retain my usual gaiety."

"Stick to interrogatives like me, Maigret." Hoch had become quite animated. "How, why, where, who? The preachers get tangled up in interrogatives, and you're soon off their hook."

"Why, Hoch, how very apt in this setting."

Thus encouraged, Hoch demanded, "What kind of a man is this John Calvin?"

"That's hard to say. What kind of persons were the saints?"

"He's a saint?"

"It is my understanding," Maigret offered, "that those who confer sainthood require that the person be certified as being monopolized by God. I understand that Calvin is very pious."

"I think he's crazy," Hoch said. "I don't mean to run him down. But he's a fool if he thinks he can make us all into something most of us don't want to be, which it would be impossible for a person to be as far as that goes."

"Speak for yourself, Hoch," Maigret said. "Master Calvin is trying to save you. I think it is quite laudable of him. A fool, a saint? In either case I don't think you should crucify him."

"I'm not crucifying him. Anyhow, they crucified Christ. Whether Calvin is a fool or a saint he runs the same risk."

"Yes, I would say it's risky being either," Maigret agreed. "The better a man is—"

"Is a fool a better man?"

"Quite often," Maigret said. "Here, Monsieur du Tillet, have a little more wine." I thanked him but said I had to go. "Will you be at the meeting of the Little Council?" he asked. "It is tomorrow, is it not?"

Yes, I told him, and that I would certainly be there. We bade one another good day, and I went off along the path that led to the shops and houses of the lower city, looking back once at the two fishermen squatting in their spot of sunlight, no doubt still discussing the difference, if any, between fools and saints.

8

I STOOD AMONG THE ONLOOKERS in the rear of the town hall. The Council of Two Hundred, their backs to us, jostled each other for places on the benches set across the room. Off to one side of this group sat the Little Council, two dozen men arrayed behind four worthies carrying silvertipped batons. "The syndics, the quadrumvirate head of the state, you might say." It was Maigret the Magnificent, who was standing beside me, his mouth confidentially in my ear. "They and the Little Council enforce the laws, keep the streets tidy, deal with plagues and foreign emissaries, and such matters. Being like me a citizen of a monarchy you'll be interested in observing a democracy at work. To be sure, the two councils elect one another and trade offices back and forth, but it's a democracy to the degree that there is no absolute authority, and they are frequently at each other's throats."

They were merchants, artisans, and suchlike. "By and large, vulgar fellows," Maigret whispered. "No education. Their fathers and older brothers were the Eidguenots." It was the name given the revolutionists who had cast out Savoy, he said. Where had the name come from? He did not know nor did anyone else, he said. "Shh, we're about to begin."

The councilmen had settled themselves. Some were leafing

through copies of "The Articles of the City of Geneva,"
which had been passed around. Others who, I suspected,
could not read, whispered to one another or stared at Calvin
on the podium, Farel beside him indicating his support.

I too stared at him, confidently erect, sure that they would
accept his rules of conduct because it was the best thing for
them. His white face starting out from his skull cap was usually strained with intensity, which drew some people to him,
yet put others off. But now his expression was carefully contained. A fool, Hoch said. Maybe he was by the bookbinder's
definition. He was going on in a vibrant voice: "We don't
think our office is bound in such narrow limits that when the
sermon is delivered we may rest as if our task is done." He
reminded them that the citizens in general assembly had
voted to live in the Reformist worship and that this meant
living under the law of the Gospel. "With it we protect the
tranquility of the community so that everything is not
tumultuously confounded." I had listened to him expound on
this matter before. "Honorable lords, the law is like a whip to
a balky ass—a constant sting to the flesh that will not allow a
man to rest in his wickedness."

There were murmurs, which I judged, were of approval.

Christian order first required, he explained, that the Lord's
Supper be observed regularly and with dignity. "Once a
month would be sufficient. The weakness of the people is
such that if the holy mystery is too often celebrated it may
become despised."

Those whose conduct marked them as unworthy would be
excluded from the Supper. The ministers of the church alone
would exercise this authority. "The Lord has put the weapon
of excommunication in the hands of his ministers so that they
can cut off the disrespectful as rotten members."

Some of the councilmen exchanged glances.

Unworthy conduct would be dealt with quite simply. The
Little Council would appoint persons known for their up-
rightness to watch over their neighbors. If they observed

instances of misconduct they would inform the ministers, who would then exhort the offender to mend his ways in the name of the Lord. If it was apparent that he intended to persevere in hardness of heart, then the ministers would arraign him before the general assembly so that everyone would know that he had been denied further communion with his Lord. "There may be some who will laugh and not care. It will devolve upon the government, then, to punish such contempt for God and his Word by exercising various means to deny them further traffic with their fellow men."

A sudden scraping of feet interrupted him. John looked up. It might have been that the councilmen had chosen this moment, as one man, to arrange themselves more comfortably on their benches.

"There are certain sly citizens who would corrupt our city by other means," he continued. "These are the papists who steal outside the city to make confession to some priest, those who choose the kingdom of the pope over the kingdom of Jesus Christ." To deal with them it would be required that all inhabitants make their confession of faith in the Reformist church or suffer banishment. In the document before them the councilmen would find a simple confession of faith. It would be becoming for the honorable lords each to sign the confession, setting an example for all, and afterwards to appoint certain ones of their body who would see to it that every citizen did likewise.

A scraping of feet was so loud that I felt it must now come from an uneasiness of minds rather than of bodies. But the councilmen stolidly turned pages, while John swept through his remaining propositions.

There would be no celebration of feast days such as Christmas and Easter, which were of Roman origin and unnecessary, since the Word of God was to be celebrated every day. The ministers of the church would judge whether people were morally fit for marriage. Children would be taught a simple catechism, which he had prepared, and present themselves at certain seasons to be examined. Psalms would be sung to lend warmth to public worship. He came to the end.

"They will not swallow it," Maigret predicted. "There is Jean Philippe on his feet. Leading merchant. He'll oppose it."

But Councilman Philippe's objections were astonishingly mild. He merely said that the practice of having citizens report on their neighbors' wrongdoing had been tried in Basel, and he happened to know that it was not a success.

A man stood up who was just visible over the heads of his seated colleagues. "Henri Aubert, an apothecary," Maigret confided, "a very upright man."

"If our city is going to live under God," said Councilman Aubert, "then we must see to it that everyone lives under God. Any winking at wrongdoing makes us all guilty of hypocrisy." There were affirmative grunts.

There was some discussion over giving the ministers the right of excommunication.

"It's our church. Are we going to let the ministers say who can worship in it—or who can't?" said Philippe.

"But who knows better whether God's law is being violated than the ministers?" demanded one of the syndics. "Michel Sept," Maigret hissed.

"They don't know everything there is to know."

"About this matter they do. They've read the Bible from beginning to end, sir. Have you read the Bible from beginning to end?"

"I still say this gives the ministers authority that belongs to us."

"Oh, come on, Councilman," Aubert put in, "the Articles leave it to us in the end to banish or put in prison, or whatever, anybody who's going to be stubborn in his wickedness."

There was a great deal of arm-stretching by now, and some even stood up to pluck at their clothing where it was sticking to them. The issue was an involved one, and most of them seemed inclined to pass over it. I was not surprised, only a little apprehensive over the fact that there was almost no discussion at all over the measure to banish anyone who refused to denounce the pope. "How else can a Protestant state maintain its purity?" asked Councilman Aubert. Someone suggested that the serving of the Lord's Supper be limited to four times a year. The reason why was not clear to me, nor was the reason Calvin did not object.

"Vote, vote," they cried. They accepted the Articles by a show of hands. "Well, I never!" Maigret exclaimed. A few who were opposed were hardly noticed, and the honorable lords clumped off to their everyday business.

F AREL WAS SO JUBILANT he could hardly contain himself when we got back to the house. He embraced John and me too, shouting, "We have created the new Jerusalem," before galloping off to deliver one of his almost daily sermons. But the moment he had gone John sank into a chair, looking so miserable I thought it must be his stomach.

"No, it's not my stomach."

"What is it then?"

"I thought I would never be able to finish."

"You showed no sign—"

"Looking at their faces, what did I see? What you see in the face of a cow."

Perhaps it was just a lack of comprehension. "I think most of them didn't know what they were voting for," I offered.

"They were sinning, every one of them. Their sin was indifference."

I suggested that indifference was the sin of most men. I wondered where this was leading.

"It is not man's nature to behave becomingly," he cried out. "People have to be shown each step of the way that leads to God. Oh, I do not say that we should be borne down by unending bondage; because of Christ's forgiveness the law is not bondage. But standing in his own judgment a man will pass off hypocrisy as righteousness. Only let him weigh his life on the scales of the law, and he will see how far he is from holiness." There was a long silence. "How can I go on with it? I haven't the strength."

It was my turn to rejoice. "We will go to Strasbourg. Come now, John. You have done what you can. Leave the rest to Farel. He is already celebrating the birth of a new Jerusalem."

"You are sneering."

"No, no, I'm not. I love you, that's all." Why could he not understand that my only concern was for him?

"You must love God first, above everything else."

"Why do you say I don't?"

"If you do, then confess it to him, that his will must be done."

"I shall pray to him that he take you away from this city before you are destroyed by it—"

"See, Louis, you do not put God's will first."

"Then how do you pray?"

"I ask for strength to do what he wants me to do."

"I will pray to him as a child to his father who cares about him." However else could I pray, only knowing my own need, never knowing exactly what God intended for me?

W HAT GOD INTENDED FOR ANY OF US became no clearer to me in the days that followed. Was it from God that John and Farel got instructions to go again to Lausanne and interfere in Bern's business?

Bern had installed its own man as chief pastor there—after all Lausanne was in their jurisdiction—but it meant that Pierre Viret, who had evangelized alone and for so long in the Pays de Vaud, was put in a subordinate role. Bern's man was Pierre Caroli, a graduate of the University of Paris and once a doctor in the Sorbonne. He had been in Geneva a little while after Farel's ascendancy, then had obtained a pastorate in Neuchâtel.

"A suave, cunning man!" Farel said. "Utterly dissolute. I know him; his conversion was never genuine. John, have we labored to establish our pulpits in order to turn them over to hypocrites like Caroli?"

"Besides," said John, "It's no way to treat Viret."

The two of them went off to reverse Bern's egregious action.

I did not accompany them. I had had enough of the affairs of the Reformist movement for a while; I wanted to think about my own. Was my association with John coming to an end? I walked up and down the city's streets; walking had become my only diversion. One night I passed the windows of Hoch's bookbindery and saw by the light inside Hoch at work and two other figures sitting beside him, one of them Maigret. Our house across the street would be empty except for the cook, and looking for company, I presented myself at Hoch's door. "Come in, come in," said Maigret. "Let me present my good friend the Seigneur de Montchenu." He was a portly man dressed as fashionably as Maigret himself. I knew of his seigneury in Savoy.

"Hoch is binding copies of Calvin's articles for the council," Maigret said.

Hoch was trimming a single folio. "I've only had a few so far from the printer," he said. "Nobody seems to be in any hurry."

The seigneur picked up a folio delicately, scanned it but made no comment. Maigret said abruptly, "I've missed your friends lately."

I told him they were in Lausanne.

"They think it wise to be away at this juncture?" I didn't know what they thought, I said. "Do they think they can rely on that vote in the council?" he pursued. I pointed out that they had had a large majority. "But some of the councilmen are having second thoughts," he said.

"About what?"

"A number of things, such as having people inform on their neighbors. And the ministers not only barring people from the Supper but proclaiming why."

"What's the difference?" Hoch interjected. "The Supper is only fiddle faddle."

"But think of having your naughtiness announced far and wide. It might not bother you, Hoch, but suppose you were one of the lords of the council in the public eye." Hoch shrugged off the possibility.

Fiddle faddle! I could not let this pass. I told Hoch angrily that it was Christ's promise that we would be forgiven.

"I'm a skeptic in such matters," said the wicked man. "I'm a—I heard this somewhere. I'm a skeptical optimist," he said, assuming a look of profundity.

Maigret entered the discussion. "*That's* fiddle faddle. If you're skeptical, what are you optimistic about?"

"I think I'm all right the way I am."

Maigret turned away from the foolish man. "There are certain councilmen who are now saying they will run Calvin and Farel out of the city."

I demanded to know who they might be.

"Philippe for one."

"He didn't object very loudly at the meeting."

"He knew he didn't have the votes."

"I gather this Calvin has acquired some enemies," Montchenu said. "Being a French refugee in this uncivilized place, does he have enough influence—we can speak freely, can we not, none of us being a Genevan?—to overcome these odds?"

The question was addressed to the whole room, but I answered: "He believes God is on his side."

"Well, if he is, that sometimes suffices."

Hoch continued to trim folios while I studied Montchenu out of the corner of my eye. By entering into a casual conversation with the man I discovered that we had mutual friends in Paris and that he moved in court circles. "What brings you to Geneva, Seigneur?"

"I'm on a holiday, idling."

He appeared to have done a lot of looking about, however. "The walls at Cornavin Gate—fascinating design. How old would you say they are?" he asked Maigret, with whom he seemed well acquainted.

"Oh, quite recent. They put them up when they were revolting from Savoy."

Montchenu began chatting now about some of the citizens he had met during his holiday. "A number of splendid people . . . Councilman Sept. Do you know Michel Sept?"

"Hardly at all," I said. I remembered that Sept had been one of those who had supported the Articles.

The seigneur finally departed with the kind of wave of the hand affected by the nobility, as if leading a charge. I surmised that he was an agent of the king. François would have a continuing interest in affairs in Geneva, I suppose, it being so close to his borders. I had the anguish of my uncertainties to think about; my heart would have me back in Angoulême one minute and clinging to John's side the next. And since I did not encounter Montchenu again, I had forgotten all about him by the time John and Farel returned from Lausanne.

9

I WAS SHOCKED AT THE ACCOUNT they gave me of the Lausanne convocation, when at length they got around to telling me of it; for some days I heard nothing, except that Caroli had been bested, so occupied were they and indignant at how little had been done about the confession of faith. No more than a handful of the councilmen themselves had signed it, and only a few copies had been distributed around the city. John walked up the hill to the town hall with his purposeful gait to remind the syndics that the law was explicit; everybody must sign. The syndics were sympathetic, but they were mild men—like Michel Sept—who had risen to their position largely by virtue of their seniority on the Little Council. "They whined that they were doing their best," John said. "When I reminded them that it took only a stroke of the pen, they said, 'Oh, naw' "—he mimicked their flat, provincial speech—" 'it takes more than that.' "

I told him of the conversation I had had with Maigret.

"Maigret"—he searched his memory—"what a nightmare; there was a man at the inn with the absurd name of Maigret—Maigre? Oh ho, it was something like that—the Magnificent. And a bookbinder from Zurich."

"The bookbinder is now right across the street from us stitching together copies of the Articles."

"What is this Maigret's business, Louis?"

I told him that I could not figure it out, but that I thought he might know what he was talking about. "Oh, it makes no difference," John said shortly. "I know what is facing us." Since his return from Lausanne his self-confidence had become towering.

One evening at supper Farel remarked, "We should have anticipated Caroli's treachery, John," and I finally heard the story of the convocation.

I knew that Christians had contended with each other in the past, but I had long wondered if any age had seen such a falling out over Jesus Christ, even Catholics against Catholics and Reformists against Reformists with burnings and woundings, as though each side stood against a mortal enemy instead of their all being Christians alike. Why did it have to be? I guess there was weakness in me that prevented me from sharing in the passions of the times.

Presbyteries from Bern, Basel, Zurich, and Strasbourg had flocked to Lausanne, for the idea of the Geneva pastors questioning Bern's right to replace Pierre Viret with Pierre Caroli had agitated the whole community of Swiss and German Reform; even Luther's legate Melanchthon was there from Wittenberg.

Caroli, I gathered, had not waited for John and Farel to attack him but had immediately attacked them. He had got hold of a copy of John's confession of faith, and noting that there was no explicit statement in it of God, Christ, and the Holy Spirit being One, had accused them of antitrinitarianism. Farel was quite violent at the recollection. "Picture it, Louis, Caroli in his foppish dress pointing a finger dripping with rings at us and fairly screaming, 'How can such men command any standing with you?' He demanded that the convocation not even listen to us until we prostrated ourselves in contrition and agreed to include in our confes-

sion the ancient creeds affirming one Godhead. We refused.
He thought then he had our head on the block."

Why had they refused? It seemed like something they
could easily concede, since they believed in one Godhead, of
course.

"Because it was my desire, as I told them," John said "to
keep the confession simple so as not to confuse the unedu-
cated people of Geneva with a lot of theology. Simplicity was
what we wanted, the simplicity of the Word of God. And
furthermore, I said that we would under no circumstance
insert anything into the confession at the request of a person
so disreputable as Pierre Caroli. I'm afraid I didn't have my
temper in rein."

"You spoke with justifiable emphasis," Farel assured him.

"The fellow fell back on scorn and insinuation," John went
on. "He dragged up this book, this stinking carcass of antitrinitarianism. 'The book of this Spaniard Servetus,' he said,
'has apparently infected certain of our pastors. It also would
substitute simplicity for true orthodoxy.' Can you imagine
the wickedness of this fellow, Louis—inciting Melanchthon
and the others to doubt us—this murderer steeped in the
blood of saints!"

I wondered what saints John had in mind. Himself? John
had quoted forthwith from his *Institutes,* he said, which had
many references to the Trinity.

"He explained the Trinity with such logic," Farel put in, "as
had not even occurred to some of the others."

"I pointed out that Caroli, when he had a pastorate at
Neuchâtel, had advocated prayers for the dead, a practice
related to the Romanist fantasy of purgatorial suffering. He
taught that eternal punishment may be alleviated by prayers
for the departed, as if God's judgment, already made, can be
appealed. I said that anyone who held to such a notion could
not be thought of as having been truly converted to our faith.
Guillaume then delivered the coup de grace. He described
Caroli's loose living at Neuchâtel and his sordid conduct in
Paris. He was stricken. He did not lift his voice again."

"It was the end of the rascal," Farel said. "The convocation adjourned, Bern sent their man Caroli packing, ruined and disgraced, and Viret was installed as chief pastor in Lausanne as he deserved."

I commented that John's reputation was growing.

"Growing!" Farel exclaimed. " 'This is a lion you have in Geneva,' they said to me afterwards, as if I didn't know it." And he threw his arms around John, as he was accustomed to do in such moments of exulting, saying, "My son, my son, whom the Lord sent to me!"—so proud he was of the apprentice who had become his master.

BUT HOW UNAWARE THE TWO OF THEM WERE of the ominous color of the clouds that were gathering in Geneva. Whole neighborhoods, almost as one man, had refused to sign the confession; none of the German merchants in the rue des Allemandes would put his name to it. John and Farel blamed this on the Little Council's lack of will, and they continued to go almost daily to the town hall to exhort the syndics. On one occasion the syndics ordered the police to round up as many people as they could, march them to St-Pierre and order them to sign the confession or leave town. But so many refused that to have banished them all would have quite upset the city's business.

John and Guillaume and the blind pastor, Eli Corauld, of whom I saw little and didn't care if I never saw him, excommunicated a number of persons, but the Little Council made no move to punish them further. The three preached with increasing vigor and frequency. But I noticed however, that their congregations were almost exclusively lower class women, bedraggled creatures one can imagine burdened by drinking husbands.

John fared better with the children of the city. Gathering

groups of them around him in St-Pierre, he had them intone his catechism: "What is the chief felicity of man?"

They answered in their treble voices: "To know God and have his glory shine forth in us."

"Why dost thou call this man's chief felicity?"

"Because without it we are more miserable than the brute beasts." . . .

He instructed them in the singing of psalms. My acquaintance Maigret and I stood in the doorway of the church one morning watching him wave his arms, trumpeting the nasals through his long nose and urging, "Louder, louder, with joy. Sing in a way to move the hearts of men."

"One must admire him," Maigret said. "So dauntless. He must know how much he has made some people detest him."

"I doubt if he does," I said. "And if he did, it wouldn't make any difference to him."

"No, you're right," Maigret said, and added, "Your friend is the moral man, whose fate it is to be widely admired and just as widely hated." He looked pleased with himself for making an utterance which, I must say, was quite profound.

T HE STORM BROKE AT THE END OF THE YEAR when the *bise* chilled people to the bone as they hurried along the streets so wrapped up in coats and shawls that they were scarcely recognizable as human beings. On the second floor of the house in the rue des Chanoines we were eating supper, John as usual pecking without interest at his food, when Councilman Aubert, the apothecary, shaking wet snow from his hat, came tramping up the stairs and cried out, "You're going to be notified—I heard it and rushed over to tell you—the Little Council has voted that from henceforth you are not to deny the Lord's Supper to *anyone*."

Farel leaped to his feet. "We cannot accept this."

"The vote was overwhelming. Even men who have supported you voted for it," Aubert said.

"We will go there immediately." Farel flew about the room. He was looking for his cloak, his red beard shaking convulsively.

"No, no," Councilman Aubert begged. "You will only provoke them."

"*I* provoke them? It is Satan who provokes them. They are ordering us to betray God. We are told to participate with fornicators and drunkards and blasphemers and papists at the holy table."

"I know, Master Farel, but the city is in a regular stew. People come to my place for medicine for their indigestion. Don't stir them up anymore. Not at this point."

"At what point then? Do we wait a few weeks when the general assembly chooses new syndics? The present ones say they are for us, but they have done nothing."

"They will be replaced."

"Will the new ones be any better?"

"Worse," Aubert admitted. "Philippe will surely be one of them."

"Guillaume, we will wait," John said. "The next time for the Lord's Supper is Easter. We will be shown by then what God would have us do."

But when Aubert, shaking his head, left us, we sat with our backs to the stove in silence. Farel beat his hands together, looking suddenly miserable. John wrapped his arms around himself trying to keep warm. I sipped the last drops of my wine, and our wretched servant-girl picked up our plates, most of our supper still left uneaten, and shuffled off, complaining, "What's the use of cooking?"

"That's the way I feel," Farel moaned. "Serving up the Word of God day after day, you too, and poor Corauld, trying to nourish them, and they puke it up. Oh, John, my spirit flags—"

"Shall I tell you what I thought about last night when I couldn't get to sleep?" John interrupted.

He had risen from beside the stove. Sometimes during ordinary discourse he would begin talking in sermon sentences, his face, which except in moments of anger was strangely sad, lifted and transcendent. He spoke to the cold, silent room that way now. "I asked myself, lying there, why are men like beasts and women so full of lewdness and vanity? Why is the world so full of scorn? I will tell you, and you must believe it. It is God's way of leading us to grace."

I heard the distant shouting of a great many people and went to the window. John was not to be interrupted. "From bestiality and lewdness and scorn, we learn," he went on. "We learn that those in God's keeping will not perish. Remember how the apostles were so despised and how they too were enclosed in a little room in Jerusalem, trembling like lambs with the whole city against them? But the Holy Spirit appeared to them. Let the dogs bark; let the devil raise up troubles for us—we leave ourselves, all things, to Christ, whose spirit enflames us to defy and overcome the world and all its corruption."

The shouting outside had grown louder. I saw a crowd at the foot of the rue des Chanoines. "They are coming this way," I said.

"Let me tell you what else I thought about." He now spoke conversationally. "I thought, we must make the chapel of St-Pierre into a classroom and start training young men in theology. You only have to look at Bern to see the need for instruction in doctrine. I see Geneva becoming the seedbed of true Protestantism, students from here going out across all of Europe."

"John," I cried, "look—men and women. Some of them are masked."

Their shouts and catcalls now made quite a din and we heard one awful blasphemy: "The Word of God is bullshit!" And with that there came the explosions of arquebuses and shot rattled against our street door. What might not have transpired then if a half dozen police, wielding halberds had not come charging down the street! The mob scattered into alleyways.

"Wild beasts," Farel choked. "They help us thus to grace? I want to spit them out."

"You are saying that if men and women are contemptible they do not deserve our least effort for their sake."

"I am tempted to say so."

"Guillaume, we must not consider men of themselves."

"How then?"

"We must consider them, even the most wicked, as bearing the same divine image of God in Christ. It is the image that wipes out all transgressions. It is why we must love, not hate."

From most men it would have sounded hypocritical. As he spoke I was moved almost to tears. It was moments like this when I felt so devoted to him, to have him repel me another time by his air of infallibility. I thought of Maigret's remark about moral man.

The room had grown unbearably cold. The fire in the stove had turned to ashes, and I called to the servant-girl but got no answer (she was probably cowering in her room), so I took a basket and went downstairs for some coal. When I got back, John was writing and Farel was pawing through his unkempt beard. I rekindled the stove for them and went off to bed and lay there thinking of this philosophy of the divine image, realizing after a while that I could not really comprehend it. So everyone must be loved and forgiven because everyone bore a physical resemblance to Jesus Christ, that is, they had two arms and two legs and stood erect, not bent over like animals. Even when they acted like animals? I had a vision of Jesus, his hands pierced by nails, hanging on a cross, mutilated by humanity with the same image as his.

THE CITIZENS OF GENEVA ASSEMBLED regularly twice a year, otherwise only at times of crisis. In November they met to fix wine prices and to elect a presiding judge of the civil court; in February they met to elect the syndics. St-Pierre was crowded for the February meeting as it never was for John's preaching, with men standing shoulder to shoulder wrapped in their cloaks against the dankness inside the stone walls. It was Aubert's advice that John and Farel stay away; their presence might provoke trouble and anyhow, not being citizens, they could not vote, so I was delegated to go and observe the proceedings. I stationed myself nervously just inside the main door. Almost before I knew it, four men whom I knew to be among John's and Farel's most vociferous enemies, Jean Philippe and three of his cronies, a certain Ami Chapeaurouge, Claude Richardet and Jean Lullin, were elected by a vote, evidently foregone, because it was carried off with a waving of arms like tree branches in a storm and a thunderous stamping of cold feet.

Chapeaurouge pushed forward, chest out, and shouted: "We demand that the councils expel certain of their members. Why? Because they are guilty of treason," and he rattled off several names too fast for me to catch, except for one, Michel Sept, whom, I remembered, Seigneur de Montchenu had asked me about on the night I had met him at Hoch's. "We have found them out," Chapeaurouge continued to shout. "They would sell us out to the French."

"It's a lie," Sept cried from the middle of the crowd.

"Oh, it's a lie, is it? Do you deny meeting with a Seigneur de Montchenu, you and these other councilmen? Do you deny Montchenu has been consorting slyly with the Frenchmen in our city?"

"What Frenchmen?"

"This fellow Maigret. What does *he* do, what's he up to?"

I did not wait for him to name me. I heard Sept screaming, "That's no proof of anything," as I fled in panic. A few chance encounters with Maigret, one chance meeting with Montchenu—and everything observed! What had I got myself into? I arrived out of breath at our house. "Those who supported you have been overthrown," I cried. "Some of them may even go to jail." My friends sat there like two blocks of wood. I told them of Chapeaurouge's charges.

"Are we too to be accused of treason?" Farel asked. "I've never laid eyes on this Montchenu."

"I haven't either," said John. "And surely these jackasses know that the French government would make bonfires of us if they could get their hands on us."

"I don't care. No Frenchman is now safe in Geneva, not even I."

"God will protect us," John said. "There is nothing to fear, Louis."

I protested that I was not afraid for myself, ashamed and angry to have him know that I was. After a while, by leaning out the window, we could see the crowd beginning to emerge from St-Pierre. Some of them passed our house on their way back to their shops. They glanced up at our windows but made no comments that we could hear, from which I derived no encouragement, feeling rather that there was something ominous about their attitude.

But nothing transpired the rest of the day—no arrival of any police—while John wrote, read passages from the Bible, and exhibited a calm that was either bravado or utter trust in the Lord.

The next morning he went as usual to preach at the cathedral, and I followed him up the hill, telling myself I would stand outside and if the police appeared during the service, slip inside and give him warning. A courageous plan. I was huddled against a wall feeding crumbs to the sparrows and thinking more ardently than ever of Angoulême when Maigret, the last man I wanted to see, appeared beside me. I gave him a curt greeting and started to move away.

"Don't run off," he said. "I'm all right; you're all right. I went to the Little Council after the assembly." He looked amused and self-important. "I enjoy considerable prestige among certain older councilmen who know of the part I played some years ago in the overthrow of Savoy, it being I who urged François to make the feint into Savoy which caused the duke to pull back from Geneva, thus saving the city. I told the council how reckless Chapeaurouge was with his charges. The reason Montchenu was here was because François is giving some thought to favoring Geneva with his protection, and the seigneur was simply sounding out a few leading citizens like Sept on how they felt about it."

But even listening to Montchenu might be seen as treasonable.

"Treasonable? Oh, pshaw. A protectorate would be much to the city's advantage, surrounded as it is by a countryside controlled by Bern. Why, Bern, you might say, already has Geneva halfway down its gullet. Does Geneva want to be swallowed up whole by the German-speaking pigs of Bern? God forbid. They all speak civilized French like we do in the towns around us, and a joining of all under France's protection would have heaven's benediction, I am sure."

Well, I had never dabbled in politics, I told him.

"It's true that Montchenu inspected the city's fortifications, as Chapeaurouge told the council, but he was looking to see how they would stand up against the Bernese, if it came to that, not the French. Actually Sept and others told Montchenu nothing to encourage him, quite the contrary. Oh, mercy me, everyone is so stuffed full of the spirit of independence nowadays. Anyhow, that was the end of it."

I told him I must go and hurried away, looking furtively to right and left.

I HAD ONLY TO GO DOWN to the wineshop in the lower city, about as far as I cared to venture nowadays, to hear people on the street discussing John's Articles, and I could feel the impending crisis, which indeed arrived, precipitated by Eli Corauld. I was inclined to avoid the man if I could; blind people made me feel uneasy, and I was repelled by his

fanaticism. He had been a monk in France who had been
infected by Reform and had followed Farel to Geneva, where
he had been assigned to preach at the little Church of the
Madeleine at the foot of Cathedral Hill. There he had been
delivering opinions on any matters that came into his head
when the Little Council issued an order forbidding ministers
to preach on political matters—a drastic order, indeed, considering how often politics intrude on religion and vice versa.
John read the order aloud to Farel and Corauld, who stood
there clutching his long blindman's staff. John, up to that
day, had maintained an air of serenity—an attitude that must
be characteristic of martyrs, I thought; my friends were
surely headed for martyrdom. But now he waved his arms
and shouted, "We will preach as we are directed by God not
men."

There was a second order. He and Farel bent their heads
over it while John read it aloud for Corauld's benefit. "This
was inspired by Bern; I know it." They were to use only
unleavened bread at the Lord's Supper; brides were to be
allowed to dress themselves in a particular fashion if they
liked; the ministers must conduct special observances of
Christmas, Easter, Ascension, and Pentecost. Roman practices, to be sure, I thought, but traditional things that would
not corrupt anyone and brought joy to many. But to these
Reformists unleavened bread was an irrelevancy, a bridal
dress a frippery, and celebration of the feast days pretentious,
having no more to do with the true worship of God than the
painted images they had stripped from the Catholic churches.
True worship was preaching and praying and singing the
psalms.

"We are not inclining our necks to Bern." John crumpled
the paper and threw it across the room.

Corauld left. I heard him descending the stairs, threelegged
on his staff, and heard the door slam behind him. I heard his
voice in the street and looked out the window. I suppose he
thought the double affliction of being blind and old made
him immune to any further assaults in this world. His staff

leading the way, he shuffled along shouting: "Does your Little Council think heaven is a realm of frogs that croak at their direction? Aah, aah, your magistrates melt like wax in Bern's breath." His staff went *tap, tap.* "Your syndics are a quartet of drunkards." He tilted his bald head back in the way of the blind, as though listening. We were about to go down and intercept him when some women gathered around him and led him off.

The crisis still might have been avoided by less obstinate men. The action the council took in the case of Corauld was, under the circumstances, quite reasonable. They ordered only that he was not to preach again. But the next day he groped his way into the Church of the Madeleine, and while the police waited at the door, called upon heaven to punish those who would try to censor the Word of God. They let him finish, then seized him and dragged him away. I could pity him; I could picture his feeble hands feeling up and down bars and stone that informed him of the predicament he was in.

On the evening of that same day I waited alone in our house. John and Farel were at the town hall. I thought of being in Angoulême when I might be returning home after vespers to have supper with my father who would show me his newest books. We would fondle them together. In the morning I would go to the cathedral to help in the services of Palm Sunday. And I was still thinking of all this when John and Farel returned.

"They spoke words with no meaning," John said to me. "They said nothing that affects us."

"They demanded that we follow Bern's instructions," Farel said, as though appealing to my judgment. "They told us again that we were to admit everyone to the celebration of the Lord's Supper. We demanded that they release Corauld, and they said they would only if we dismissed him. John said to them, 'Before God we will do none of these things.' They said, 'Then before God we forbid you to preach,' and John said to them, 'I do not know the God you call on.'"

"Was that where it was left?"

"That is where their insane talking ended," John said.

"Corauld is left in prison. And you will follow him there through your stubbornness. What are Bern's instructions that you cannot swallow them?"

John looked surprised but not angry. He said to Farel, "I have sometimes wondered if we have gained anything in opposing these petty things thrust at us by Bern. We have lost everything if our little church in Geneva is dispersed. Certainly these things from Bern do no harm to our souls, Guillaume. Could we not swallow a little unleavened bread?"

Farel was silent. John's demeanor abruptly changed again. "But if we allow the state to impose its authority on our church," he declared, "that is the crux; we surrender the dominion of Christ."

I prayed that night to a number of my favorite saints. The week passed with John and Farel making visits to Corauld's cell, but with no untoward incident. It was Easter morning. Farel went off as usual to the Church of St-Gervais on the other side of the Rhone. John went to the cathedral, where I followed him. Would he be immediately seized and dragged from the pulpit? There were no signs of any police, and John, wearing his cloak against the cold that the walls could not shut out, looked down calmly on a large congregation, many of whom were drawn more by curiosity, I was sure, than their faith. He preached—there was no interruption—on a Christ who was human and suffered as any man would suffer the agony of torture and death. "If he had not, what a small thing it would have been for him to have gone to the cross with nothing to fear as if in a sport. This is proof of his boundless love for us, that he did not shun death no matter how much he dreaded it. It is he who died as men die in mortal anguish, who has risen this Easter day to appear before God as our mediator."

The time had come for the eucharist. But the communion table was bare, no cup of wine appeared, no tray of bread, and John suddenly trumpeted: "My brethren, the devil has seized the councils. Evil has infested the city. In this strife, with all this mockery, it would be a blasphemy for us to offer ourselves to our Savior to partake of his body and blood that are the symbols of the sacrifice he made for us. Therefore, brethren, there will be no holy table on this Easter morning." He made a wave of dismissal, and drawing up the skirts of his coat climbed down the steps of the pulpit and walked past the silent people, those few who still believed in him and those who had come only to take his measure.

The heralds proclaimed another meeting of the assembly the very next day. I stood behind John and Farel, who were staring out the window. The citizens were trooping up the hill again. We said little or nothing to each other, not daring to speculate as to the purpose of the assembly. Mid-morning. Aubert arrived out of breath. "They voted to expel you for disturbing the peace of the city."

Expel them! They would go forthwith before the Little Council.

"It won't do any good," Aubert moaned.

Farel beat his breast in rage. Were they not trying to maintain the kind of peace that God would have in the city? Was that a crime against these people to be thrown out for it? The Little Council must not bow to the rabble.

"They will not listen to you."

"We will go," John said. "God will make them listen to us."

In less than an hour he was back, alone. Farel had gone to his own apartment. John walked confusedly about picking up and laying down books and papers. "No, the dogs would not listen," he said suddenly. "You will not believe it. They said they would deal with us mercifully, not put us in prison. But we must be out of the city by sundown."

I saw his stricken countenance. I knew what he must be thinking, to be driven out like some miserable beggar, denied any hearing before the assembly, any kind of trial, denied a martyrdom. I could think of nothing to say, and when he showed some sign of pulling himself together and began gathering up his papers a little more methodically, I made an effort to gather up my own small possessions. We were thus occupied, in silence, when several bailiffs arrived and after presenting a paper of some sort, started stripping our rooms of the furniture the city had provided. Our servant-girl, standing in a corner leaning on a broom, looked in pityingly. I could have beaten her for her expression.

"As I told Guillaume," John said, "if we were serving men we are badly repaid, but we are serving a Master who will reward us." He was a little more composed.

I asked what was going to happen to Corauld. "He has been released. Friends will take him to Lausanne. Like Paul we will shake off the dust of our feet against them. Farel will go to Neuchâtel. You and I will go at last to Strasbourg."

Oh, yes, so I would go trailing along like a dog at his heels. The moment had come for me. "I am going to Angoulême," I said.

He straightened up from a pile of books. "You are going to desert me? Well, I expected it."

His words were a blow, and I turned on him in a fury. "You expected it?"

"Because you have never freed yourself of Rome, from its tyranny."

"I should subject myself to John Calvin's tyranny."

We were shouting at each other while the bailiffs continued to remove the furniture.

"The Word of God is not tyranny; it is freedom."

"Who says it is the Word of God? You do. Does that make me free?"

"Read the Bible, you ignorant papist."

"How can you think you alone have understanding, or any more of it than any others? I am ignorant. You are puffed up, and God is reproving you this very minute—" But I could go no further; I was close to tears. I picked up my saddlebags, now packed, and rushed down the stairs. When he yelled after me, "God keep you, Louis," I did not answer him.

The April rains had made a quagmire of the road that followed the Rhone, my way home. What must the passes of the Juras be, which he must face going north! God help *you*, John Calvin.

PART THREE

Jeremiah heard the Lord say,
"Stand in the ways,
and see,
and ask for the old paths,
where the good way is,
and walk therein."

May God uphold me,
I am become the leader
of the Reformation.

10

I DID NOT GO TO STRASBOURG, as I had told Louis I would. I went to Basel. But did it matter where I went? Wherever I went, I would be alone, in loneliness that was like a black tide, engulfing me as I walked past the lighted windows of houses at nightfall, or contemplated the clouds embracing the April moon, even as I smelled the sweetness of springtime or listened to the sociable voices of the family that had taken me in. Defeat has no company.

I relived those last days in Geneva. And our flight. And a day of terror when Guillaume and I were swept off our horses trying to ford a stream—saved by men whom God had posted on the opposite shore, who made a chain of themselves and pulled us out. We made our way first to Bern, where we found no love, but only concern that the confusion our departure had caused in Geneva might encourage the duke of Savoy to return. We did not mention the blame Bern must bear for this. We went before the Bern ministers, deeming it expedient to lay our case before them that it might be understood by the whole Reformist community, comporting ourselves with more humility than we actually felt, and even admitting that we had been stubborn and possibly imprudent in trying to preserve the sacredness and independence of our

church. The ministers decided to our satisfaction that we
were, after all holy and innocent men, and they dispatched a
herald to inform Geneva that it was their desire we be taken
back. We would have gone, however fearfully, but the
Geneva council, aware of the herald's mission, would not let
him inside the gate.

Farel had gone to Neuchâtel to take a church. Why had I
come here to Basel? To rejoin Nicholas Cop? I don't know. I
found that Nicholas had returned to Paris with François's
forgiveness, extracted by Dr. Cop, no doubt, while he was
tending one of the king's notorious diseases. What little
money I had from selling my books in Bern was all but gone
when I threw myself on Simon Grynaeus, in whose house I
now languished. Poor Grynaeus could not be otherwise but
charitable towards a fellow pastor bereft of all his old companions. It was true; they were all gone—even Louis, leaving
me so sorely wounded, he whom I had loved so.

Would blows never let up? I met a man from the Piedmonts who told me Olivétan had died. However, the man did
not know any of the circumstances. Dead in the mountains
among the people who were so pure and white, like the
edelweiss, you said, dear Olivétan. Oh, lucky man you are,
but I am left to mourn. Then news came that old blind
Corauld had died in Lausanne, that it was suspected he had
been poisoned. O God, I prayed, is it your desire that I be
deprived forever of all those who were ever close to me?

I would have shaken myself loose from Basel; I would have
gone on to Strasbourg, but that city was no longer the pleasing prospect it once had seemed. "You must come to us
immediately," Bucer was pleading. "Our French refugees are
without a church. They don't understand our German." I was
repelled as of old, more than ever, by the thought of public
life, of preaching and pastoring, shrinking from everything,
imprisoned in despair.

One day there arrived at Grynaeus's house that humble
housekeeper of the du Tillets' library, Brother Titus, bringing me a packet from Louis. I sat him down and rushed off to
my little room to discover a sack of coins and a letter. Joy, oh

joy! Louis would be begging my forgiveness, telling me he wanted to come back to me. But wait—"You must come to Angoulême," I read. He would receive me with open arms. He himself had returned to his canonry at the cathedral. "You must also return to our mother church. Can you really think that you have a true vocation in God in what you have been doing? You were called to it by men who have no authority from God." Could I believe what I was reading? "What right did they have to say that the church where you all learned your Christianity is not God's true church? My advice to you now is to come to Angoulême, and not to publish anything for a while but just to sit and think about a lot of things you have not thought of yet."

I hurled the money across the room. When I had calmed myself so that I could hold a pen, I wrote: "Olivétan and Corauld are both before God now to justify me to him. When you and I come to that same place, then we will find out which of us was separated from him. And all those like yourself who think your foolish words condemn me—it is you who will be sentenced. God's true agents will testify as to who has been schismatic."

I crawled around the room gathering up the coins scattered about and thrust them and the note at Brother Titus.

Several weeks went by when my rage subsided, leaving me as usual ashamed of myself. I forgave Louis. If I could only see him again, and I was thinking how I would take his hand and tell him I forgave him when another letter arrived from Angoulême, this one brought by a merchant on his way to Zurich. It was just one sentence: "You had better not write me again unless you can use modesty and temperance." Louis, who had been so devoted to me, who had been so dear to me! One sentence, a sword plunged into my heart. There was no comfort in the knowledge that it was Louis, not I, who had been at fault.

There is never any comfort in simply knowing that one has been right and that one has been dealt an injustice. I heard reports that the church in Geneva had virtually fallen apart after our expulsion. I got no satisfaction from it. Platter, who

had printed my *Institutes,* and who had recently been to
Geneva brought me one such report.

"They found some pastors. I don't know where they got
them; Bern may have supplied them. But they do little more
than keep the churches open. They'll admit anyone at all to
the eucharist. They're tolerated because they keep out of the
city's business. The taverns are wild, open all night. The
council didn't bother to rescind any laws, people just don't
pay any attention to them. The whores are back on the rue
des Belles Femmes. As for your leading citizens—ho, they
set an example of scandalous living. The outstanding man in
town is your old enemy Jean Philippe. After his term as a
syndic expired he was elected captain general of the militia."

I was indifferent; it was as though I did not hear him,
drowning as I was in the black tide.

"God, who found Jonah, will know how to find his rebellious servant Calvin. . . ." It was a letter from Martin Bucer,
impatient at my continued refusal to join him in Strasbourg. I
thought of Farel exhorting me the same way that night at the
inn. I heard Louis questioning the authenticity of Farel's admonishment. How did I know Bucer spoke for God? But I
knew he did. He was so well known for his piety, and for his
great *Evangelienkommentar* on the divine hand at work. If I
could only withdraw from men. But Bucer said I could not.
Oh, duty, duty; the little congregation of French in Strasbourg needed me. I thought of Christ's perfect example and
how the strength of God's summons is in the greatness of the
pain it promises.

So I went, carrying my trembling spirit like a poor lamb in
my arms.

THEY PAID ME A FLORIN A WEEK. My fellow exiles, who
met in a church once occupied by Franciscan monks, were
almost as impoverished as I. At Bucer's suggestion I rented a

house, which, while exuding rotten timbers and cold stones, nevertheless had a large number of rooms that I could let to students attending Johann Sturm's nearby academy. I hired a cook-housekeeper who was so notorious for her slovenly habits that I was able to get her cheaply. "Madame Sow" I called her, although not to her stupid face. Five students came to me to shiver in their rooms and suffer near starvation in this miserable household while I recalled for them what I had endured in the refectory at the College de Montaigu in order to get an education. They must accept all things with a glad heart, I told them, yet my own heart was filled with strife. Yes, strife with God. Trying to obey Christ's command to love, I stood revealed in hypocrisy. The most trivial acts of people roused my anger. I heard myself shouting at one of my boarders, "Where else can you live so cheaply? Besides Castellio, you are a lazy pig." To Sebastian Castellio everything—Greek, Latin, philosophy, mathematics—came easily; but his marks were a disgrace. He departed after a few weeks.

By concentrating on the things of God I thought I might turn God's attention from my lurchings. I threw myself into my pastorate. After revising the German Reformist service to suit me I translated its Latin into French for my flock. They loved to sing, and so that music and orison might be properly joined I compiled a number of psalms for chanting (I liked dabbling with verse), set them to music, and led my congregation in making joyful noises, as I had led the children of Geneva. I delivered exegeses on the books of the New Testament and taught classes in theology at Johann Sturm's, and edited sermons and lectures into commentaries that I got published, thus earning a little extra income.

I could almost forget myself in evangelizing. I had the power to convert men, and in this cosmopolitan and commercial city, where people were always arriving from distant cities and strange influences, I brought a number to the true faith. I turned one man from Liége away from the evil beliefs of the Anabaptists and had the satisfaction of seeing him and his family join our little church before he died of the plague.

I worked long nights on the second edition of my *Institutes*. I dreaded giving myself any respite when I would have to see myself for what I was, so unstable, so racked by perversity. God continued to harass me, dealing me one blow without warning. I was summoned by Bucer one morning to a meeting of the ministers, where I was informed that Pierre Caroli was begging to be taken back into our church. He had actually returned to the papist church after his expulsion at Lausanne, but now he was here in Strasbourg pleading for forgiveness, carrying a letter of endorsement from Simon Grynaeus no less. What did I think? Think? I could only pour out my anger at the ministers, these geese, who were not able to discern hypocrisy wiggling through the grass. I stormed out of the meeting.

Several days went by when I heard nothing more of the business until one night, after midnight, when I had gone to bed, I was aroused by Bucer's servant. He carried a document which Bucer in a note requested me to sign, as had all the other ministers. What a scurrilous nighttime conference must have occurred. They had also obtained (this I could hardly believe) the signature of Guillaume Farel in Neuchâtel. The statement said they were ready to accept Caroli's confession, which included the sentence (and at this I was even more incredulous): "I leave to God's judgment the offences by which I was forced to desert the Protestant cause."

Throwing a cloak over my night clothes I rushed out of my house and through the dark streets to Bucer's house. I threw the paper on the floor, demanding: "Do you think I am going to sign this mockery?" And I went on shouting in French while Bucer stared at me, waving his arms and muttering in his German, which I neither understood nor wanted to. I got enough control of myself to say everything all over again in Latin. Why did they not let me see this before they all signed it? I would die before I put my name to it, I told him. I strode out of his house, and becoming aware of Bucer following me, ran to my house and slammed and locked my door. Still trembling, I wrote a letter to Farel: "If I had had you face to face, I would have turned all my fury on you." I was seized then by a paroxysm of weeping. I lighted a candle to show me the way to my bed in this miserable house that resounded with the grunts of Madame Sow and the snores of Johann Sturm's students, sighing as I put the candle down, and sat rocking on my bed, moaning "Oh, the wild beast in me!"

WHEN HIERO ASKED, "What is 'God'?" Simonides said, "Give me a day to think about it." Then he asked for another day, and still another day, and doubled the days, and said at last: "The longer I ponder it the more obscure it seems." The philosopher does not know. He is like a traveler at night who sees far and wide in a lightning flash, but then is plunged into darkness again. God has no visible form; in the valley of Horeb only a voice was heard. But I know his likeness; it is in man, not in man's body. The body does not care whether man surveys the heavens or counts the stars or measures the space that lies between them. The body does not care whether man joins past to future, or knows right from wrong. These are skills of the soul. God's likeness is in man's soul.

What a comic character I am, sniveling at my lot and trying to comprehend his actions. It is to try to comprehend nature itself: heaven and earth created out of nothing, *creatio ex nihilo,* as all motion of days and nights and months and years are adjusted to the miracle of divine power, all things great and small. Infants nursing at their mothers' breasts have tongues to preach God's glory. There is no need of orators. We submit our judgment to his glory as a thing beyond guesswork, not as a thing of miserable man's superstition but of the felt power that lives and breathes in the mystery.

When I try to say all, I have yet said little. I can think beyond what I can utter, but still my mind is overwhelmed.

I WOULD SIGN THE STATEMENT because even men like that rascal Caroli should be forgiven, but only on condition that Bucer remove Caroli's impudent statement blaming Farel and me for his treason. Bucer agreed, and I signed.

But I was left in despondency at the way men in whom I had confidence had disregarded me, feeling never more estranged from my friends than now. I sat brooding in my room, notes on God's glory and mystery scattered around me, the grey afternoon darkeningly at my window, thinking of our Savior and his words, "This is my body, take, eat . . ." and thinking how the Holy Supper is corrupted by both the papists and Martin Luther, who talks of a corporeal presence that can be touched, chewed, and swallowed—how monstrous!—trying by such wizardry to unwrap a mystery wrapped in mystery. God is here and yet he is not here. We only know that we are given nourishment for our faith and that the bread and wine cannot be taken in by unbelievers any more than rain can be taken into a rock because the hardness of wickedness leaves no opening for God's grace. I was thinking of this in the gloom of this late afternoon when I heard a knocking, knocking, knocking at the door. I went downstairs and pushed past Madame Sow who was yelling, "Quit it. I hear you," and opened the door. There stood my beloved brother, Antoine, and my halfsister, Marie, who threw her arms around me so that I was engulfed by her dark hair, all mussed up from her throwing back her hood. We could say nothing to each other, only laugh and laugh. I had not seen Antoine since the night we parted at the river, and Marie, not since my father's funeral—a child then, now a woman who came just up to my nose.

We conversed in my room out of earshot of Madame Sow.
Our brother Charles had died. I was astonished that this news
affected me nowhere near the way the deaths of Olivétan and
Corauld had. But we had never been close. There had been
an intemperance about him that had frightened me, for I saw
in him the passion I must try to suppress in myself. Oh, the
dark blood ran through all us Cauvins, excepting gentle Antoine, our mother's child. Charles had died excommunicate,
like our father, in violent disagreement with the canons of
the cathedral. There had been a settlement of the Cauvin
estate, Marie's mother had married again, and Antoine had
brought with him the small part of the settlement belonging
to us. He and Marie had come to be with me. He would set
himself up as a printer, having learned the business in
Paris—all this came tumbling out—and she would take over
the running of the house. She assured me of it.

I COULD NOT SAY, after several weeks of Marie's "running"
things, that my domestic affairs were any better organized
than before. But did it matter? I heard sounds of joy in my
world. She was like a bird that sits on a branch and sings and
sings without reason. My glum boarders (down to four after
Castellio's departure) greased their hair and danced around
after my sister, my little bird. Madame Sow, when she realized that her careless ways were not imperilled, was heard
to laugh, and I preached with new strength and conducted
the singing of the Psalms most vigorously. Marie's cheerful-
ness was not all of her. Such kindliness came with it. When
my stomach kept me awake all night and unable to get out of
bed in the morning, and I had propped myself up in order to
do some writing, she would come into my room as the sun
came in the window, bringing me a pot of hot water and
kissing me on the forehead.

But merciful heaven, what thoughts began to come to me! Was not loneliness easier to bear than these images? I had written in the *Institutes* that the only true wisdom we possess is knowing God, and ourselves, and to know ourselves means to make a terrible descent into an abyss. What did I find at the bottom of this pit? Wilfulness, stubbornness, intolerance, violence, and now, fantasies of pleasure made more monstrous by the circumstances. And these images—as much as my stomach—left me sleepless.

I was desperate. I took recourse, in order to rout passion, in writing an analysis of my condition.

"By our nature and lusts aroused in us," I wrote, "we are doubly subject to women's society. The condition is there in the handful of Adam's dust, and it is only needful to have our eyes opened to have the mischief begin." But God forbids fornication. A few men free themselves from the dilemma by using a power that God gives them: they castrate themselves that they may devote themselves wholly to his work. But the rest of us, including myself, must struggle with our passions. I continued, calmly, on my analysis: "Some men say in their struggles: 'With God's help I can do anything.' Yes, but chastity in celibacy is also a special grace the Lord bestows on only a few. In most of us lies the vice of incontinence, and let no one think while his heart is burning with lust (as I had written elsewhere, citing the admonishment of Jesus), that so long as he does not touch a woman he is innocent.

"One must conclude that in all this God has a purpose, and that men go against him if they do not accommodate themselves to what he has given them or denied them. He cursed men with lust. Why? So that they would not lead a solitary life, which is a condition against his intention. He forbade man to fornicate so that, in a fellowship sanctified by Heaven, man would take a wife. Therefore," I wrote in triumph, "when a man's power to tame his passion fails him, let him recognize forthwith what the Lord requires of him. And for maidens and widows anxious about remaining holy," I added, "the same rule applies. Paul has said it, 'Better to marry than to burn.'"

I thereupon regained some equanimity. I determined to get married immediately.

But I had no idea where to find a suitable wife. I could think of no one in my congregation, and Madame Sow was beyond consideration. I would appeal to certain of my friends for help. Having arrived at this decision I began to feel quite sprightly, so much so I composed some verse. Doggerel, it might better be described, making an odd item lying among my notes for sermons.

I am not one of those lovers who are so insane
As to be smitten by a female figure, thinking to gain
Happiness from this.
There are more enduring elements to bliss.
Oh foolish men who are willing to embrace
Besides the lady the vice behind a pretty face!
The only graces to my taste—
Is she modest, is she chaste?
Will she think about my health?
A dowry?—'T would not be amiss, a little wealth—
All this I think about, not how prettily she is dressed.
Know you, dear friend, of such a one with whom I might be
blest?"

I sent this appeal to Farel—in more becomingly sober prose. I also solicited the help of Master Bucer, who was married to an ex-nun by whom he had sired thirteen children.

Farel responded promptly. There was a Madame Goullet who was a member of his congregation, whom he described as a person of great enthusiasm for the Reformist cause. She was in her forties, Farel thought, which he hoped would not be a drawback.

"She sounds worthy enough," Antoine said, "but one does wonder why she has been overlooked for so long." It did raise a question.

Bucer produced a Fraulein Schwarz, a lady from a well known family of bankers. I wondered about this. Would not her wealth, so far above mine, make her feel superior to me?

"Herr Schwarz, her brother, holds you in the highest esteem," Bucer said. "So much so that he would attend your church instead of mine—he was quite frank about it—but for the fact that he speaks no French. Neither, I have to confess, does his sister."

I inquired whether he thought she would apply herself to learning French, and he said he would ask her. He reported back that Fraulein Schwarz wanted a little time to think about this. "In that event I will erase Fraulein Schwarz from any further consideration," I told Antoine, who was interesting himself greatly in the enterprise, as was my little chicken, Marie.

We had heard from the pastor of a church in the country—my quest had become widely known—of a lady of so generous a nature that the search could end forthwith. I sent Antoine off to make her acquaintance, and if the lady came up to Pastor Ziegler's description, bring matters to a conclusion. I was growing impatient.

He rode off on a mule into the hills, and returned several days later to announce that we had been grievously deceived. "She is generous all right," he said. "So generous—I began to suspect and made a few inquiries—that she allowed Pastor Ziegler, who is himself married, to get her with child. He wants very much to be rid of her." Antoine's indignation matched mine. "Oh, John," he urged, "think again of Fraulein Schwarz. Doesn't her brother call here day after day? He has sent us a cask of wine. He has read your *Institutes*—he stumbles through Latin—and he says he is learning French."

"But I have no thought of marrying Herr Schwarz."

"But he says his sister is also beginning to say a few words in French."

"Does he say that?"

"I understood him to say so. John, think of the dowry she would bring with her. You have seen the Schwarzes' house, the wide staircases, the paintings, the tapestries on every wall."

I had thought of all that too much, I told myself morosely. "Lord," I begged, "help me escape from the Schwarzes."

My sprightliness had left me. I had never imagined that so

many problems would lie across the path of such a simple matter, and I was wondering where to turn next when Marie said to me "There is one right under your nose, Brother John. She comes to your church. She is the gentlest person I have ever met. She is a widow; her husband was an Anabaptist you converted when they came here from Liége."

"Johann Stordeur. He died of the plague."

"Yes. She still mourns him, but she is sensible about it and struggles along as best she can with two little children. She is young, as delicate and pretty as you are old and skinny." She patted my cheek.

How old?

"Thirty-one."

"I am also thirty-one."

She laughed. "But you have grown old looking for a wife. Speak to her, John. Before she was married she was Idelette de Bure. I must go to the door, John, I see him in the street; it's Herr Schwarz again."

"Tell him I am working on my sermon."

That Sunday morning, I hurried out the door behind the pulpit in order to greet Johann Stordeur's widow as she came out of the church. From my brief examination I saw that everything about her was probably as Marie had said, which I might have recalled. It was Marie's undertaking to have her to our house several times for supper, and I was impressed by her graciousness in overlooking our miserable surroundings. She helped Madame Sow in clearing the table and exhibited the modesty and humility one admires in a woman. It was clear that she cherished the memory of her husband, but it was also clear that this pretty little creature could become attached to me. After a month of such association, which included some walks together, I had to own to a thrill of emotion when she first addressed me as "John."

But actually faced by the prospect of wedlock, I pulled back. I reviewed the temptations that were responsible for pushing me this far. Was I going to admit that I lacked the strength to serve God worthily and virtuously without a wife

for a crutch? I had managed to live without indulgences—
except for a moderate amount of wine—since those days of
debauchery connected with Princess Marguerite's soirées. I
also thought of acquiring two children still too young to be
boarded at school, the boy placid enough, but his older sister
given to spells of wilful behavior. Then I reflected on those
nights of anguish and the passion that assails a man when he is
not expecting it, the insidious smell of a woman's hair, and
loneliness, and I had to confess that I was no better than any
other man in this respect. I summoned my dear friend Farel
to ride down from Neuchâtel and marry us.

Self-committed? No, I was freed, freed and out of the
abyss, and so joyous that God must have felt it was meet to
caution me even while the flowers that Marie had picked—
which I permitted Idelette to wear at our wedding—were still
fresh. I was seized by a fit of coughing in the middle of a
sermon, and staggered home, to find that Idelette had already
taken to our bed, having been seized by the same catarrh and
fever I had. I crawled in miserably beside her, and there we
lay for several days. When I was a little improved I had Marie
bring me my writing materials.

"What are you writing?" Idelette asked weakly.

"A letter to Farel," I said. "I owe him our thanks for per-
forming our marriage ceremony." I had much to say to my
friend about my revived spirits and the perfect union I had
made. "We lie side by side, coughing and groaning on our
sick bed. Our illness, I know, was ordered so that our wedlock might not be over joyous and exceed all bounds."

But nothing could suppress the joy I felt at being one, once
more, with God.

W HAT DOES IT MEAN TO BE RECONCILED? It is to be
serene, to be confident again, to be able to dismiss all things
that distract one from God's work.

I now was able to dismiss the memory of Geneva. It would remain forgotten, not ever to be recalled—no, not even by this man appearing at my door this morning. What did he want? I had nothing to do with him, this man absurdly called Maigret the Magnificent, wearing a velvet cape and plumed hat, a spectre belonging to things I had dismissed. Why was he standing there? To be sure, his voice was not the drunken voice of the man in the inn that dreadful night, but was very earnest: "Have you had the latest news from Geneva, Master Calvin?" I had to invite him in. "If I may—" and he deposited his hat on a pile of books in one corner, the only space available for such a headpiece. "Your foes have been vanquished. As a matter of fact, Jean Philippe has been decapitated."

He took a chair, and observed: "The consequences of arrogance. I will omit much of the background, but I must inform you of the part concerning the treaty, since that was what brought about Philippe's end." He lavished some care on a long grey moustache. He was not to be hurried.

"First, the treaty," he said. "Some years ago in gratitude for help in overthrowing the duke of Savoy, Geneva granted Bern certain rather unusual rights in the duke's old holdings on Geneva's outskirts. To wit, Bern could impress the males in these holdings into its army, collect any fines that Geneva might impose, mind you, and pardon persons who had been sentenced in Geneva's courts. The Little Council decided one day that its predecessors had been remarkably stupid to sign such an agreement and sent some emissaries to Bern to renegotiate it."

What did I care about any of this? So my enemy Philippe was dead; my mind that morning was on matters of more importance. Bucer had asked me to go with him to a colloquy called by Emperor Charles. Ever beset by both Suleiman the Turk and François, Charles was still trying to make peace with his Protestant princes and screw his fractured Germany together again. Although I expected little to come of it— nothing had come of other recent colloquies—some Roman and Lutheran theologians worthy of my time would be on hand, and I was looking forward to it. I was thinking of that, not of the inconsequential demise of Philippe. But my visitor's voice was insistent.

"They sent Ami Chapeaurouge and Jean Lullin—you will recall them, they along with Philippe and Claude Richardet were the syndics when you and Farel were expelled. Ah, that tragic occasion." His expression was lugubrious. "They returned, announcing they had obtained a new and satisfactory agreement. But they were hardly back when a Bern bailiff rode into the holdings and impressed three youths into the Bernese army. Look here, what's this? And the Little Council ordered Chapeaurouge and Lullin, rather belatedly, to let them have a look at the treaty. The two fine emissaries did not have a copy, besides, it was written in German, they said. Could they read German? Well, no, they couldn't. Good heaven, what jackasses! And when the council did obtain a copy from Bern and got it translated, they discovered hardly a thing had been altered, hardly a tit or a tat."

"I can scarcely believe it," I said, my mind still on the colloquy which was to be held in Regensberg, close to the great forests of Bavaria, which I was looking forward to viewing.

"But it is true! What happens? The power of the Philippe faction was always balanced on a pin, there had been riots over a number of things they had done like raising the wine tax. Now the streets rang with denunciations. Chapeaurouge and Lullin, hauled before a magistrate were accused of treason and sentenced to death, and might have lost their heads forthwith if Philippe had not provided them with an armed escort and rushed them off to Bern—heedless of public opinion."

"I presume that was why he was executed," I tried to hurry the story along.

"No, that's getting ahead of things." The man regarded me eagerly. "You must hear the rest, Master Calvin. As it happened there was an archery shoot the next day." I knew of this Swiss sport, archers shooting at a stuffed bird, a popinjay, tied to a stick. The sport was innocent enough in itself but always attracted large crowds that made a day of it and ended up in drunken roistering. This occasion was no exception, I gathered, and Philippe and Richardet coming out of a tavern overcome by wine, had met a councilman who had made a speech against Chapeaurouge and Lullin, and slew him. "A large crowd saw the deed and pursued the two murderers over the bridge to St-Gervais. Philippe they caught and dragged off to jail. Richardet eluded them for a while, but they found him hiding in the house of a friend. He tried to get away by lowering himself out a back window on a rope. But he asked too much of the rope—he was grossly overweight—and plunged to the ground to die of his injuries the next day even as the council was having Philippe's head cut off."

Maigret leaned back in his chair, shaking his head. I asked if that was all he had come to tell me. "No, Master Calvin." His eyes were pleading and he folded his hands prayerfully. "I have come to beg. Geneva is near anarchy. One cannot sleep with drunken parties in the streets, banging on one's door, even breaking one's windows. There are riots over nothing. Thieving. Raping—women are not safe at night. Slayings. The councils, much less the ministers, can do nothing to suppress the violence that is abroad. The good people of the city—there are many such—can only pray that God will send them a prophet to lead them out of their wilderness. They are going to ask you to return."

I heard myself shouting, "No, no, nothing can persuade me to go back to that place, Monsieur Maigret. Why did they send you? You're not a Genevan any more than I am."

"It would help, they thought—my being French like you. I also enjoy a reputation for being able to arrange things."

I demanded to know who "they" were.

"Ami Perrin for one. He is a leading merchant. The merchants are especially dismayed at all this tumult, their property being in constant peril."

"I have no business with merchants," I told him. "My vocation is with the church."

"But God would have men live in peace and enjoy their

property in safety." He was quoting from my *Institutes!*
"God would not have men live like rats in straw." My own
words recited to me. "The council met and resolved—I swear
this is true, you cannot be indifferent—the exact words: we
must implore that great and good man John Calvin to return
to us."

I groaned, feeling the pains in my stomach that were the
ever ready companion of any distress. Had God chosen this
unlikely person to convey his desires to me, as he had once
chosen Farel and Bucer? It could not be. "I have a pastorate
here in Strasbourg. I am immediately engaged elsewhere. I
leave in a few days for Regensberg."

"But after that? You cannot say no, Master Calvin." the
man—oh, he was an actor—was almost in tears.

"I must have time to consider." What was I saying?

He sprang to his feet. "I will return to them with that
message, a message of hope," he cried. "You will hear from
them. I know God wants you to listen." And before I could
say another word he clasped my hand and donning his hat
swept out the door.

I heard from them several days later. It was the kind of
message composed in committees: "We pray you very earnestly that you would transfer yourself hitherward to us, seeing that our people greatly desire you among us, and will
conduct themselves towards you in such sort that you shall
have to rest content." It was signed: "Your friends, the Syndics and Council of Geneva."

I wrote an account of it all to Farel. "I would rather submit
to death a hundred times than to that cross on which one has
to perish daily a thousand times over," I wrote in despair.

I SAT SLUMPED OVER THE HEAD OF MY MULE, thinking as
we crept along of how many roads I had already ridden since,

a boy, I had left Noyon for Paris—journeys to Orléans, to Angoulême, to Basel, to Italy, to Geneva, so often journeys in fear. I thought especially of the one that had taken me to Strasbourg only two years ago, all alone. I had company now. In the little cavalcade that I had led out of Strasbourg to take the highway south along the Rhine were my brother, Antoine, and sister, Marie, and my wife, who was pregnant, and my two stepchildren.

Antoine and I sometimes rode side by side at the rear, letting the women set the pace. I hid my own thoughts, bantering him: "Don't look so dejected, Antoine."

"Why shouldn't I? It was so promising. I was getting work for my press. And you with a devoted congregation, pleading that you wouldn't leave them." It was true, they had wept when I told them. I had wept too. "A perfect life for you," he rushed on. "Time to write and study, to complete your second *Institutes,* becoming recognized as the foremost scholar and preacher of the Reformation. Is that not true?" It was true. My colleagues at Regensberg had accorded me this standing. It was one reason why, they said, I must do this thing I was now doing however much I shrank from it. I must not stay withdrawn from the center of the battle.

"So you could not even stay at Regensberg until the colloquy ended," Antoine lamented.

"They were getting nowhere," I told him. "So many fruitless hours of argument. I was wasting my time. Oh, not all was wasted. I made one dear friend, Luther's close companion, that good and gentle man, Philip Melanchthon. He is trying to save Lutheranism, Antoine, before Luther destroys it with his intemperance. Has Luther lived too long? But God has his purpose, as in all things."

"Which you never tire of saying."

He made me think of Louis du Tillet, but I did not love him any the less for that. We rode for a while in silence.

"I still don't understand why your decision was so sudden."

"It was not sudden. All the while at Regensberg I prayed. I tried to find a pretext for avoiding the thing I had to do. I found excuses for myself, all the excuses you've given. They might suffice in the sight of men. But I was aware all the time that it was God with whom I had to do, who sees through all crafty maneuverings."

The journey was long. We followed the valley of the Rhine and turned eastward into the Jura passes, stopping frequently at inns, because we did not dare to travel at night without an escort. The women and children were near exhaustion when one day (it was in the month of September in 1541) we were met by a company of mounted militiamen, a herald, and commanding them, Ami Perrin, leading merchant of Geneva. With the herald announcing our arrival, we rode through Cornavin Gate, where a large crowd had gathered. They began to cheer and run alongside us, shouting my name.

I got right to work. The next day, established in the same old, narrow-faced house that Farel and I had occupied in the rue des Chanoines, now quite crowded with my expanded household, I plunged into the composition of a new set of ordinances, having given this much thought during our long journey.

11

GOD PROVIDES US WITH CIVIL GOVERNMENT to protect our welfare and to insure the security of that other government, which is enthroned in his church. Civil government stands guard while the church informs it with moral principles. If either fails the way is left open to unrestrained wickedness, which imposes a tyranny over people as oppressive as the tyranny of some murderous king.

Farel and I had tried to lay a foundation for a community of such divinely ordained dimensions with the Articles of 1538, which, however, had proved to have some deficiencies. The people must be brought more directly under the discipline of the church—not an easy task, of course. And since I would need the cooperation of the civil functionaries, my first step was to enlist them not only in formulating additional, necessary church laws but in providing means of enforcement.

Accordingly I asked the Little Council to appoint some of its own members and members of the Council of Two Hundred to assist me; they met with me daily in a chamber of the town hall. Also in attendance were the ministers then occupying the city's pulpits, three men of little merit supplied by Bern, whom I meant to get rid of as soon as I could. The councilmen on my committee were donkeys, with that animal's ignorance but also its determination, for I must not forget, their fathers had unseated the duke of Savoy and his bishop, and they themselves had removed Farel and me not so long ago.

The most eminent among them was Ami Perrin, who had the self-indulgent countenance of a rich youth and consumed overmuch of our time telling pointless stories, encouraging us to laugh by guffawing in our faces and grasping our shoulders. I could never be quite sure when to take him seriously; during a discussion of the ministers' role in society, which, I explained, was to declare God's will, he inquired: "Why does God not appear himself to declare his will, or use his angels for that purpose?"

I decided he was serious, expressing in this childish fashion his dislike of having any mortal tell him what God would have him do. I answered good humoredly: "Angels, Master Perrin! But congregations would be terrified by such majestic presences." And I went on, "Listening to the preachments of other, puny men is a test of one's obedience to the Lord. It is, moreover, a test of our love for one another, to recognize that another fellow being has been struck by holy fire and bears the true faith." I avoided his gaze. One of our three ministers was notoriously immoral, one was heretical, and the third drank too much. "They must also be pleasing to their flock," I added. "Oh, they must be pleasing to their flock. Love means acceptance."

For the rest of the morning Master Perrin wore a dark look.

We ministers would stand at the top of the church's order. We would declare God's will in sermons every Sunday beginning at daybreak at the ringing of the church bells, and on into the afternoon, at St-Pierre, and the city's other two churches, the Madeleine and St-Gervais; and every Monday, Wednesday, and Friday morning.

"Must people then go running from place to place all week listening to preachments?" one worthy inquired. "When will they get their work done?"

"They will work better with God's Word in their ears."

A company of twelve elders, "godly, grave and pious men," I prescribed, would form with the ministers a consistory charged with censuring immoral behavior and making fraternal corrections. It was a flaw in the articles of 1538 not to have provided for such a body. And finally, in the church order, would stand twelve deacons chosen for their spotless reputations, who would manage the churches' funds and see to the care of the poor.

A school must also be established (I pressed this vigorously) to teach language and worldly science, headed by a learned academician but having as its highest duty the teaching of sound religious doctrine. The school would be under ministerial supervision.

I made certain compromises, profiting from experience. For the Little Council, while vowing its deepest respect for me, insisted nevertheless that it must approve my appointments of ministers; and that elders and deacons must be members of the councils and chosen by them; the consistory would have the authority to excommunicate, a dilution of the minister's power since the consistory included twelve laymen. I was not happy about these twelve having a part in the decision to excommunicate, but I promised myself that they would agree to cut off whom I found to be unfit, and if they defied me, I would depart. The Little Council could impose punishment on recalcitrants; I had always been ready to agree that civil or criminal punishment should be the prerogative of the government.

Curiously, in compromising with men I knew for the most part to be donkeys, I had produced a document in close conformity to my theory of the two governments in man, which separated the political from the spiritual and placed each under the appropriate authority, civil and religious, but retained the point that man's conduct is a moral question intruding on both jurisdictions. I had provided the means of investing the political authority with moral predications, and I was satisfied with the document, which the Council of Two Hundred approved.

Martin Luther sang of God as a mighty fortress. I had

raised a fortress manned by the church and government under God.

"I T WILL RESOUND AROUND THE WORLD," Maigret proclaimed. He had become a visitor whom I enjoyed; he was a useful informant, and I was also pleased at his increasing piety, which might have been due to intimations of morality—underneath his elegant dress was an aging man—although I did not doubt his sincerity.

"Our affairs are not very visible beyond the Juras. Bern, Zurich, some of the other cantons have remarked on it—and Strasbourg on account of my associations there—"

"Oh, the world may be preoccupied by the same old bloody doings; those two elderly cocks, the king of France and the emperor of the holy Roman Empire dance around each other, and England's big cock slays his counselors and takes women to bed, and their subjects are too busy gulping down their sorrows to think of much else." I thought too of that other despot, Pope Paul, hurling his spears around Christendom, issuing an index of heretical books, reviving the inquisition, trying to organize another meeting of his ecclesiastical eunuchs, others having failed, in order to bring about the extermination of Protestantism. "But one day they will all perceive," Maigret went on, "that what you have set up in Geneva is a new thing on the landscape—scarcely visible, like the little monument surveyors put down to mark what deeds-of-sale call 'the place of beginning.' What I see then are churches filling that land where such a faith is preached that men will recognize it as forming the pillars of government. Isn't that it, Master Calvin?"

I could not but be impressed by this image. "With God's help, Laurent." (I used his Christian name in our intimate conversations.) "Yes, societies where churches will exercise

such influence as to set Protestantism in everlasting opposi-
tion to the monarchism of Rome. What you have said is that
we have a beginning—a beginning of a parliamentarianism in
which God holds the deciding vote." His was an excellent
point and reminded me of Olivétan seeing the beginning of
"Calvinism."

The Geneva government acted worthily. Heaven, having
removed those rascals Philippe, Chapeaurouge, Lullin, and
Richardet, had put power in the hands of honest persons.
Michel Sept, alas, had died, but Aubert the apothecary still
held office, and the majority of the councilmen gave off an air
of being grateful for my presence. It was the presence, of
course, of the Holy Spirit which inspired these men who had
once ceased to govern because their bowels had turned to
water. I found it good to lecture them occasionally, using
excerpts from the Bible and my *Institutes,* sometimes quoting from Lucius Annaeus Seneca: "The licentiousness of
cities will sometimes abate through discipline and fear but
never of itself."

"Only sometimes, Master Calvin?" they inquired; "we have
vowed to banish it," and they acted, in fact, with great ear-
nestness, jailing persons who laughed during my sermons and
exiling immoral persons. An ancient she-goat said she intended to marry a youth of twenty-five. The council
threatened her with banishment, and she wept and fumed,
but that was the last we heard of her obscene plan. Thieves,
murderers, and rioters they ordered beheaded.

A few troublemakers wanted to strip the consistory of the
right of excommunication and instead refer each case to the
Little Council. I flatly rejected the proposal. "If this is done,
I will leave," I told them, which put an end to that. In the
ensuing months, the city marvelously settled down.

This was not to say that Satan did not continue to practice
his vocation by cunning ways, enticing people to various extravagances and folly. Some there were who served banquets
of twenty to thirty plates and side dishes piled high with
sweets. How Satan must have chortled over such misuse of

God's gifts. I persuaded the Little Council to pass an ordinance limiting banquets to three courses and four plates a course, which was more than sufficient. It was the devil's idea too to inspire the bourgeoise and even some of the lower classes with a love for loud and unbecoming costumes. I could not see them laying out their capital in order to ornament themselves in gold and silver cloth, furs, feathers, lace, and the like. Men as well as women! "Just look at yourselves," I exhorted my congregations. "Men dress up like young women as though they grieved over the fact that God had not made them women and would like to renounce their sex. And women dress as if they would carry an arquebus instead of a distaff or as if they were playing in a farce and trying to attract the glances of men who would say excitedly, 'Who's that? Can it be Madame So-and-So?' It does not matter in what member you are unchaste; the Father loathes all immodesty of body and soul." How should they dress? "In clothing that simply protects you from cold and heat," I told them. I noticed that Maigret began appearing in less sumptuous array.

THE COUNCIL OF TWO HUNDRED had voted me five hundred florins, twelve measures of corn, and two tuns of wine a year, which was not very much, considering the household I had to support. They also presented me five feet of velvet cloth for a cloak, which I could use, the one I had worn for the past ten years having become quite threadbare. And they furnished me (at an investment of 120 florins; they were at pains to tell me) a hickory chest, a maple bench, a chest for my papers, some straight chairs, a sideboard and a wash basin—all on loan, they hastened to say. They also paid to have the household items we had acquired in Strasbourg brought down to us, which arrived safely over the mountains in answer to Idelette's prayers.

All this was an improvement over Strasbourg where there had been times I wondered how I was going to provide food for my family, and hadn't even money to send messages. This was partly my fault; I was often in debt as a result of helping others who were more in need than I. But I say, a curse on pastors who feed themselves and don't feed their lambs. Christ sent his apostles out without gold, and formed his church without gold. The church and its servants have money not to keep but to distribute.

I do not consider poverty a particular virtue, nor do I think people sin when they make money. Money is sinful when it has been acquired in ways contrary to God's commandments and is used to indulge a man in luxury and vanity. But the profits of our labor come to us as from the hand of God, so that to condemn money as such is to blaspheme God. The judgment hangs on the use a man makes of his money, and its chief use is charity. As for him who has nothing, he should thank God for his existence and the wonderful things God has surrounded him with.

One of the things I rejoiced over was the little garden behind our stone house. There Marie grew peas and beans. Idelette helped, although not very much in the weeks before her baby was due. From the garden one saw the Juras, Mount Saleve, and the lake and the Alps. The heart knew no impoverishment, only rapture. In the vines, in the trees, in the hills, I saw God tending this earthly life. The sunshine and the rain attested to his passing by. The stars at night cried out of his existence. The smallest blade of grass, the beautiful order between day and night—everything was like a painting of his majesty.

I saw too how God made our rapture deeper by visiting us with sadness, as in one of those paintings (the comparison is inadequate) in which the artist brings out the brilliance of the sun by putting in areas of darkest shadows. Darkness came into my wife's and my life a few weeks after our son Jacques was born. On a morning I would not forget I had gone to celebrate the baptism of another little creature God had sent into this world, and in the church in St-Gervais I stood in a circle of faces and inquired, "What Christian name have you chosen for this child?"

"Claude," they informed me.

It would not do. A small matter, perhaps, but another example of Satan's guile. Claude was the name of a so-called saint in the papist idolatry. I had made public a list of names that were acceptable to me.

"It's my baby," its mother screeched. "My pain and agony!" Women are inclined to exaggerate.

I tried to soothe her. "Here is a fine name. And one at the very top of my list—Abraham."

"Abraham! It is a name for a Jew. Besides, it's a girl baby." It seemed to me that Claude was in fact usually a boy's name, but I was about to suggest Sarah when the company that had assembled to see me wash away the sin in which the child was born set up such a tumult, even shaking their fists at me that I bowed to their desire. There are times when we must temporize.

Moreover I had a sudden premonition that Idelette had need of me. When I arrived home our little Jacques was dead of a convulsion.

I tried to console my poor Idelette as we wept together. "God is a father too and knows what is best for us."

More often than not, children pull parents apart. Idelette's two children, Johann and Judith, stood between us, despite my efforts to be a father to them; such is true of many families and not only where a stepparent is involved. But a dead child draws parents together. Idelette and I were never so close, our devotion never so bright as now against the darkness of our lost child.

So my hands were full of my family as well as of the city. The security of a household is fragile; illness and death are not the only trespassers. One day when my sister Marie was

walking home from the fish market in the rain, a young man
discovered the pretty face under her shawl and was so smitten he had been running after her ever since.

"Now they want to get married," Antoine told me. Who
was this interloper on our peace; what did he do? He was
employed at the city's board of audit, a more pretentious
sounding job than it was since he was only a minor account-
ant, and a rather undistinguished young man, I thought.
Charles Costant was by no means the person I would have
chosen for her. "But she is not your daughter, John," Antoine reminded me.

I could not deny that. If she had been my daughter would I
have forbidden her to take this step? Perhaps I would. Young
people cannot be counted on to do wise things, always in a
state of revolt, as they are, and ready to defy their elders
simply on principle. I thought how God had found it necessary
to send Moses down from the Mount with particular instructions to the people of Israel to honor their fathers and
mothers, and look up to those who had been placed over
them and treat them with honor, obedience, and grateful-
ness. God lights up a father with the spark of his own splen-
dor by sharing the title, "Father," with him, and those who
violate parental authority are monsters. Didn't God say to
Moses, "He that curseth his father and mother should be put
to death"? To be sure, we can say that such punishment was
prescribed when the very survival of the tribes of Israel de-
pended on the unity of its families, which could only be
maintained by authority. But was the danger of fragmenta-
tion resulting in the death of a society any less today than it
was among the Israelites?

I pondered all this, yet gave my consent to the marriage
even though it was not asked for. I myself married them,
making sure that they understood the sacredness of the vows.
Anyhow, my little songbird was gone.

She was replaced in our household by another female,
whom Antoine brought to us, a silent creature who existed
much to herself, sitting at our table scarcely opening her

mouth except to eat. This she liked to do, goodness knows, which accounted for her plumpness. But I must say she was pretty, and good natured, which I suppose was what prompted Antoine to marry her. Anne was her name. It was in her favor that she was the daughter of a seigneur, Nicholas Le Fert.

Antoine had got himself fairly well established as a printer, although not yet well enough off to move his wife and himself into their own house. He had set up a press in the back of the shop where this uncouth fellow Hans Hoch had his bindery, an arrangement Maigret had suggested, though I was not enthusiastic about it. I was not exactly drawn to Hoch, and as I said to Maigret, Antoine's moving in with him had something of the odor of a consortium with the devil. I spoke only half in jest.

"Hoch is a scoffer," Maigret admitted. "But not a convinced one. His scoffing is largely a pose. The arrangement will facilitate the publication of your writings."

My writings, in fact, were pouring forth. What drove me on at such a pace, still in my early thirties, afflicted an inordinate part of the time with indigestion and migraine headaches, so that I counted myself lucky when I could get four or five hours of sleep at night? Did the thought of death press on me? I did not fear death; I only worried that I hadn't enough time left to do what I had to do. The council had given me a secretary to help me keep abreast of my obligations. Young Jacques Baudoin peered at his writing tablet through frog's eyes, writing furiously as, more often than not, I lay abed in the early morning composing the thoughts that had marched through my head during a sleepless night. He was a veritable engine who rarely missed a word, although I could tell from his sallow, wooden face that he had little idea of what I was saying.

Once I did detect him trying to suppress a smile. Inspired by a recollection of my gullibility as a child (God forgive that credulous woman, my mother), I had addressed myself to the subject of relics. "The world, instead of discerning Jesus

Christ in the Word," I dictated, "amuses itself with his sheets and shirts, and splinters from the cross. What foolishness prevails. There are enough splinters around to fill a ship. And people, Romanists, that is, gather around admiring the bones of the saints, which are all actually trash. Witness the leg of a stag preserved as an arm of St. Anthony. They are unable to make up relics of the virgin's remains on account of their doctrine of bodily assumption. What do they do? They try to indemnify themselves with samples of her milk. She could not have produced all the milk displayed in towns, convents, and nunneries if she had been a wet nurse—period, Baudoin. Or a dairy. Foolishness is compounded. At a church in Aix-la-Chapelle you can see a shirt of the virgin that only a giant-ess could fill, and right alongside it the shoes of Joseph which only a dwarf could squeeze into. Care at least should have been taken to maintain a better proportion between the shoes of the husband and the shirt of the wife. . . ." It was not one of my more dignified essays, but I gave it to Antoine to print. He reported that Hoch had read it with great glee. Baudoin and Hoch—well, we cannot always choose our audiences.

I translated into French the first edition of my *Institutes,* which was selling very well now. Maigret saw to it that copies were smuggled into France. Some were seized, we learned, and on orders of the president of Parlement burned on the steps of Notre Dame. But a few undoubtedly found their way into the hands of my countrymen. Oh, Lizet, you never should have let John Calvin escape from you!

My treatises on the New Testament made their orderly way across Baudoin's tablet. And hardly a day passed when I did not find it incumbent on me to prompt people to sober thought and behavior. Princess Marguerite had taken under her wing the deplorable Libertins, insane people who indulged themselves in every immorality on the argument that anything was justified since all things originated with God. The sect had become quite widespread, even finding adherents in Geneva. "Do not take personal offense," I wrote this foolish woman. "When a dog sees anyone assault its master, it barks and stands at bay. Seeing the truth of God assaulted, I would be remiss if I remained dumb. You would not have me betray God in order to favor you." My tone could not have been more restrained, but I waited in vain for a reply.

I must write the councils of Bern, Zurich, Schauffausen, and Basel, and demand that they appeal to François, as I had, to cease his persecution of the Waldenses. I must also write to Melanchthon, for I heard that Luther had let loose his invective at the ministers of Zurich because they had published posthumously Zwingli's ideas on the eucharist. "Your Master Martin," I advised him, "is letting himself be carried beyond all bounds. If we throw away our independence for fear of irritating him, then it's all over with our church." I let him see a certain melancholy that had overtaken me. "My beloved Philip, I almost lose courage when I reflect how much at so unseasonable a time these intestine quarrels tear us asunder." Hoping to restore some peace, I wrote to the ministers of Zurich: "Be tolerant of Luther in spite of his intemperance. Flatterers have done him much harm. Only try to remember the energy he has expended on the overthrow of the Antichrist." I indited a suggestion to Charles V that instead of trying to reconcile the Protestants of Germany with the Roman church, he himself sever his relations with the pope.

I PROPPED UP MY HEAD ON A PILLOW in order to bring into better view the man who seated himself on a stool beside my bed, whose somber clothes matched his despondency— Sebastian Castellio, who had quit the room I had rented him so cheaply in Strasbourg chiefly, I think, because I had chided him for his laziness. I had discovered him when I arrived in Geneva, teaching in the city's school where he had risen to the office of rector. I had accepted him with misgivings.

"I and my family cannot exist on what the council is paying me," he was saying. "If I had known how penurious these Genevans are I never would have come in the first place."

We had been over this before. I could do nothing about it except tell the council they were in a way of becoming like the pope robbing his priests, the way they squeezed both teachers and ministers. I knew the revenues were available if those councilmen who saw to the collection of taxes had not treated themselves and their friends with special consideration. In some matters I had little influence, being neither an officeholder nor a citizen.

"They at least pay the ministers more than they pay me, although," he added morosely, "I admit it's enough for what I do—spending my time caning little boys. Master Calvin, recommend me for a pastorate."

I tried to lift his spirits. "You are teaching these little turds discipline which is of supreme importance."

"Nominate me for a ministry," he insisted. "You're short of preachers. You've swept three of them out as though they were bats in a chimney."

I would not deny that. I had banished them to country pastorates; Master Champereaux because he was never sober, Master D'Ecclesia because he mocked me, and Master Ferron because he had a weakness for chambermaids. I had found some more reliable men among the French refugees who were coming to us.

"We can get by on what a pastorate would pay us," Castellio groaned.

I also groaned, inwardly. To make him a minister of the Word would be to act a lie, for he accepted or rejected doctrine as it suited him. This I told him.

"You mean I don't agree with you on every tittle of Scripture," he said angrily.

I reminded him that I had heard him ridicule the teaching that Christ descended into hell. "But it is incongruous that Christ wrestled with fear and the devil after his crucifixion," he cried. "He was divine. Furthermore that statement in the creed is nowhere to be found in Scripture."

I told him that it was found everywhere, that Christ prayed with tears and loud cries, that the people heard his fear, that he cried out, "My God, my God, why hast thou forsaken me?" And I asked him, "Is there a more terrible abyss than to feel estrangement from God? He bore this—the cross, death, hell—in order to bring us life. You say the struggle was incongruous, and you deny that he descended—then you debase the meaning of his sacrifice."

"I can leave the whole clause out of my confession and still believe."

So long as he rejected or questioned any part of the Word, then he could not be trusted to preach it, I told him flatly, to which he retorted, "No papist was ever more rigid. Isn't my faith enough?"

I challenged him to a test of his faith, asking him if he accepted the doctrine of election.

"My parents were peasants," he said. "I am inclined to believe chiefly what I see—like the miracle of lambs being born on our farm in Dauphine. I left the Roman church because I saw it slaying anti-papists. I'm a matter-of-fact man. I'm aware of such mystery as that of poetry, being a professor of literature. But I cannot see into anything as mysterious as divine election." His voice rose tremblingly, "I don't accept it. I don't reject it. I don't know."

"And you don't have the faith to support the logic of the matter."

"I thought logic was to support faith. Logic leads me in the opposite direction to this doctrine. How can we believe that God elects some for damnation and others for salvation even before they are born or know what virtue is? Logic does not bring me to this doctrine of despair that says no acts of righteousness will save you. According to Ezekiel, God said, 'I take no pleasure in the death of the wicked but would have the wicked turn from his way and live.'" And he clapped his hands as though he had scored a point.

But he had missed Ezekiel's meaning, that God would show mercy to the repentant but that repentance takes no decision out of God's hands. "It is God who wills the repentance."

"I'm lost in your reasoning."

"You're lost," I agreed pityingly. I cross-examined him. "Do you not believe that God has an overall plan?"

"Yes, I do."

"Do you not believe that the plan is changeless?"

"We must presume it," he said unsatisfactorily.

"But you reject it when you say you can take God's decision for you, for heaven or hell, out of his hands."

"I do not say that. I say I reject the hopelessness that comes from knowing I may not have a chance for salvation." He asked slyly: "Are you one of those elected to be saved, Master Calvin?"

It was a childish question, I told him.

"Because it is so obvious that you are—"

"It is obvious that no one can know."

"What, not even you, so clearly a good man?" he asked.

I disregarded his sarcastic tone and explained to him that if we are repentant, if we do the will of God, we can be sure it is God working in us and that his purpose can be the fulfillment of a favorable plan for us; and that if we continue in wickedness we have quite likely been abandoned.

"And where does Scripture make this clear?" he asked.

"All of Scripture is testimony to his infinite wisdom and his knowledge of all things from even before the beginning." My head had started throbbing; I wanted to bring the discussion to an end. "I will try to find you something somewhere else, Castellio."

"Yes, send me out of the city, like Champereaux put out in

the fields. Purge the city of my dissolute mind, because Castellio defies Calvin, Castellio does not accept a doctrine of hopelessness, nor does Castellio accept every last thing in Holy Writ." The man was now in a rage. "I accept what testifies to a merciful and forgiving God. I only reject that writing that turns from him. They were mortal men who wrote the Bible. I do not deny the truth was often revealed to them. But they sometimes wrote wickedly, out of the pit of human passion. Read the Song of Solomon, oh, thou most moral man!" He snatched the Bible from beside my bed and leafed through it. "Read of Solomon and his Shulamite shepherdess lost in lust." And having found his passage he began to intone: "Let him kiss me with the kisses of his mouth. His left hand is under my head. His right hand doth embrace me. My beloved is mine and I am his, and I would not let him go—"

"You are abridging, which is devil's work," I shouted. "Besides, you blasphemer, it is an allegory of Christ and the church."

"Are sacred allegories written in lewd images? A garden shut up is my sister, my bride, a spring shut up, a fountain sealed, he said. I was asleep but my heart waked, she said. It is the voice of my beloved saying, open to me, my sister, my love, my dove, my undefiled." I tried to seize the Holy Book from him, but he backed away. "The joints of thy thighs are like jewels, the works of a cunning workman, he said. Thy navel is like a round goblet wherein no mingled wine is wanting. Thy belly a heap of wheat, thy breasts two fauns. O love for delights thy stature is like to a palm tree. I will climb up into the palm tree, I will take hold of the branches—"

"Put down the Book!"

"Make haste, my beloved, she said, and be thou like a roe or hart upon the mountain of spice. . . ."

God forgive him. How he sinned, his voice reeked with sin! He would have to leave Geneva. I had enough problems with my church and the city without having to deal with a blasphemous rector. I lay abed, my head throbbing worse than ever after he had left my room.

"THE WOMAN FIRST HAD CHILLS, they said, then began shrieking, and was delirious and coughed up blood as black as your stove." It was Baudoin, trembling as though he himself had chills, who brought me this report. The woman was the wife of a butcher in the Bourg-de-Four. I say it profits us nothing to search for God's purpose as we see people around us suddenly struck down, whose sins are no greater than others', children who have had no chance to redeem themselves from Adam's crime along with notorious malefactors whom you might expect to have incurred God's wrath—all slain without seeming discrimination. If the black plague that had come to us showed any favorites, they were the poor. The wealthy were able to flee. The houses of the rich became blank, shuttered walls. Carriages filled with the well-to-do rolled through the city's gates headed for country estates. Those who were left, muffled in scarves and using whatever vehicles they could obtain, rushed the afflicted to our hospital. It had once been a Dominican monastery and stood close by—oh, dreadful convenience—the Champel burial ground.

Soon after the outbreak the Little Council came to me. One of my pastors, they pleaded, must go to the hospital to minister to the stricken. Governments are always filled with piety at moments like this, although I would not take anything from the worthiness of their request. "I will go," I told them. But they forbade it. "No, no, Master Calvin. We cannot risk losing you." I was in anguish, agreeing with the council that my first obligation was to the survivors of the calamity visited on us, and yet wondering whether I was not rationalizing the fear that held me as it held everyone. My pastors were terrified—with one exception. Pierre Blanchet, the youngest of them and the one to whom I was most devoted, came forward and offered himself, and went daily to the hospital carrying an assurance of God's mercy and grace to the dying.

There was little the city could do but isolate the victims and quickly bury the dead. An effort was made to stop the plague's spread. A number of citizens came before the Little Council to swear that they had seen certain women, known to be possessed, smearing doorknobs with the pus of suppurating buboes. The council seized at least thirty such creatures, and after extracting confessions that they had practiced witchcraft in this abominable fashion, ordered them drowned or burned to death, in some instances hanged and left hanging as a warning.

Viewing some of these bodies in the trees near the bridge to St-Gervais, I thought how Satan, in the case of murderers, rapists and the like, is a voice from outside urging them on to their deeds, but in the case of witches actually inhabits his victims. The bodies, clad only in undergarments, bumped about in the wind, freed of Satan at last. I stood praying for the souls of these creatures who had been chosen to carry out God's unfathomable will.

Blanchet had died, having caught the fever only a few days before it could be said the pestilence had subsided.

12

I NOTED AROUND THE TIME of my thirty-fourth birthday that four years had passed since my return to Geneva.
I had given up any hope of living, as I once dreamed, a
life of serene study and contemplation. My little house was
a public place. When Idelette's children were home from
school it was filled with their noise, especially Judith's
and her friends', until I would storm out of my room
and shake the walls—most unbecomingly, I confess—with
my shouts for quiet. Idelette tried to make my room a
refuge for me, but it seemed there was always someone at the
front door, someone of the consistory, or the Little Council,
or an emissary from Zurich or elsewhere, or some French
ex-priest whom I must refresh with a glass of wine and whom
just as often as not we must take in until he found a place to
live, or some member of my congregation who owed a large
sum of money for medicine for his wife. I could not let him
go to jail; I could do nothing but refer to the purse I kept in a
chest drawer, which Idelette would then discover held only
half (or nothing) of what she was counting on for the house.
But she would stand guard over me if I asked her to. I'd hear
her whispering, "Master Calvin is ill."

"Oh, poor man."

"He will be all right. You may see him tomorrow." I kissed her and assured her the Lord would forgive her for telling so many lies. She herself was never in very good health and got little help from a series of maidservants, who came to us and left us in a flighty manner. Madame Sow, trailing disorder, had at least always been on hand.

Despite all this, I had reason to be gratified by what I had accomplished. I had restored some decency and morality to the city. Also, at the request of the council, who recognized my familiarity with the French Code, I had reviewed the city's civil law. I had finally given up the idea I could legislate a perfect state on earth, for perfection can never be found in any community of men, the insolence of some being so great and their wickedness so stubborn, the most severe ordinances cannot restrain them. But one can try to create a condition of tranquility wherein religious worship is secure. Then the wicked may be subdued by their own consciences as God's law shows them, as in a mirror, the impurity and insanity of their self-confidence; before that image their bravado may diminish.

I actually recommended few changes in the city's code. The revolutionists, as I have observed, had been very diligent about passing laws; some of the punishments prescribed, I thought, were excessively severe, so my chief recommendations were directed at ameliorating them but making sure that they were enforced, and at insuring everyone equality under the law, however idealistic I knew this might seem.

I also helped resolve the dispute with Bern in the matter of jurisdiction over Savoy's former holdings, a dispute that had dragged on, threatening at one time to bring the two cities into armed conflict. Our negotiations ended happily with Bern surrendering most of its claims.

I also strengthened my own forces. My countrymen were arriving in considerable numbers, seeking refuge from François, and from these I was able to recruit several men of great virtue, not the least of whom was Michael Cop, Nicholas's younger brother. Nicholas himself had returned to the security of an academic life. Once again must I ask God to forgive him, as the Sorbonne had from its contrary motivation? But Michael possessed a more stalwart character, having such zeal for the Reformation that he set an example for all of us.

All in all, that year of my thirty-fourth birthday, I was in a position of some power, and so I dared to undertake a piece of business that cried out for action. I advanced on it with some trepidation but with no less determination.

Pierre Ameaux was a member of the Little Council who had inherited a family business making playing cards, and in this wise was profiting from gambling, which was prohibited. I confronted the council with their colleague's obliquity. I was not opposed to all games as such. I enjoyed a go at quoits in my garden, and Maigret and I occasionally played *clef,* wherein one slides keys across a tabletop to see who can come closest to the edge without going over. But playing cards for money is quite a different thing, impossible to pursue so that God is not in one way or another offended. People begin taking his name in vain, they practice fraud, they lose their tempers and no one can keep his perspective. How many marriages do we not see broken up as a result! "As in drinking," I pointed out to the council, "it is best to refrain from gambling altogether." Ameaux must be forbidden to sell his playing cards in Geneva. I supposed we could not prevent him from selling them elsewhere.

Ameaux cried out that he would be ruined. I pointed out that he could use his manufacturing facilities for some other paper products, but he began weeping, protesting over and over that he would be ruined, which showed how profitable his illicit business had been. I said that what he was doing was just as wicked as usury (which was not to be confused with lending money at legitimate interest for purposes of production, a practice approved by Scripture), and while everyone was sympathetic with Ameaux's distress, the council voted that his exploitation of men's weakness and vice must cease. Business should never be based on immorality.

.I felt some pity for Ameaux when, shortly thereafter, his marriage disintegrated. It was through no fault of his own. Some of the citizens, chiefly the wealthier ones, had been corrupted by the scurrilous philosophy of the Libertins, and among them was Ameaux's wife. Madame Ameaux had abandoned herself to the lust that was virtually a religion with these people, and went about looking anywhere for fulfillment. She even took to harassing me, so that I had to give orders to my household not to let her in the door. Ameaux sued for a divorce.

The case, which would normally go before the lieutenant of justice, was preempted by the Little Council, which, I suspect, wanted to enjoy a recital of Madame Ameaux's activities. The councilmen turned to me for advice. Divorce was not a matter that I was able to approach with too much certainty. The Roman church's doctrine that marriage is a sacrament is manifestly absurd—making of copulation a sacrament! But on the other hand, matrimony is a compact holily made, the reflection of a man and woman's sacred union with God that cannot be easily put aside. While these thoughts contended within me, I kept putting the council off. Ameaux sat in council meetings fuming over their repeated postponement of his suit. He could not, as I had, shut the door to his house on this shameless woman so long as she was his legal wife. The council could have acted, but they didn't. I suppose I should have been pleased that they deferred to me so helplessly in this matter. As a consequence, Ameaux, already resenting the part I had had in curtailing his business, now held me wholly to blame for his marital troubles. Oh, wholly to blame, although it was certainly not I who had indoctrinated Madame Ameaux in her amorality.

I still could have retained some sympathy for him if it had not been for an incident that now gave a new shade to the situation. Both the council and I got a full report of it the morning after it happened from a supposed friend of Ameaux, who had been a witness; friends are not always to be trusted when they are possessed of some scandalous news. The report was that Ameaux, at a supper party in his house, having drowned himself in wine, began to revile me, describing me as an evil man preaching a false doctrine, sticking my nose into everybody's business and leading the Little Council around by its nose, and this on top of the fact that I was a foreigner ("a base Picard" he called me), and that my ambition was to be the pope. A pope in the Reformist church!

The Little Council ordered Ameaux's arrest and he was brought to trial for libeling me and making treasonous statements about the government.

I was disturbed to see that he had some defenders on the council, some individuals who thought that he should be pardoned and let go, or at the most given some mild form of punishment: he had already suffered much anguish and after all, he was their colleague. I listened to this without comment and listened in silence as the Little Council, completely confused by its own speeches, decided to turn the matter over to the Council of Two Hundred. Some days later I sat in the town hall as the Two Hundred decided that Ameaux should be punished. And his punishment? He must appear before both councils and on his knees ask them, Calvin, and God to forgive him.

I spoke out then. I spoke as the head of the consistory, representative of that government that is enthroned in God's church. I poured out my anger on their wooden heads. "Because I am Christ's servant," I declared, "in dishonoring me Ameaux has dishonored Christ." I would not be present at the charade they suggested. In fact, I would not enter a Geneva pulpit again until proper amends had been made to the name of God. Ameaux must do penance before the whole city. The Two Hundred was a sea of gaping faces, a sight I turned my back on and left the hall.

In this way, by showing how determined I could be, victory became mine. Aubert, the apothecary, brought me the news that the Two Hundred had retracted its decision and turned the case back to the Little Council, and that body had immediately imposed a sentence more commensurate with Ameaux's crime, a sentence I could accept.

The very next morning the *guets* in their bailiffs' uniforms appeared at the door to Ameaux's cell where their captain read the Little Council's order. He would strip down to his undershirt, then crawl on his knees down the hill from the jail to the lower city holding aloft a torch, and at certain designated places he would pause and pray loudly for God's forgiveness. From the lower city he would proceed in the same manner across the bridge to St-Gervais and up to his doorstep.

The company of bailiffs, members of the Little Council including the syndics, the consistory, and I accompanied him. I steeled myself against pity. We moved slowly, paced by the progress of the half-naked Ameaux, a wretched, three-legged creature holding aloft the lighted torch. A little trail of blood appeared on the cobblestones. But he had brought his pain and humiliation on himself, and I perceived the salutary effect the sight of him had on the crowd that had gathered to watch. A few of them jeered at the officials and us of the consistory, but most were quiet, and when we stopped at the place du Molard there was complete silence. There Ameaux uttered his repentance: "Forgive me, O Lord, for my offense." He turned his eyes upwards to me standing next to him, as though begging me to prompt him, which I did, having written the prayer he was to recite. "Cleanse my heart forever from my wicked thoughts."

By the time we reached the bridge, he had the words well in mind but each time his voice became less audible. "Louder," the captain of the bailiffs ordered.

"Never mind," I said, "God can hear him."

Myself, I was feeling sick. Would the agonizing journey never end? I prayed silently both for Ameaux and for the strength to carry me on. We crossed the bridge. The shopkeepers came out and stared at us. We proceeded through mean little streets, past people who, here in St-Gervais, were distinctly hostile, until we reached the unfortunate man's house, where he collapsed, dropping the torch that guttered out in a puddle. Someone, I suppose a neighbor, darted forward and helped him to his feet and into his house. The bailiffs cleared a way through the crowd and we all of us proceeded quickly back across the bridge.

An unruly and uncouth neighborhood, St-Gervais. I had another taste of its humor several Sundays later when I went there to preach the first of a series I planned on the deity of our Lord Jesus Christ, taking my text from John ("In him was life and the life was the light of men"). I would repeat the sermons at St-Pierre. When I arrived at the church in St-Gervais I had to shoulder my way through people gathered around the door, who shouted at me, "We're not listening to you this morning," and they might have prevented me from going in if I had not shown them that I was not to be intimidated. Inside was a modest congregation which, for its part, was ready to listen to me, I was happy to see, and quite upset by what was going on outside. "We will pay no attention to them," I said. "They are worse than beasts." "Is that so," someone shouted from the door. "You're the beast, Calvin." The ushers closed the door in his face and I went on with the service. But when it was over, there were the same people outside and they followed me to the bridge ranting and raving at me. It took the police to disperse them. And it took a manifestation of the Little Council's resolve to maintain tranquility to subdue the yelling and marching around that erupted that afternoon. The Little Council dispatched workmen to St-Gervais who began nailing together a gibbet. Their hammering became the only sound in the neighborhood on that Sabbath day.

I suspected that Ameaux was behind the agitation, and although pity has no place in our hearts when Christ's name is calumniated, I did allow compassion to rule me and incline me to forgiveness. I put aside the uneasiness I felt about divorce and recommended to the Little Council that Ameaux, who, refractory man that he was, had nevertheless suffered much and should be granted his petition. The Little Council complied immediately. I did not expect Ameaux to be grateful, nor was he, judging from the gloomy air he assumed whenever we happened to meet.

T HE MONTHS WENT SWIFTLY BY in struggles, in triumphs, in mourning, in work—how long would God give me, borne down as I was by my afflictions? I thought especially about the seeming capriciousness of death, which tested people's love for him (my own love remained immutable) when word came that Luther was dead, brought down by a stroke in Eiselben, where he was born, and that on the wall beside his bed he had scratched, "I was your plague when I lived, papa; when I die I shall be your death." An optimistic man. Pope Paul continued to survive to act and plot against us. Oh divine inexplicableness, cutting down a saint and leaving the Antichrist to grow in mischief! What struck me with the greatest force was the realization that the giants of the Reformation were now gone—Zwingli and Oecolampadius having departed long since—and that only men like gentle Philip Melanchthon, Bucer, Farel, Simon Grynaeus were left, all worthy men but none of them capable of sustaining what Luther had begun. My thoughts fluttered like a crippled bird looking for refuge. Our cause no longer had a thunderous Wittenberg; Zurich, Strasbourg, Bern were divided and parochial. Was our beginning to be our ending? Who was to be our leader? One night I told Antoine of my thoughts. He put his hand on my shoulder. "The answer is plain to you, John," he said.

I knew it was—I, buried in these mountains, still in my thirties. God give me strength! "You have said it, Antoine.

God uphold me; I am become the leader of the Reformation."

T HE RUSHING DAYS TURNED INTO THE WINTER of 1547 and the time of the February elections. I did not attend the voting of the Council of Two Hundred, not wanting to seem to impose my presence directly on their politics. That afternoon, when I heard knocking, I went down and admitted little Aubert, whose face, purple with cold, was screwed up in consternation.

"Perrin succeeded in getting more than a dozen of his friends elected to the councils," he said breathlessly. "They reelected him after he made a speech deploring the way Ameaux was treated. He laid all the responsibility on you. 'Are we going to let this holy Picard put us all on trial?' he ranted. I myself was reelected only by a hair. And Perrin— you never heard such devotion to the city and valor as he affected—was made captain general. Oh, Master Calvin, things are bad, and I do not know what we are going to do."

He left me to return to his store. I went up the hill and let myself into the emptiness of St-Pierre. I had not asked for this life. Whenever I had to face such as Pierre Caroli, or the city's councilmen in public, my legs would turn to water. I was able to put on a bold countenance because God supported me. I fell on my knees at the foot of the steps to my pulpit and prayed aloud: "O Lord, is it not your wish that I bring the city into your way? Is it not your wish that your Word prevail?" The hush, the shafts of light through the windows, the very stones vaulting heavenward, all were an affirmation. "O Lord," I asked, "is it not your wish that I go on doing what I am doing?" I heard God say, "You are my servant."

PART FOUR

"Gird up your loins,"
God said to Jeremiah.
"Speak to them
all that I command you.
Be not dismayed at their faces.
I have made you into
a fortified city
against the whole land.
They will not prevail against you,
for I am with you."

How confounding, that
I, Maigret,
should become
Calvin's secret agent!

13

"My DEAR SEIGNEUR MAIGRET, why do you continue to live in that dungheap?" This inquiry, Monsieur Devereux, my solicitor, always appended to his communications when forwarding to Geneva the rents he collected from my small seigneury. I would answer: "It is edifying to narrow one's point of view. On a dungheap, in the raging of flies, one has a mirror of the confusion of the whole world." I am given to such turgescence, I am afraid. The truth was, the income from my seigneury near Nemours was not adequate to support me properly in Paris—I had a shameful love of ostentation—and I would have died of boredom living in Nemours. I had come to Geneva one winter when the king's first secretary, Le Maçon, a warm friend, had enlisted my services in gathering information about Geneva's revolt against the duke of Savoy, who happened to be the king's uncle and was cordially hated by him. I had stayed on, finding I could pick up a little extra money representing Geneva merchants occasionally in Paris, where I had many excellent connections. But lately I had developed a more compelling reason for staying that I wouldn't mention to Devereux because it would have simply confounded him.

I was thinking of this one morning as I opened an invitation to dinner from Madame Belthazar, who was known as Widow Belthazar, her husband being only recently deceased. I certainly would attend. Ah, yes, Madame Belthazar, I certainly will attend. The reason for my continuing to remain in Geneva was that I had become wholly converted to Master Calvin's doctrines, which I recognized as a universal reproach—a conversion that confounded even me in the light of my once feckless life. I had become devoted to the man, the first attachment I had felt for anyone since a stage in my late forties (this one romantic but also moving me deeply) when an aunt brought four of my female cousins to visit me, towards the oldest of whom, I think it was the intention, I should bend my interest. But it was the youngest, half my age, lovely Louise, so anxious to learn, whom I instructed tenderly in the woods around my estate. She had died that autumn. Now, even at sixty I would find myself moved to tears at the memory of her. I must forget all that. I stood ready to serve Master Calvin in any way I could and one way was to be his confidential agent, a kind of work at which I had some experience, and if I do say so, not a little talent.

His enemies were people to whom my social standing gave me access. They passed as patricians in Geneva, but pah!— they were really bourgeoisie, acting the nobility, gallivanting between town houses and country estates, dressing up in Paris fashions, and making jokes about the Reformation. They were the jackals who had pleaded with Calvin to return only because they were terrified lest anarchy wipe out their properties. They were as disorderly as the meanest rascals in Geneva. I could guess what Widow Belthazar's dinner would be like.

I put a leash on my little pug, who reminded me of Madame Belthazar in looks, and set out for my morning constitutional, which took me along the rue de Rive where, as I was passing the Perrin mansion the newly elected captain general and his wife emerged and got into their carriage. "Where are you off to?" I inquired.

"We're off to the country. We're having a hunt," said

Madame Perrin. "A pity you could not come, Monsieur Maigret."

I might have reminded her that I had not been invited, but I was willing to put it down to some confusion in her guest list. "But I will see you next week at Widow Belthazar's, will I not?"

They shouted back, "We'll be there," and while Barbarossa, my dog, barked hysterically, the driver lashed his horses and they went flying down the street, people jumping out of their way and turning around politely to doff their hats.

My walk took me up the hill to Hoch's bindery. "God be with you," I said to that unreconstructed fellow, and passed through the disorder of his shop to Antoine Calvin's printing press in the rear. Antoine was proofreading what turned out to be a communication Master Calvin was sending to each member of the Little Council, and Antoine gave it to me to peruse.

"It is to be recognized," I read, "that when people are incited by drums and fifes they begin hopping about frenziedly, hugging and kissing. Therefore, be it enacted—"

"He is quoting there from an ordinance against dancing enacted many years ago," Antoine explained. "And as you see, after quoting, he proceeds with his own comments."

I read it out loud—words have more meaning for me when I read them out loud. "It is the truth, crowds dancing are like unbridled calves (isn't it *calfs,* Antoine?—no, I guess not). All control, honor, and shame are lost. Perhaps intercourse does not take place, but there is an opening to it, an announcement of Satan's introduction. I request that this ordinance have your attention and that it be determinedly enforced."

Calvin himself came in just then. "This is a nettle you're grasping, Master Calvin," I said.

"Can anyone deny the truth of what I write?"

"No one," I agreed.

He was not there to chat. He had come only to make sure that Antoine had finished the letters which he wanted dis-

tributed to the councilmen, and he hurried off, head bent
forward in his usual manner. Since Barbarossa was showing
the ill effects of the smell of warm glue from Hoch's quarters,
I too departed on the end of the leash constraining the admi-
ral of the Turkish navy.

On the evening of the party I put on my best plumed hat,
had my servant give me a good brush, exchanged a look with
myself in the long mirror at the bottom of the stairs and
issued forth. A score of people, all of them well known to
me, were at the widow's for what was truly a banquet involv-
ing numberless dishes all served to the accompaniment of
fifes and drums. Sure enough, having drunk a great many
kinds of wine, the diners began to jiggle in their seats, and
had scarcely finished their sweets before they were leaping
up.

As usual, Madame Perrin was the ringleader—Franchequine Perrin, a raucous woman with the voice of a peahen. She was the daughter of François Favre, a notorious
rake, I reminded myself as I sat watching her performance;
once charged with raping a farmer's wife, Monsieur Favre had
told the judges, "It wasn't his wife, it was his daughter," and
had gone off to serve a brief sentence cackling incorrigibly.
Tum-ti-tum and *wheetle-tee-tee*—now Franchequine Perrin
was dragging Ambelard Corne, the draper onto the floor.
Oh, dear, Corne was an elder, president of the consistory, in
truth, and now quite crapulous. And as the evening wore on
he became altogether abandoned, bobbing like a rubber ball
in a whirlpool of women's gaudy skirts. So all the men, Captain General Perrin, the Chautemps brothers, the great lout
Pierre Vandel, Philibert Berthelier, Jacques Gruet. . . . I had
seen enough. My departure was precipitated by Franchequine Perrin screaming at me, "Why don't you dance,
Magnificent?" and dragging me into her embrace, which I
suffered for a moment before excusing myself on account of
the gout. I said goodnight to the disheveled Widow Belthazar, and left, long before, so I would judge, the party was
due to break up.

I spent a sleepless night. The one with whom Calvin most

significantly would have to deal was Captain General Perrin, and I thought about him as Barbarossa twitched in his sleep beside me. I was, of course, well acquainted with Ami Perrin. I had probably transacted more business in Paris for him than for anyone else, besides having been his emissary to Calvin in Strasbourg. I knew something of his background—of his father, a peddler, who had accumulated enough money to get his wooden plates and glassware off his back and purchase a shop in the place du Molard where he had prospered, enjoying much admiration for being self-made. What kind of a youth was his son, who had inherited his business? One of the minor officials in town hall whom I cultivated (it is the little mice who know all the crannies in the government) had put me onto an old record in the police files. Shortly after the town had freed itself of Savoy, but while the Roman Catholic Bishop Baume was still clinging to his see, there arrived on Guillaume Farel's heels another Reformer named Bocquet. Unaccountably—perhaps to show the disdain in which they held the bishop—the Little Council gave Bocquet permission to preach in a Franciscan monastery in the rue de Rive. There he appeared to exhort the sullen brothers of St. Francis. According to the report, one night a half dozen youths sauntered past the monastery wall.

With a little imagination I could conjure up the scene: one of the youths perhaps crying out, "What's that noise?" . . . "What noise?" . . . "A noise of some kind of violence" . . . "Has it to do with Bocquet, do you think?" They thereupon hurled themselves at the door.

They beat the first monk they met with the flat of their swords, and when another tried to intercede, one of the youths fell upon him shouting, "What have you done with Bocquet?" I did not have to make this part up; it was all in the record of complaint filed by the father superior. The youth would have murdered the monk (I could picture the fellow lying on the floor in a pool of blood) if the father superior had not rushed in swearing that Bocquet was nowhere around that night; the noise they heard was the cook chasing a chicken for tomorrow's dinner, and finally persuaded the intruders to sheathe their swords and depart. The youth responsible for almost murdering the monk was Ami Perrin.

There was no prosecution. Ami's father by this time was an influential man. I reflected on the fact that his son, who had grown up to inherit both his property and the prestige that always goes with property no matter how obtained, had some decidedly dangerous characteristics when he was young, and so far as I could see he had undergone no change. While Barbarossa growled at being disturbed I lay there turning this way and that.

WHEN I GOT TO HIM in the morning, Master Calvin was still in bed writing, looking wraithlike in his white nightcap. He said to me: "I am instructing the ministers in Neuchâtel on how to answer an ass at Johann Sturm's academy, a Chaponneau, who would divide the essence of God from Christ. I have written them that they have only to turn to Augustine." He took up a paper and read: "In substance, the Father is the same as the Son. Of himself, the Son is called God; in relation to the Father, he is called the Son. And again, on the other hand, of himself, the Father is called God; in relation to the Son he is called Father. When what is spoken relates to the Son, the Father is not the Son. When the Son is spoken of in relation to the Father, he is not the Father. When what is spoken relates to the Father and the Son as self-existent, this is the Father and the Son, the same, the one God. Now your little masterling, Chapponeau, may ask in what manner are the Father and the Son in the beginning—are there two beginnings? You can answer: by no means. As the Father is God and the Son God, so each is the beginning, not in two beginnings but only one beginning."

I waited patiently for the opportunity to tell him of the revelry at Madame Belthazar's.

He looked distressed. "Do you know how much I dislike doing what I have to do?" he asked. "Farel used to police the inns at closing time. I think he relished the work. I shrink from it." I felt a little chagrined, wondering if he would rather not be informed at all of lawbreaking. "I am one to defend doctrine and contest against heresy," he went on, "not to get drawn into these evil little things." He laid down his letter to the ministers of Neuchâtel. "Why must I do it? God, who knows of my shrinking from it, will forgive me because he knows that I will obey him nonetheless. Why must I? Because we are like children in a household in which the father is always present, and being in his love requires good behavior. God is like that, always among us. People drinking, women cavorting around like rutting goats; it is an affront to our Father." He sighed deeply and climbed out of bed. "We will assemble the consistory."

So it came about that my hilarious friends, and I (the role of a secret agent is not an easy one) were asked to appear that very afternoon before the pastors and the elders. They might have simply refused, but apparently they were not yet prepared for open defiance of the Ordinance of 1546. They stood in fashionable array before the chancel in St-Pierre, the whole lot of them (I noticed that Ami Perrin was missing) managing to convey an attitude of idle curiosity as to what the consistory would do, all of them being so prominent. Only President Corne showed any contrition; shaking from head to toe, he confessed to having broken the law. But the others denied that they had performed a single figure.

"Amberlard Corne has confessed that he was dancing," Calvin said. "He would not have danced alone. Moreover, we have heard from a witness that there were fifes and drums and that there was dancing of an abandoned sort."

"What witness?" Madame Perrin demanded. I kept a wooden face.

Calvin, who meanwhile was counting noses, inquired: "Where is the Captain General?"

"He had to go to Lyon on business," said his wife.

"That is regrettable. His presence would have set an example to others, who would know that the authority of the consistory extends without partiality to everyone who breaks the moral law."

"Authority to do what?" asked Pierre Vandel.

"To impose excommunication and remand you to the Little Council."

"Nobody broke any law," Madame Perrin declared. "And he is a liar who says anybody did." Our peahen's wattles shook, and she began to screech: "You want to drink our blood. You want to drive us from town. I say this to you, Master Calvin, if you don't look out, what happened to you before will happen to you again—"

"Such threats have no weight with me," Master Calvin said. "If I am banished from the city again, so be it. You ought to know by now who I am, one to whom respect for our Father is so dear that nothing will make me flinch from maintaining it. And I will lay aside my duty only with my last breath. Does that answer you, Madame Perrin? I say it in order to make it manifest to all of you that I intend to proceed firmly."

"Amen," one of the ministers, Abel Poupin, ventured to add, drawing Madame Perrin's fire on him. "Go back to France where you came from, you swineherd!" One of the elders admonished her, and she put on a contrite air then, and said in a flutey voice, "I'm a modest woman not used to speaking out."

"I suggest that in the language of abuse you have no match," said Pastor Poupin.

"You slanderer, you liar, Poupin," the lady—if we may call her that—screamed again. And she laughed scornfully as Calvin, the other ministers, and the elders moved into a circle briefly to confer, whereupon Calvin announced that yes, they all agreed that the entire guest list at Madame Belthazar's party should be barred until further notice from communion with our Lord, and must appear before the Little Council to see what civil punishment that body would mete out.

I did not relish being excommunicated, although I trusted that my position would be understood in heaven. Nor did I enjoy being sentenced with the others, the next day, to two days in jail. However, I put on a look of penitence and took my place in the procession that filed out of the Little Council's chamber in town hall to be herded up the street to the ecclesiastical palace, now the town dungeon, all of them sniggering and digging each other in the ribs, except Corne, who wore a look of anguish, and Madame Peahen, who kept kicking one of the bailiffs.

I quietly accepted incarceration in a basement cell that must have once been a groom's quarters by the smell. And there I sat that night, sleepless, with nothing to placate my stomach but a little bread and water, when I heard a rustling outside my cell and looked up to see two figures stealing along the corridor. One I identified as a matron of the jail, and the other, what's this?—Franchequine Perrin holding her cloak over her face. I considered raising an outcry but decided against it; she would gain nothing by fleeing. Where could she go? She would not want to exile herself forever from Geneva. I think she was merely acting like the fowl she resembled which likes to show how difficult it is to keep it cooped up.

As a matter of fact, she did not get very far. Master Calvin told me later of the circumstances of her recapture. It seemed that Pastor Poupin himself happened to be walking near the south gate when she came into view dressed as a man and mounted on a horse. She might have ridden by without his recognizing her, but she could not refrain from hurling imprecations at him, and he quickly called on the police to stop her.

I wakened abruptly having just dozed off, at the commotion that attended her return to jail.

Three days I spent in that odiferous hole. When we were let go we naturally attracted some gawkers who had never seen quite that many of the town's patricians emerging in one body from jail, a spectacle they seemed to enjoy.

I learned later that we left behind, incarcerated, the captain general. How had he got there? He had thought better of skipping off and had returned from Lyon to appear before the Little Council in a jocular mood, which some of the Little Council shared with him, to accept a sentence handed out by his friends almost apologetically.

T HE AFFAIR GAVE CALVIN NO PLEASURE, leaving him mostly anxious that people understood that his zeal was for their own welfare. He composed a letter to Perrin, which he let me read, containing a suggestion that he and Perrin talk things over. "I would consult with you not only over your salvation but your name," he wrote. "How odious would be any imputation that you consider yourself unrestrained by the common law. There have been remarks leveled at me to the effect that I must take care lest I stir up slumbering fires, and that what happened to me eight years ago might happen to me again. Unworthy treatment of me by some parties will not cause me to fail in my duty. These observations do not refer to you but that member of your family who is nearest to you. That is why I suggest that you consult with me in order to clear your name, and also that I may impress upon you the necessity of obedience to God and respect for the common order and polity of the church."

"Do you really intend to send this?" I asked him.

"Of course." He did not even inquire why I would have any doubt about it and expressed his surprise as days went by and Perrin did not reply. "Well, I trust, anyhow, that we have heard the last of his impudence," he said.

But we hadn't. One afternoon I dropped by Master Calvin's house to find Pastor Poupin there in a state of extreme agitation. He had just come from preaching a mid-week sermon at the Church of the Madeleine. Leafing through the Bible on his lectern with the intention of putting a mark at the daily lesson, he had come upon a note. It began: "Poupin, you pig." It went on to state that if he and the other ministers continued to interfere in the life of the town they would meet the same fate as Monk Werli. He had scarcely been able to get through the service. "Who is Werli?"

I told him, and of Werli being stabbed to death at the time of the revolution. And I allowed myself to indulge in some reminiscences about those tumultuous times when an effort had been made by the Catholic sympathizers to retaliate for Werli's death by poisoning Guillaume Farel's friend Viret, an account that added nothing to Poupin's composure.

Calvin decided that the note must be turned over to the authorities. It took little time to ascertain who the author was. One of the people who had been jailed was Jacques Gruet, a hanger-on in the Widow Belthazar's circle, who had been one of the more antic carousers at her party. He was always spouting queer ideas and enjoyed a vaguely sinister reputation that seemed to fascinate the widow; he had once poisoned a neighbor's dog, and he was, in fact, suspected of having supplied the poison that was put in Viret's spinach soup. He was a Savoyard, and the note was written in the patois of Savoy. He was seized, and a search was made of his house.

In his garret was a long scribble written in bad Latin which described Christ as "a seducer full of wicked presumptions," who deserved to be crucified, whose miracles were only sorceries and whose coming into the world had brought nothing but confusion. Apparently he was in the habit of jotting down every bizarre notion that occurred to him, for the police also turned up notes stuck in his desk, under his pillow, even scattered around the floor. *"Why can't I dance if I want to? Or fornicate? Who are these Frenchmen who are invading the city and telling us how to behave? The city belongs to the Genevese, to us, and to our fathers,"* he had scrawled, who himself was a Savoyard. *"Disaster impends. Thousands of citizens will be slain in a fratricidal conflict if the city continues to be ruled by the brain of one melancholy temperament."* He was obviously possessed.

His subsequent confession was conclusive. He screamed
out on the strappado, they told me, that Savoy would avenge
him. The duke would march on Geneva where he would find
allies inside its gates. Gruet was a cooked goose. Well, not
cooked, precisely; they took him to the execution grounds at
Champel and cut off his head. I witnessed the event, ex-
periencing my usual misgivings; I wondered if it were not
possible to punish an affront against God without doing such
violence to his handiwork.

I was more disturbed, however, by a violence I sensed
rather than saw. I was sure there was something more than
madness in Gruet's behavior and that Franchequine Perrin
was in on it. My servant Charles, whose one good eye was
enough for him to maintain a watch on our neighborhood,
informed me that the morning Poupin found the note, Gruet
had breakfasted with Franchequine's old man, Favre. My sus-
picions of her and her family were shortly confirmed by a
note she wrote the Little Council, which was soon on
everyone's tongue. Anabaptists scorned taking marriage
vows, she wrote, and since Madame Calvin had had children
by one of them she was a whore and should be banished from
the city. The letter made no reference to Gruet, but we know
how women will resort to irrelevancies when they are beside
themselves.

"She is a beast!" Calvin cried out. "Traducing my poor wife
in order to attack me—"

"The wild beast goes for the throat."

That her husband also was up to no good was soon evident.
He had no sooner emerged from jail than he formed a
society—recruited from the wilder youths of the city, I
noticed—which called itself *Les Enfants de Genève* and
paraded through the streets shouting anti-Calvin slogans.
Two of Perrin's cronies, Philibert Berthelier, whose prestige
rested on his father's martyrdom in the revolution, and Pierre
Vandel, who never failed to attract attention by the medals
and gold chains with which he festooned himself, led these
marchings, which caused a certain demoralization of some of

the lords of the councils, enough so the Perrinists almost succeeded in winning a majority at that year's elections.

The rivers froze, ice rimmed the lake, Ami Perrin greeted me with great bonhommie whenever we met, sometimes stooping to pat my dog (although I judge my connection with Master Calvin was now widely suspected since I was no longer invited to dinners), and Calvin went on writing and preaching with his habitual disregard for his physical resources. He suffered that winter from such a cough that he was unable to draw a breath without pain, an affliction that was not alleviated by his despondency, which was caused not alone by his adversaries in Geneva. The Reform movement appeared to be almost in ruins in its very birthplace as the Emperor Charles divided and cut up the Protestant princes of Germany piecemeal. He said to me one day: "I do not even try to think what the issue may finally be. Do you know how you close your eyes at the onset of some pain like the cut of a surgeon's knife? Sometimes I close my eyes and repel as much as I can all my reflections." He clenched his fists. "I fix my eyes on God alone."

In the dead of winter he set off on a journey to Zurich, which was not calculated to improve his cough. But Zurich was being threatened by the forces of the triumphant emperor, and he must exhort Paster Bullinger and the city's fathers to stand fast for Christ. I could see him bending his thin body against the icy winds along the Rhone. But he returned reassured; Zurich would resist to the last man, if it came to that. He got back as the willows along the lake were taking on the yellow pallor of spring.

GOD'S MAN! From where but heaven could he have derived his strength? Another man might have tried to dance cunningly around his enemies, trying to achieve his ends by

cultivating public acclaim. Not Master Calvin. Let anything
touch on his moral convictions, even when the matter was a
minor one, and he threw himself at it head on.

It was April and near the time of the arquebusiers' annual
shooting match. Now what was this! The militiamen, who
included a goodly number of the rowdy *Enfants,* petitioned
the Little Council to let them wear slashed hose at this widely
attended event. An odd fashion, when you thought of it,
cutting slits in the breeches to reveal the colored under-
socks. But the Swiss mercenaries had adopted it, liking the
cock-a-hoop effect, and since fashion follows fame, slashed
hose had become popular all over Europe. I had to admit that
I had once fancied the style myself when my thighs were of
such proportions I could afford to draw attention to them.
But there was no gainsaying it, the effect was immoderate,
and it was forbidden to display the hose in the city. Calvin
strode into the town hall where a group of arquebusiers had
gathered around Captain General Perrin, who himself had
sponsored their request and was slapping their shoulders and
guffawing with them.

"I do not have to remind you, my lords, that slashed hose
are against the law," said Master Calvin to the Little Council,
his voice hoarse from his persistent cough. "The petition
before you is inspired by silliness and vanity—wanting to
costume yourself like a coxcomb!—and scarcely reflects the
seriousness of the militia's mission, which is to defend our
city." The young men whistled derisively. "It would appear,"
he went on, "that Captain General Perrin merely intends
rather to lead his men in dancing at balls." There was a great
hubbub, out of which a vote finally emerged. It was close, but
the petition was turned down, and Perrin stormed out of the
meeting followed by glowering arquebusiers.

They held their match dressed in somber upper and nether
hose. The town, which was always crowded with people in
from the country for the event, seemed to be in a particularly
rebellious mood that night, I noticed walking up to Calvin's
to play a game of *clefs* with him (I insisted that he occasionally

allow himself some diversion), and I remarked that slashed hose was a small matter to be allowed to arouse such resentment.

"It is not a small matter," he said. "Besides the need to uphold the law, it was necessary to make an example of these men. Isn't the attitude of our young people deplorable enough? If you don't grant them what they ask for, then they threaten to go from bad to worse. Does that mean we are to grant them every license under the sun?"

"Certainly not. But I was thinking also of your relations with Perrin. I think it is not prudent to mock him, especially in public."

"This comic Caesar and his Penthesilia!" he said. "I will not suffer them to subvert my ministry," and he snapped the key so that it spun over the table and across the room.

14

I T WAS A TRIP I HAD NOT LOOKED FORWARD TO—at my
age one likes to remain, as much as possible, motionless—but
here I was a mule's day's journey from Paris, clumping along
with a clerk who was on his way to Calais. He did little to
relieve my tedium, being one of those fellows who runs on in
an unpunctuated voice, dropping names—should I know
him?—but I never quite caught the name. Although as we
were passing the woods of Fountainebleau I did catch "François"; my companion felt that it was appropriate to mention
sepulchrally that the most Christian king of France was dead.
He had, in fact, been dead for a month.

Unmourned by me. François had stood for everything I
had come to deplore. I had once been conducted by my
friend Le Maçon on a tour of the palace at Fountainebleau
and allowed to view this repository of pagan symbolism,
wrought by Italians and evoking nothing but profligacy and
licentiousness. I was allowed to peek into the bedchamber of
François's poor queen and into the chamber of Madame
d'Etampes, his mistress—both under the same roof!—the
room of the latter adorned by a fresco of starkly naked
women. I was shown the Galerie François, large enough for a
herd of elephants to cavort in, and I briefly entertained a

fantasy of the beasts brushing off Rosso's caryatids with their
hindends, plucking off the golden chandeliers with their
trunks, and leaving a debris through which no Christian piety
would ever shine.

As I approached Paris I thought of how death had overtaken England's Henry that same winter, requiring God to
deal with both these royal whoremongers and murderers in
the space of two months—not that I doubted his competence
to do so, although my faith was a little shaken by the thought
of the Emperor Charles still eluding judgment. Cock-of-
the-walk, the Protestant princes surrendering to him, marching unopposed into Wittenberg over the grave of poor Martin Luther. But away with these reflections; like Calvin, I
must fix my eyes on God. I reminded myself that my only
remaining interest in François was over the fact that his demise
accounted for my having to make this trip.

The Little Council had decided that it was incumbent upon
it to send an emissary to Paris with greetings to the new king,
Henri II—a mission calling for considerable tact, as I said to
Calvin, considering Geneva's proximity to the border of
France and the number of Henri's subjects who had been flock-
ing to our city for refuge. And who did the geese choose for
this delicate role? Captain General Ami Perrin, thus giving
this stupid and treacherous rascal every opportunity to make
mischief. John (I had come to address him as such, a privilege
he allowed very few others) asked me to follow him to Paris.
"You must keep an eye on him, Laurent." I must say the
assignment came a little tardily. Perrin had a lead on me of
several weeks.

I SAID GOODBYE TO MY TRAVELING COMPANION, the
clerk, grateful that I was not destined to accompany him to

Calais, and rode through the streets of Paris where a royal coffin draped in black velvet must have passed not so long ago on the way to the Cathedral St-Denis, trailed by prelates, chevaliers, soldiery, and ambassadors (including our worthy Ami Perrin, no doubt). I pulled up at the house of my friend Antoine le Maçon, whose offer of a bed I readily accepted.

We dined in a nearby tavern. He avowed knowing next to nothing about Geneva, only that a sour-faced anti-papist was trying to run the place, "by Holy Writ," he said cynically. He had got that from Perrin no doubt. "I know he wrote a Lutheran book because they burned it here in front of Notre Dame."

"The flames from that burning will consume France some day," I said ominously.

"You've become a Reformist? What are you doing in Paris?" he pressed me.

"Personal business. I'm largely idle these days." I avowed my own ignorance of the new king and his court, where, it turned out, Le Maçon still served as first secretary even though his old employer was gone—expiring ingloriously, he told me, of complications induced by syphilis and bellowing out to God to forgive him for his manifold sins. Madame d'Etampes, whom he had barred from his deathbed because of his appalling appearance, had gone to her bedchamber where she writhed on the floor and begged the earth to swallow her.

"Oh, Antoine," I said, "it is like the old days when you and I traded so many confidences." I filled his glass, and lowering my voice in the crowded tavern asked, "What of the new king?"

"He is ruled by the widow of the Seneschal of Normandy, Diane de Poitiers."

"You're making this up, Antoine. She is old enough to be his mother."

"Don't you know of young men infatuated with their mothers? She began mothering him when he was freed from prison in Madrid, poor little thing. He needed mothering, his own mother being dead and his father not liking him very much—"

"I never liked him very much either."

"To have your father deliver you to the Emperor Charles as a hostage, then have him marry you off at age fourteen to a little pudding like Catherine—it is bound to affect one's humor. And let us do justice to Diane. When little Henri arrived at puberty she took him between her legs and assauged his natural savagery."

"He once raped a Piedmontese peasant, a virgin," I recalled.

"Furthermore, she has observed the proprieties—she still wears widow's weeds—and she has seen to it that Henri goes occasionally to Catherine's bed. France owes her something. The Medici has produced two for the royal succession and is ripe with another."

"I knew the widow distantly. Quite rich—"

"Her husband left her considerable property, and Henri gives her a rake-off on his sales of royal appointments. He also showers her with jewelry, his latest gift being the crown jewels that his father gave Madame d'Etampes. Yes, very rich, and a woman of great strength."

"Her strength is not in her looks."

"No, it's in her Catholic faith. She'd be an archbishop if she were a man, and if she got her hands on your Calvin that would be his end. Whoop! Off to the stake! They say that her bed is a seminary where she instructs Henri in anti-Protestantism between his gasps of passion."

We addressed a fresh bottle of wine. "Antoine, dear friend," I said, "you must have run into a certain Captain General Perrin recently—an overdressed bumpkin who was sent here to convey Geneva's greetings to the new king."

"So that is why you're in Paris."

Oh dear, had I gone too fast? "We've never had any secrets from each other," I reminded him.

"I got him an audience with Henri. He's pushy. Is he one of your lords?"

"He's our leading dry goods merchant."

"Can he be believed?"

"By no means."

"He brought Henri the intelligence that Geneva is threatened with attack by the emperor."

"There is not a modicum of truth in it. Zurich may feel threatened, but Zurich is on the other side of the mountains and right under Charles's nose."

"What are we to think of the request he made?"

"Without knowing the nature of it—"

"You must protect me—"

"You will be protected even if they put me on the strappado," I promised, shivering nevertheless at the thought.

He whispered: "He wants the king to send him back to Geneva with two hundred horse."

"Two hundred horse! To begin with, where on earth does he think the city would quarter two hundred horse? It's already crowded with refugees."

"They are to help defend Geneva."

"Has this been decided on?"

"You will protect me?"

"To the death."

"The idea was not original with your captain general. Certain persons talked to him when he arrived and they proposed it, but he embraced it immediately."

"Who are they, Antoine? I am fascinated by all such detail."

"There were several, all of copious Catholic faith. Among them were the cardinal of Lorraine and the duke of Guise, whose son, incidentally is married to Diane's daughter."

"What is their purpose?"

"They would like to annex Geneva to France, and they are opposed to Protestantism."

"Do they have Henri's ear?"

"They have the ear that is closest to his, sharing as it does his pillow."

I stood up, if a little unsteadily. "I must get some sleep, Antoine. I must be off at daybreak." Supporting one another, we made our way out of the tavern. The first thing in the morning, mounted on a horse—mules would be too slow—I was galloping south for Geneva.

I rode every mile of the way in apprehension. Antoine Le Maçon was a gossipy and mischievous man who liked spilling the soup, but I could not rid my mind of the fear that when he woke up in the morning he might regret his indiscretions and send agents in pursuit of me. Powerful persons were involved in this affair. And Perrin—I could predict his every move. He would discover a plan of Charles's, to march across the mountains, and in such an emergency, as captain general of the militia and supported by the French cavalry, he would repose all authority in himself. The councils, with no way to assert themselves but through a few bailiffs armed with halberds, would be rendered impotent, Calvin and his pastors would be banished, and Geneva would find itself a protectorate of France with that rascal Perrin as its governor. It was with thanks to God that I came safe and sound to Cornavin Gate. I reached home and fell into bed exhausted.

By morning I was able to make my way up the rue des Chanoines and report to John. We agreed, there was no question that the matter was one requiring immediate action, and that the best course was for me to inform the apothecary Aubert, keeping John's involvement secret. I repaired to Aubert's shop, and he went off, breathless with his news, to inform the Little Council. Before the day was out they sent for me.

Aubert made a very moving speech. "Once before," he said, "our gracious friend, Monsieur Maigret, was instrumental in saving Geneva from her enemies when he persuaded François to move against Savoy. Now our enemies are François's son, and my lords, one of our own, and we thought, trusted, citizens. We owe Monsieur Maigret our gratitude."

The speech impressed them, but they wanted to know the source of my information. I told them that I had been sworn to secrecy, but as they all knew, I had many friends in Paris, and my source was someone not too far from the king. How did it happen that I was in Paris? The question was put to me suspiciously by that popinjay, Pierre Vandel. I happened to be there on personal business, I told him shortly. Was I acquainted with the duke of Guise or the cardinal of Lorraine? Vandel eyed me darkly. Slightly, I said.

I could see that they were greatly agitated. They asked me what steps I thought they should take. I told them they should station militiamen at Cornavin Gate to take Perrin into custody when he appeared and bar the way to any French cavalry.

Several weeks went by while the city stood in a kind of state of siege. Then one morning my servant came to me to report excitedly that Captain General Perrin had been arrested at Cornavin Gate and taken off to jail. I put a leash on Barbarrosa. I would go out and take the temper of the town, since the news of Perrin's arrest would have spread like wildfire, and I opened the door to find two policemen standing there.

"Where are you going, Monsieur Maigret?" one of them inquired.

"Why, out for a walk."

"You will have to walk in the direction of jail, Monsieur Maigret. You are under arrest."

I let these oafs see my astonishment. "On what charge?"

"The instrument in my hands says treason."

Treason! I paced around the cell to which they relegated me (the same mean cubicle I had occupied before), while I adjured the guards, when I could get one to stop and listen, to fetch one of the lords of the Little Council. After some hours, Aubert appeared. "The Perrinists have turned the tables on us," he lamented. "An official from Bern arrived this morning to say they have evidence it was you not Perrin the duke of Guise and the cardinal of Lorraine communicated with. He said they had this from their own ambassador to Paris. At least half the Little Council believed him."

Why, I implored Aubert, does Bern lend itself to such deceit?

"Perrin has good friends there who have no love for Master Calvin. They would purge Switzerland of him," Aubert said. "Perrin is an ally." (An emetic in my book.) "They must save his life."

To that end I must be destroyed! I was overcome. I questioned whether I had the fortitude to walk the road to Champel. "Now what?" I moaned.

"You are not dead yet," Aubert said encouragingly. "There are councilmen inclined to disbelieve the Bernese ambassador. The first syndic, Maisonneuve, is among them. There was much argument, but the decision arrived at was to have the Council of Two Hundred try you both for treason at the same time. Truth will conquer, Monsieur Maigret."

But I was a lamb beside this Genevese lion Perrin, and worse, a French lamb. I closed my eyes. John had never known things to be in such disorder as this. I felt the cut of the ax, the flames devouring me. But like John, I would keep my eyes fixed on God.

And so I did, and I saw how God has many unusual ways of preserving his servants, even by compounding disorder to the point where only he could compose it.

As the trial proceeded under the shaky direction of Monsieur Lambert, the public prosecutor, it became apparent that political power, not justice was at stake. My dear John rose courageously to testify that I was a man of proven integrity—the captain general himself had trusted me in the past to carry out sensitive missions for him—and that it was he, Calvin, who had sent me to Paris because of his doubts about Perrin, confirmed by the information I brought back. The court was in an uproar at this. Perrin, who brazenly glared at me from across the room, scoffed at my story while insistently repeating the one put forth by the Bernese ambassador who, significantly, was not present.

With little weighing of evidence (admittedly there wasn't much), the courtroom became a storm of factional outcries, Perrinists demanding that I be executed, Calvinists demanding that Perrin be put to the stake. At one point, Madame Perrin, sweeping past me, spat in my face.

The storm erupted from the town hall into the streets. A mob collected in the courtyard. We all ran to the windows. People were yelling at the council and at each other, some demanding that Perrin be freed, others, I was happy to note, demanding that I be set free. Many, waving swords, pressed up to the door where only a handful of bailiffs barred the way. It was then that I saw John leave the courtroom, his face pale under his black cap, and the next I knew he was outside facing the mob. I heard his voice:

"Don't you know that to threaten the workings of civil law is to threaten God's kingdom on earth?"

Some shouted: "We don't hear you, Calvin."

"Disperse!" he ordered. "I say, disperse."

Instead, they surged towards him and began pulling him about while the bailiffs stood there in attitudes of helplessness. He wrenched himself loose, raising his arms over his head. I heard his voice: "Do you have to shed blood? All right, begin with mine. God is my witness. Here is my body for your swords."

They gawked at him. They began sheathing their swords, those in the front ranks turning away, and as they did the rear ranks followed. And jostling one another ill-temperedly, they shuffled off.

"The Lord has intervened," John said quietly when he reappeared in the chamber. "He does not want to see our city plunged into civil strife. He would lay a reconciling hand on us. Put aside these arguments now, and let us return to our work and set an example of living peacefully together without any more recriminations. I for one am ready to withdraw anything I have said about Captain General Perrin."

"As for me, I think what Master Calvin says does him credit," Perrin responded pompously.

Monsieur Lambert presented a summation of the testimony and the evidence. "After all," he said, "there was not very much, and the French horses have not materialized." I myself doubted that they would now. Monsieur Lambert disavowed any further interest in pursuing the case, and on motion by Maisonneuve, the council voted to dismiss all charges.

I was profoundly relieved (it is not amusing to have one's very existence threatened), but I knew that a crisis had only been postponed.

15

I N THE MIDST OF MY RECOLLECTIONS of Cousin Louise I would sometimes find myself thinking of the unhappiness I had probably been spared by her death, a thought that was not to my credit, I admit, but men are wholly self-centered, and I had observed so often, among my friends, the sorrow that involvement with women can bring. I saw such sorrow descend on John.

His domestic situation was at best more than I could have borne. Idelette was ill in bed oftener than she was up and about, and so lacking in firmness as to be quite incapable of disciplining her two children. John breathed with relief when they left in the morning for school, and shut himself in his room when they were home. I do not doubt that the stern visage he presented when he emerged only increased their churlishness. I have found it to be true, that men who know what is best for society are unable to cope with their families. But it was Antoine's wife, Anne Le Fert who was the most serious problem.

She and Antoine continued to live with John for a year or so after they were married. There was an animal-like quality about this woman, who said very little in company, smiling timidly, but constantly hunting with her eyes—men could sense the search. Were the Le Ferts, whose head was a decent, honest merchant, accursed? Anne's sister Jacqueline had been murdered, the body, with stab wounds over the heart, found one night in the place du Molard, certainly the devil's work. She had not been robbed; she still wore an expensive necklace and rings. I wondered if she had had the same miasmic aura that Anne had, a woman with a want that needed constant filling. I am sure it was what had intoxicated Antoine, who confused it with love, whereas his real devotion was for his brother. Where he found ecstasy was in printing John's books and tracts. He would return home late at night, tired out, to the bed where Anne lay waiting for another kind of ecstasy. I felt some sympathy for her, in spite of myself, living in this crowded, God-haunted house.

Antoine and she finally moved into a house of their own just off the place du Molard. I did not see much of her after that, only when I happened to encounter her chatting in front of some shop with Jean Chautemps, who was supposed to be employed at his father's paper mill but spent most of his time in roistering, drinking, and hanging around the streets. He was a severe trial to Chautemps, Sr., a decent man like Le Fert, a member of the Little Council and treasurer of the hospital. He had two other sons who were, if anything, worse rogues than Jean. One could see again how women produce difficulties with their fecundity.

When I saw Anne in converse with Jean on a street corner I would think how like attracts like. I was not surprised when I heard that the pair had been arrested. Antoine had returned one night to find Jean at his house. I do not believe he found them in bed, because the presentment, which I took pains to examine in the council register, stated simply that Chautemps was found in the house of Antoine Calvin "at an indiscreet hour." The pair was released after ten days in jail, when it was noted in the register that there was "nothing evident but only presumed . . . Madame Calvin vowed to live honestly henceforth . . . Monsieur Chautemps promised he will no more frequent her house."

I am not one of those who immediately rush to friends with expressions of sympathy when what they are really there for is to hear all the details of the disaster. But after Anne was exonerated, and while the Perrin crowd continued to roll the affair around on their malicious tongues, I stopped in at John's house. I found him quite cheerful. We talked about sundry matters, including some recent slurs that Franchequine Perrin had been casting at the consistory, and he said he sometimes wondered which one, Madame Perrin or her husband, was the most iniquitous. I said I had no doubt about her influence on him being so profound, and I added, "I long ago concluded that women are at the bottom of everything, certainly of things that cause us pain." He asked if I was referring to Antoine's wife, and I said I had her in mind, along with others, of course.

He was undisturbed. "The affair is closed," he said. "Anne came to Antoine begging him to believe the best of her and telling him in what reverence she held the marriage vows. In a way, Antoine can be grateful to her for affording him the chance to show his Christian spirit. He quickly forgave her."

I inquired if he had also.

"I was in a rage at the woman. You have seen me lose my temper. Or have you? I do my best to suppress the fire that seethes in me on certain occasions. But Antoine was an example to me. Yes, I forgave her."

He sometimes surprised me by sudden humility. Well, I would forgive her too. But I thought, we shall see; I could not believe that she had got the devil off her back.

WOMEN SUCK MEN TO THEM, then betray them or wrap them in so much devotion that the poor husband is left in despair if the creature happens to become ill and dies. I could not say which I thought might be the harder to bear, losing

one's wife through treachery or untimely death. I mused on
this in the light of Idelette's sad state, wondering how John
would bear up if he lost her. And late that spring when he was
plunging into another revision of his *Institutes of the Christian Religion* and needed all his thoughts for this, she died.

Antoine, who was at his house that night, told me how she
had suddenly called to him and said, "John, I am thinking
about my children." He said to her, "I will take care of them."
She said she had commended them to God, and John said
again he would watch out for them. "Pray with me," she
whispered, and as they prayed she came quietly to the end of
her limited resources.

I sat with him one evening after he had buried her. Above
us rose God's Juras, somewhat overweeningly, I thought, and
so did he because he looked at them in consternation and
began to weep. "Throughout her illness she was never
troublesome to me. I have lost the best companion of my life.
She was my strength."

I remembered his telling me once how he thought death
should be regarded, and I thought it was appropriate to remind him of it. "A friend had just had a grandson, you told
me, and you wrote to him that you wished you could be with
him so you could both laugh together over the howling infant. It was your idea that laughter be the first note we hear
when we begin life so that we remember to laugh when we
leave it."

But there was no laughter now in the wretched man's
face.

S ORROW, SORROW—BACHELORHOOD HAD SPARED ME SO
much of it, while John had so much to bear already. Railed
against, insulted. Some people named their dogs "Calvin"
and shortened it to "Cain." Sacristies in France circulated

venomous lies about him. At a rumor that he was dead the priests of his birthplace, Noyon, held a service of thanksgiving. John did laugh when that story reached us. But he found no gratification even in knowing that such hatred was provoked by his increasing influence. I knew his dejection, preaching God's love, which everyone should share, while men rejected him more and more. From the high pulpit in St-Pierre's he spoke to his congregation one Sunday morning: "My days are swifter than a weaver's shuttle and are spent without hope. O Lord, show me why you contend with me." It was the lament of Job.

A new year began. Perrinists won a majority in both councils and elected Captain General Perrin a syndic. Oh, where was God these days, John?

PART FIVE

"For your sake I have suffered rebuke,"
Jeremiah said to the Lord.
"I sat alone
because you filled me with indignation.
Why is my pain perpetual
and my wound incurable?
Will I be altogether unto you
as waters that fail?"

I see the shadows
of all the people
who would sit in judgment
on me.

16

I SPENT THE WHOLE DAY trying to catch up on my correspondence while my little engine, Baudoin, scratched away, looking up at me with his frog's eyes whenever my voice faltered. I was determined not to flag before he did. But, as I wrote Bullinger (with whom I had recently reached an agreement on the sacraments that greatly angered the Lutherans), I sometimes was so exhausted by constant writing that I felt an almost positive aversion to dictating a letter and wished that others had some of his moderation as would enable them to cultivate a sincere friendship with less letter-writing. My friends in France were particularly importunate; well, they were suffering at the hand of that devil Henri so courageously, I could not neglect them. I thought of a Monsieur Venot being stood for six weeks in the pit they called Hippocras's Cup and telling his torturers, "You waste your time, messieurs," before they put him to the stake.

I must write Farel and tell him that his latest book disappointed me. But first, what did Guillaume think of the college of cardinals taking almost four months to elect a new pope? "Julius III ought to be an extraordinary monster seeing that the best workmen have wrought so long in his creation."—Back to the book. "I am afraid, dear Guillaume, that the involved style and tedious discussion will obscure the light which is really in it." One did one's friends no favor by praising them undeservedly.

Somerset must have a letter, pulled down from his peak, as he was, deposed as little Edward's protector. I reminded him that prosperity sometimes so dazzles our eyes that we cannot see why God chastises us, but we must honor God as we would a physician who pursues a course of healing not according to our liking but as he knows and judges to be best. He had sent me a ring once belonging to his mother in gratitude for my several letters of advice. I thanked him for it. He had achieved much as England's regent in getting rid of many vestiges of papist practices.

Baudoin looked up to inquire who the new regent was. The earl of Warwick, I told him, whom I did not trust. We would have to rely on Archbishop Cranmer to increase the gains Somerset had made. Baudoin lighted some candles; daylight did not last long through my narrow windows. I must rebuke Melanchthon for accepting so readily the so-called interim agreement the emperor had rammed down the throats of the Protestant princes. Why hadn't he the courage to resist it; did he want peace before all else? He didn't fear death; was it then the goading of the people around him?

I must again urge Nicholas Colladon in Paris to come to us with his family. Worthy Frenchmen, causing me to rejoice, were arriving in goodly numbers, one being Theodore Beza, whom I had sent on to teach Greek at Viret's college in Lausanne. Ah yes, I owed Viret a letter; I had overlooked him too long. Also Seigneur de Falais, son of the duke of Burgundy and kin of the Emperor Charles, had come to us, as had the mayor of Noyon, the noble Laurent de Normandie, and Paris' eminent printer Estienne, and Guillaume Budé's widow and her family whose son Louis was helping me on my commentaries on David and Solomon.

"You will still find people here, dear Nicholas Colladon," I dictated, "who are unmannerly enough; you will meet with some sufficiently annoying trials. In short, do not expect to better your condition except in so far that having been delivered from miserable bondage of body and soul you will have leave to serve God faithfully."

The day had expired, and I was already late for the meeting of the Venerable Company of Pastors, so I dismissed Baudoin and took myself off to the chapel of St-Pierre's, where, since the meeting had begun, I sat down quietly in the rear among the townspeople. They were always welcome to attend. Michael Cop was expounding on the doctrine of election. "Those who are not regenerated by the spirit of God," he was saying, "continue in a state of rebellion because obedience is a gift accorded only to the elect."

I saw a certain Jerome Bolsec rise from the benches. He was a Carmelite monk who had studied medicine, fled from France to Italy, and recently lighted in Geneva. He had ingratiated himself with Jacques de Falais by curing the seigneur's maid servant of cancer. Or so it was said. Now he announced modestly enough that as a physician he knew something of life and death, and he vouchsafed agreement with a great deal of what I taught. But then he launched an attack on the doctrine of predestination. "If a man has faith, God will grant him salvation," he bellowed. His little black beard quivered with excitement. How could anyone accept the doctrine, he went on, that it did not matter what good a man did if God had not already chosen him? Where did this notion come from?

I stood up then. I said that the notion came from St. Augustine, among others.

He was momentarily taken aback at my presence, but rallied to shout, "Our election depends on our faith and faith originates within ourselves. You also affirm, Master Calvin, that God wills all things. Including sin? They why did he punish the people of Sodom? What injustice—to destroy them for doing what he destined them to! I know where you got this: not from Augustine but from the ancients who laid the blame for all things on Jove."

I was determined not to lose my temper. I answered that

sin could in no way be applied to God, but this did not hinder him from exercising his power through Satan and the wicked, making them instruments of his wrath in some cases to teach the faithful patience.

But Bolsec began to harangue the townspeople then, who, I saw, were finding more excitement in a meeting of the Venerable Pastors than they had anticipated. "The city has been agitated lately by accusations of treachery," he orated. "But that was a little thing. I say Calvin has been betraying you in your faith. The Church of Geneva has been false to you. Don't be deceived by it any longer." And before he could be apprehended he was gone from the chapel.

"So THERE YOU HAVE IT, MY LORDS." Ami Perrin, addressing the Little Council, did not try to hide his glee. "You see how these Frenchmen are not only eating us out of house and home and pushing up prices; they are showing so much natural treachery they will bite off each others' noses. They have been asking that we make them citizens. How could we ever trust them? How could we know they aren't plotting against us?"

The council was meeting to take action against Bolsec, who had been arrested, his fulminations at the meeting of the Venerable Pastors being cause enough, but he had further threatened the tranquility of the city by proceeding for the next several days to several taverns where he had repeated his impieties and his rantings against our church.

Captain General Perrin was not through. "Who brought these Frenchmen here?" he demanded. "Why, Master Calvin."

I did not answer the clown. I and the others of the Venerable Company were there to witness against Bolsec, whose impostures took precedence over Perrin's blatant irrelevancies. Bolsec sat in the prisoner's dock looking almost demure, and when he was called upon to defend himself he stated coolly, "You have only to read Calvin's *Institutes of the Christian Religion* to find everything I said about his libeling both God and mankind confirmed." Some councilmen admitted that they did not clearly see through all the points that were raised. "It is quite simple," said Bolsec. "According to his doctrine you were condemned before you were born and no amount of good behavior is going to save you."

I said it was not simple at all, but that Bolsec was right, my doctrine was set forth in the *Institutes.* It was furthermore part of the teachings of Martin Luther and the warp and woof of the evangelical religion.

"This I deny," said Bolsec. "The ministers of Basel and Zurich and Bern do not accept it. Ask them, my lords."

"Very well, ask them," I readily agreed.

Bolsec was returned to jail to await their replies, and I went home and composed a letter as coming from the Company of Pastors to the ministers of the three cities. That would make our position clear: "We have no reason to entreat your confidence in so many words. The *Institutes of the Christian Religion* by our own brother Calvin is known amongst you. It is not needed to record with what reverence and sobriety Master Calvin has herein discussed the question of the secret judgment of God; the book is its own bright witness. We are anxious to have this plague removed from our church so that it may not infect our neighbors when we have got rid of it ourselves."

The only sound coming in my window was the watchman proceeding up the street. I could not sleep. I had finished the letter but the awful problem of predestination rattled around in my head so that I kept getting up, walking around, sitting on my bed. I set some fresh candles on my desk. God would observe this light in a night-fast world. I had the idea—a grotesque one, I admit—that I would reduce the whole subject to verse. I made a few lumbering starts, then hit a fairly good stride.

The truth, my lords, to which the prophets attest
Is that nothing falls to us except by God's bequest.
We stand before his throne, by him regarded
Either as participants in his love or already alienated,
All of us cast in an unfathomable plan, God-created—
Some to be saved, others discarded.
And if we say his judgment can be changed by a person doing
    good or doing ill
We deny his omnipotence, make him subject to our will.
Nor should we think of him as gazing from above,
Searching in the bedlam of the human race
Those whose deportment might seem to have earned his
    grace—
He has already selected them and bound them by his love.
Can we not comprehend it? Consider what we've learned.
From Christ conceived by the Holy Ghost—would we say
He was made the Son by his righteous way?
To say that this was how it was done
Is to say that grace was not freely given to the Son.
Just so God bestows on some a grace freely given and
    unearned.

Should I not admit my adversaries to the discussion? Very
well, come Bolsec, poets, other men of wit to posit:

Are we to believe that God is so feckless
As to form us exquisitely only to reject us?
You show him painting in a timeless frame
Figures of grace and figures of shame.
Your world is not a bedlam but a tableau, in fact,
Each person fixed in some specified act—
Of honorable labor,
Cheating his neighbor,
Spreading charity, committing murder—all preordained.
A few, foreknown to him, to be retained,
Most to be wiped out by the Maker's clout.
Where are justice and mercy, or do we leave that out?

We perceive God's mercy when we understand.
Let me begin. Some writers turn to Luke and the traveler's
    story.
He was robbed and left half-dead. Ah, they say, an allegory:
Half-dead, he's half-alive, thus still

Able to exercise some power of will.
It's a parable, they say, to illustrate the state of man,
Who though fallen is half-good, so able to win salvation
If only he will mind God's revelation.
But I say the story does not pertain at all
To the state of man after Adam's fall.
The true allegory would have the traveler left
Not half-alive but wholly dead, that is to say, bereft
Of all the endowments that Adam enjoyed
Before he sinned in pride, and, estranged in heart and mind,
Died leaving to all mankind
His sinful heritage: all of his seed to be destroyed,
Born as all are, depraved.
It is only through God's mercy some are saved.

Come then Pelagius and others of his tribe.

It's a rigged game.
First, poor Adam made to fail
Then down his trail
Plunge all his children headlong—
No other way to go, you say—it's wrong,
We claim.
Tell us, what must God have in mind
With a mindless arrangement of this kind?

Fools look for cause above God's will. How useless to persist
In looking for something that can't exist.

Well, come at it in another way.
You bring forth Scripture and you say,
Here's all the proof we need
To validate this awful creed.
Let's open the Book. Would you care
To point out where?

Open the Book. While there were others to choose,
God chose the Jews,
Stubborn as they were, stiff-necked,
He covenanted with them and made them his elect.
And from Abraham's yield
Winnowed the seed to plant his field:
Isaac over Ishmael, Jacob over Esau,

Ephraim instead of Manasseh, choosing each by law
Known only to himself, never disclosed to us
To whom it must remain, and remain mysterious.
The words of the Book admit of no other construction.
You doubt? Read John who quotes the Son (and none more
    truly attends him):
"None can come to me except the Father sends him . . .
I pray not for the world but for those the Father gives me."
Thus Christ reveals there are those marked off by divine
    decree,
And the rest of the world is consigned to destruction.

Come philosophers and theologians to quote from the
Book contrarily:

"God so loved the world that he gave his only begotten Son."
Would not the writer of this have "the world" mean everyone?
"That whosoever believed in him would have everlasting life." The
    author?
Your same John. Moreover, in the phrase "whosoever believed"
God seems to be saying he is to be relieved
Of having to select
Those to retain, those to reject.
Instead he merely presides
While each person decides
How to trade in on this heavenly offer.

Of course God loves the world; it was his own creation.
But divine love confounds interpretation.
John did not mean what you say he meant.
He meant, the faithful are of God's chosen element
And truly believing will feel the leaven
That lifts the spirit with hope of eternal life in heaven.
But here's the crux: true faith, or its opposite, is not left to a
    person's choosing
As something to arrive at after musing.

I am interrupted at this point by a clamor of many voices:

What! You deny free will? Then there is no shame,
And whatever we do we're not to blame?
This is what you say, do you not?
We must hold the potter accountable, not the pot?"

I say no such thing but something more profound.
Actually, of all creatures man is most free,
But human nature makes of sin a necessity.
This is not incongruous. God of necessity is good, don't we
    say?
And Satan is wicked in the same way?
Now turn this thought around.
We do not say that good in one case, or in the other case,
Is not of God's or the devil's will.
Likewise we are not compelled to sin. It's our own
    undertaking,
Our sinful errors, our own willful making.
Who wills so that evil follows can't pretend
That he is guiltless, being born depraved.
In a peculiar manner all persons are enslaved—
And free. Free, that is to sin. While it also behooves us
To remember: we cannot do good unless God's spirit moves
    us.
By this I don't contend
That we are not borne along without any motion of our heart,
But we're impelled by a force in which we have no part,
So affected by a spirit seizing us from within
That we do obey God's will and refrain from sin,
And through grace so bestowed—through its mysterious
    effect—
Salvation comes to us whom he saw fit to elect.
I do not say this grace comes all at once
But comes to us through perseverance,
Which itself must be bestowed, is of itself a gift of grace.
We come to salvation in an irresistible embrace.

But still, how do you explain discrimination?
If all souls start out bearing God's incrimination,
Why shouldn't God let all of humanity go to hell,
Leaving none to tell
The mistake that he mandated?
It wasn't our idea to be created.

You accuse God because the attestations
To his greatness and omnipotence will not permit
The understanding of your limited wit.
You ask me to explain it. I am only a man
Like you, no better able to see what no man can:
Who are we, then, to make accusations?

"Thou seekest reasons," Augustine said. "I can only tremble
   at the breadth of it,
I only see how deep it is, I cannot reach the depth of it."
Why does God save some, let others go?
There is only the answer: It pleases him to do so.

Come now some members of my congregation imploring:

Then say at least, Master Calvin, how we may know.
If we were elected or not—how will it show?

The devil with men contrives to meet
On purpose to unsettle them with doubt
And leave them weeping: "What if God in his disposing has
   left me out?" Or prod some to nag God with persistence
Demanding to know what he intends with their existence.
As if anyone could penetrate the judgment seat.
What a devilish snare,
Capturing men in torment and despair!
But I will tell you: begin with the Word and end with it.
The Word will tell you all you need to know of it:
That the purpose of election is to populate his kingdom
With a host from earth to glorify and sing of him.
These he loves, loving them as he loves his Son.
So gaze in the mirror that is Jesus Christ. Put aside all
   self-deception;
See what you see of your own reflection—
By which I mean, if you and the Son are in communion,
Then you may believe you've been engrafted in the blessed
   union.
But only attend to yourself, do not speculate about your
   neighbor,
For the greatest of all mysteries is how the Spirit moves
   amongst us.
Human eyes see many instances of injustice,
See men who seem to be exalted, perfuming the air with
   piety,
Cunningly covering up their insobriety.
And other men may seem deliberately to labor
Towards their own undoing, God's favor in no way manifest
As they wander drunkenly in the wilderness.
They have sinned. They bear all the marks of the reprobate.

But remember, God gathers some up early, some up late,
And even as like foolish sheep they flee
To come to the very brink, puts forth his hand.
Are you one of these? Hear you the voice from the upland:
"I will not cast out those who come to me . . .
I know my sheep, my Father's sheep. Nothing shall take them
  from me."
There you have it, my lords, at least you have it in part.
I've taken pages in my *Institutes* to explore the thought
Of a doctrine that seems too dreadful, so I wot.
And as hard to contemplate as to express—
Oh, predestination makes us tremble, I confess.
But as the omnipotence of God cannot be computed,
So the logic of divine election cannot be disputed.
And behold, you of faith, it should not crush, but lift your
  heart.

The horns were blowing from the corners of the city. I hid
the manuscript where Baudoin would not discover it. I would
read it all over sometime, then destroy it. I did not want to
acquire notoriety as a rhymer.

P ERSONS IN A RAGE WILL VENT THEIR FEELINGS on
whomever happens to be at hand; I am no exception. My
behavior, to my shame, is often unexceptional. It was poor
Maigret who received the full draft of my wrath at the replies
of the other cities. He had stopped by to play a game of *clef*
on an afternoon when I clutched the answer from Bern,
which the Little Council had just sent over to me. Bern had
been the last to respond. Basel had written that they were for
moderation on the question of predestination; it being so
intricate, they preferred to put the emphasis on simple faith.
(What was simple about faith?) As for Zurich, one would
have thought Bullinger and his pastors had never heard of

predestination, their reply was so lukewarm. Now here was
Bern, capping the others in its blindness.

"Keys!" I shouted at Maigret. "What have I to do with
such a fools' game?" And I thrust Bern's letter at him, unable
to read it out loud. Its superciliousness choked me.

" 'To come to the subject of dispute with Bolsec,' " Maigret
intoned, drawing himself up in the very image of a lord of
Bern and causing me to smile in spite of myself, " 'you are not
ignorant of how much vexation it has caused very many good
men, of whom we cannot have a bad opinion, who reading in
the Scriptures those passages which exalt the grace of God to
all men, have not sufficient discernment rightly to understand the true mysteries of divine election, attach themselves
to the proclamation of grace and of universal benevolence'—
such a rhapsody of words, where are they taking us?"

"Continue."

" 'And think that we cannot make God condemn, harden,
and blind any man without being guilty of the insupportable
blasphemy of making God himself the author of man's blindness and of his perdition, and by consequence of all sin.' "
Maigret stopped and stared at me, affecting to be out of
breath. "Where have we arrived at?"

"We have arrived at thinking Bolsec may have been in
error in his reading of the Scripture, but he's a good fellow
who should be forgiven. Many make the same mistake. Read
the next part."

" 'We do not believe that it is necessary to treat those who
err with too much severity, lest while wishing to defend with
too great zeal the purity of dogma, we swerve from the law of
Jesus Christ, that is, from charity—' " reading the last words
in an admonitory voice and raising one hand in mock solem-
nity.

But any sense of comedy had left me. "So the purity of
dogma is not to be defended," I fairly shouted. "Nothing is
certain. The Scripture is a *nasus cerea,* and the faith all Christians hold concerning the Trinity, predestination, justifica-

tion by free grace are things indifferent over which men may contend at pleasure. Christ would have us be tolerant of such contention. I say this is not the charity Christ preached. Error is error. We are being pulled apart not by dogma but by indulgence."

T HE MAGISTRATES OF THE LITTLE COUNCIL insisted on showing the letters to Bolsec, so he arrived at his trial puffed up with self-confidence, winking at Ami Perrin and others who in their hostility to me seemed to have forgotten that he was a Frenchman, and enjoying, to my dismay, the reassuring glances of Seigneur De Falais, whom I had counted as one of my closest friends among recent refugees, but who seemed to be infatuated with the man who had cured his maid-servant of cancer, if indeed he had. A number of councilmen would have released the doctor without further ado. But I had prepared myself. I had in my hands a Bible and St. Augustine's *Predestianone,* which I submitted in evidence, and in addition a statement signed by the Venerable Company of Pastors. It made clear that we cared not what the rest of the Swiss churches deposed, or that Geneva stood alone in this matter, if Bolsec was not banished (the most moderate of punishments) the entire company would leave the city.

This caused much debate, from which the prevailing opinion emerged that the city could get along without the doctor but not without its church. "In the long run," said one magistrate, whom I could identify over intervening heads as little Aubert, "institutions have to be preserved against men," a statement with which I was not in full accord but did not think it wise at this state to question.

Bolsec was found to have harbored false opinions contrary to Holy Scripture and the evangelical religion—a decision I would have put in much stronger terms—and banished forever from Geneva.

But it was an affair, in the time it consumed and the trouble it piled on top of my other troubles, that I could have done without.

17

T RIED BY BARKING FOXES and all manner of mad dogs, I preached at least three hundred sermons that year, two hundred of them on Deuteronomy, which Antoine printed and Hans Hoch bound, stacking the pages on his table and cackling, "You're keeping me in business, Master Calvin; I don't complain. But I wouldn't have believed there was so much to say about anything, anyhow not about a handful of wretched Jews."

I asked him if he ever saw further than his nose. Wretched Jews? Deuteronomy was God's testament to his anointed people! Hoch was like so many in his trade, printers, book-binders, who treated words as bricks to be laid in place, having no thought of the souls and consequences of words.

Secretaries were the same. I had a new one to help Baudoin, Nicholas de la Fontaine, who seemed only a little more aware than was Baudoin of the meaning of what he was writing down. But since I preached extemporaneously from notes, my sermons would have been, in fact, a scattering of bricks, if my secretaries had not gathered them together for me. It was not too arduous a task; my sermons were brief. There were some preachers who were like hod carriers climbing up to their pulpits and dumping out prolixities on

231

their congregations. I had constantly to admonish Guillaume
Farel on this score. The Gospel must not be brought into
contempt by tediousness, I told him.

Some preachers, on the other hand—I thought as I left
Hoch's shop with a bundle of my sermons under my arm—
treat words as butterflies to be chased and netted for the
delight of it, like Laelius Socinus in Zurich, trying to enchant
his audiences with subtleties and paradoxes. I had advised
Bullinger to instruct Socinus to leave off floating around
among his aerial speculations and preach the plain Word of
God.

And thinking of Bullinger, I was reminded that I intended
to chide him again for failing to stand by me in the Bolsec
affair. What a marvelous dullness: when we are pushed together into a corner we don't recognize each other. Such
obtuseness would destroy us. That and lassitude. God's work
could not wait. How much longer was Cranmer in England
going to procrastinate? All he had done was issue promises of
a convocation to frame a constitution for the English church.
How many more autumns was he going to spend making
promises? He was already old, as I had pointed out to him,
and by and by perpetual winter was going to set in on him.
Did he want to depart from the world leaving so much un-
done? Was life on this earth such a great thing if we had
nothing to show for it?

Agonizing and yet heart-stirring news had come from Lyon
where five youths (Cranmer should take note of this) had
died for Christ. Five, little more than children, who had left
Viret's university in Lausanne to make their way into France,
bearing the evangelical message in their hearts, had unwisely
confided their mission to a stranger. They had been seized,
convicted of seditious intent and sentenced to be burned, and
for weeks I had suffered with them, my physical afflictions
intensified by my sense of helplessness. I had written an
appeal to Henri, and the other Swiss cities had for once
joined me, which brought only the response that we had
better not try to run the king's business, or he would run

ours. I hoped against hope that my letter to the youths would reach them in prison. How hard it was to see why God did not intervene against the rage of our enemies, but if the use of our life was so worthy a cause as bearing witness to his Gospel, I told them, he must hold that life precious and not allow it to have been spent in vain. They were chained to a stake in Lyon's place de Terreux. The eldest, I was told, asked to be allowed to kiss the others, and whispered to each, "Courage!" Young lives extinguished so early—I wept. But the Gospel would spread across France. Those of my countrymen—who were now calling themselves "Huguenots," I suppose from the Eidguenots of Geneva—would be inspired to greater faith by the blood of the lambs from Lausanne, as the Blood of the Lamb, our Savior, waters the earth.

Cranmer and other elderly men hanging onto life as though it were something precious when it was precious only in the hands of the Lord, could learn from the courage of these children.

FAREL, ALTHOUGH HE HAD NOT BEEN SOLICITED for an opinion on the Bolsec affair, his devotion to me being so well known, had nevertheless informed the Little Council of his feelings, that Bolsec was a son of Satan, and warned that the tolerant treatment of him would inspire similar offensive actions against me. He was right. There arrived in the city a howling beast named Zeraphim Trolliet, a monk from Burgundy. He came to me asking to be made a minister, but there was something about him I did not like, and I refused him, whereupon he went to the Little Council and repeated all of Bolsec's tirades, charging that I disseminated in my *Institutes* the evil doctrine that God was the author of sin. I asked what the man was aiming at unless to acquire a reputa-

tion with the ignorant from having disputed with John Calvin. Did I have to defend myself against this particular slan-
der again and again?

"We ignorant would like to hear your case," Ami Perrin
sneered.

I said I had not meant to include the Little Council among
the ignorant, but I expressly stated my position in the *Institutes.* "Would you like to state them again?" they inquired.
Very well, and I did.

There are two causes of man's sinning, I told them. One is
open and manifest in man's corrupt nature. The other is con-
cealed in God's counsel with himself. Are we going to neglect
what is evident while trying to enter into God's secret? Now
I do not say, I went on, that God's counsel with himself does
not overrule everything even though proximate causes might
strike the eye; to say that would be to contradict the truths of
Holy Writ. But let me put it this way, I said: a man is not
nourished by his own industry but by the grace of God alone.
But a man who will not work is idle because he chooses to be,
and he deserves to starve. It is the same with doing good, or
doing evil. The solution of what only appears to be confounding is easy enough when we learn to distinguish between
sovereign cause and causes that are secondary.

They seemed to understand. At any rate, they pronounced
the *Institutes* holily done and my doctrine to be truly God's
doctrine. But then they went on to say they thought Trolliet
was a good man, by and large, who merely liked to argue and
probably should be considered for the ministry.

So did Bolsec like to argue. They were both wicked men,
and I had confirmation of this almost immediately with respect to Trolliet. Viret had given me some warning; a letter I
had dismissed, a letter wherein I described the people of
Geneva as making only a pretense of wanting to serve Christ
while desiring to be governed without him. Trolliet, some-
how, had got hold of it, and laid it before the council.

The whole business would have been ludicrous if it had not

become suddenly so threatening to my ministry. I was invited to appear again before the Little Council, and when I declined, feeling that I was not accountable to them, only to God for my opinions of the people of Geneva, they informed me that unless I did agree to appear I would be escorted thereto by a bailiff.

Farel hurried to be with me and accompanied me to the town hall. I was in an awkward position. I could not defend myself except by denying that I had written the letter, or recanting what I had said. But Guillaume was my defender. He proclaimed that there was no one more dedicated than I to Geneva and to God's work, and if I had found fault with the citizens it was because of my concern for them. I was a man who dealt severely with anyone I thought deserving of criticism, no matter what his station. I had criticized Luther, Melanchthon, Bullinger. "Even I, his dearest friend," said Farel, "have felt the chastisement of this worthy man who, however, scourges no one more severely than himself."

I sat in silence through all this, which I suppose was true enough. It did have an effect on the council, which satisfied itself by reprimanding me for not responding more promptly to its summons. Vandel ordered me: "Do your duty better the next time, Master Calvin." Guillaume put a restraining hand on my arm. Oh, I remained quiet, merely gazing at their stolid shopkeeper's faces. I searched for those who had once supported me. They were there but in retreat before the enmity that predominated in the chamber, from which I was summarily dismissed.

I prayed to God for the goodness that would make me worthy of his help.

That difficult year ended, but the new one began as a time that would face me with even greater difficulties. The Perrinists, commanding an overwhelming majority at the February elections, elevated their comic Caesar to first syndic. Twelve years after my return to Geneva, I took my measure: I was forty-four, with a miserable and vulnerable frame that seemed twice that age on occasion, and was confronted by enemies who now had the political strength, certainly, to destroy me.

They could have driven me out by barring me from the churches, denying me the house I lived in, and cutting off my mean stipend. They could have, but they did not dare. I was known all over Europe by now. If this would not have deterred them, parochial as they were, I still had a following of good people attentive to my preaching and earnest in their worship, who could not be disregarded by any faction that would try to expel me. The councils also had to consider the possibility of Savoy, or Henri, exploiting any internal conflicts in the city. I would not leave of my own volition, despite my saying several times that I would. No, they would not get rid of me except they succeeded in turning the whole population against me.

It became evident that this was what they had in mind. Maigret came to my house one evening very excited. "They are spreading a story," he said, "that Henri has sent 40,000 pieces of gold to the city to be deposited and paid out to three refugees who are supposed to be actually the king's secret agents—not named, of course—and I'll probably turn out to be one of them. The story is going around all the taverns. The gold is to be used to suborn certain officials. They're not named either, but they're known to be ones who have stood up for you. They are going to be paid to betray Geneva to France. How? Such stories don't have to include details. It's the general effect."

No proof was needed to have the story aired portentously in the Little Council, and it might have had if Perrin had not overplayed his hand. "Not 40,000 pieces of gold," he declared, "but 300,000, my lords!" This was too much for those councilmen who, whatever their politics, still retained their burgher's good sense. Such a sum was almost beyond their calculations. They pressed Perrin closely, and becoming aware of how little there was to the story beyond rumor, began to hoot goodnaturedly at their Caesar, who was glad to bring the discussion to an end. Their hoots echoed through the taverns, Maigret told me. Perrin discovered that being laughed at was only a little less painful than being pursued by howling dogs.

I could not describe the event as a triumph. I had no triumphs, except my writing. I had even seen publication of a fourth edition of *The Institutes of the Christian Religion*. Do I say *except?* To see your thoughts come to life on blank paper is the profoundest of satisfactions, which no one can take from you. Let my enemies plague me. Let the council forbid the French refugees to carry swords while *Les Enfants de Geneve* chased and stoned them. Let the arquebusiers strut around in slashed hose, as they were now allowed to do, and let the councils again challenge the consistory's sole right of excommunication while Madame Perrin and her wicked friends forced us by their very behavior to deny them the Lord's Supper. Let the taverns stay open all hours, and gambling continue and prostitutes parade in the streets, immorality now being winked at by the Perrinists in the councils. Let Bern try to dictate our manner of worship. I could endure everything. And if it was to be, I could endure being driven out of Geneva, so long as I was left with paper and pen and a candle to see by. So I told myself. Standing at bay, I had my pen to sustain me. How else would I survive adversity?

I HAD GONE TO ANTOINE'S SHOP one morning to correct some proofs and on my way out, passing through Hoch's bindery, paused when Hoch said, "I've been turning it over in my mind, whether to tell you. Do you know that camel Daguet?"

He was Antoine's house servant, a hunchback, who had once tried to steal some of Antoine's silver but had returned it, receiving my generous brother's forgiveness. Aside from that I knew little about him. "He comes in here on errands for Antoine," Hoch said, "and stops to talk—mostly about his success with the servant-girls around town." Hoch spat.

I presumed that he was informing me of a problem for the consistory, but I had a lot of business waiting for me that morning and I asked him if Daguet's case couldn't wait.

"Well a few days ago the rascal boasted that he had been enjoying the favors of a lady of the upper class. 'And very conveniently located,' he said. 'She has only to come downstairs to find me ready.'"

The mind, half attentive, arrested, tries to reject what has impinged on it. Had Hoch told Antoine?

"You don't tell a man he's being cuckolded, unless you don't like him."

"Why did Daguet tell you this?"

Hoch shrugged. "Since he was born he's suffered ridicule—only my theory, Master Calvin—and he's poisoned by ridicule and he's bound to avenge himself on anyone he can. He doesn't have a full taste of vengeance unless he talks about it."

I crossed the street to my house. The letters I had to answer, the sermon I had to make notes on, my day's work lay on my desk, but I could only bow my head over it, seeing none of it, seeing only the images of crime and passion stealing down the dark stairs of my brother's house. Suddenly I was overcome by my own guilt. How little of my affection had I given Antoine, taking for granted his love for me while I blindly piled work on him that kept him at the press until late at night. Might I not have become aware of my sister-in-law's treachery if I had visited them oftener and not been so occupied with myself? Perhaps Antoine suspected what was going on but had refrained from troubling me with it. I thought how I had pushed aside those who were closest to me so that they would not interfere with my work, sending Idelette's two children to Viret to be taught in his school in Lausanne, something I had done that very autumn, telling myself that the school in Geneva was poorly run—which was partly my fault, because I had not yet found the time to persuade the council to appropriate the funds needed for our school's improvement. I knew in my heart, the reason I had sent them off was to free me from their responsibility. The work on my desk lay untouched.

I went to Antoine's shop that night, where he was working during the hours when his wife and her lover could be making the most of opportunity. My beloved brother listened. "She has given me four children," he wept. Could he believe Hoch's story? He looked at me a long time. "Yes," he said finally. I told him that we must give her the opportunity to deny it.

We immediately set out for his house, which was dark, and let ourselves in, the key grating noisily. I shrank from the thought of surprising the pair in bed. I told him to call to her, which he did. As we stood there at the bottom of the stairs to the living quarters, a door, which led to the kitchen and the servant's room beyond, opened, and my sister-in-law appeared in a wrap. She was startled, no doubt expecting we would have gone up the stairs. No word was spoken at that tragic moment. She ran up the stairs, and Antoine slowly followed her.

I made my way through the kitchen. Daguet lay on his bed, a cover barely hiding his grotesque form, his face, which was obscenely Adonislike, turned up to me. I ordered him to get dressed, and went out to the street. It came to me as I walked towards the place du Molard that it was near here that Anne's sister, Jacqueline, had been found dead one night. I was not there to muse on coincidences. I found one of the night watch and directed him to go to Antoine's house and arrest Madame Calvin and the servant Daguet. "On what charges, Master?" Fornicating, I told him.

How often in the days that followed I wished I could absent myself from the city. I tried to close my ears to the remarks that met me on the street. Some people came to St-Pierre just to let me see the derision in their faces.

She confessed—how could she do anything else?—when

she came before the lieutenant general, Tissot, the draper,
who noticed the bedraggled condition of her gown after a
week in jail and asked, "Was there no one to bring you a
clean dress, Madame Calvin?" She shook her head. Her hair
was carelessly combed and her face, no longer pretty, was red
from weeping. She sat in chains, as did the misshapen man
next to her. Tissot ruled that they were both to be banished.

It was the last I saw of her. Antoine told me that she had
gone to her father. We had a report of Daguet passing
through Cornavin Gate alone, except for the devil, who rode
in the pack on his twisted back.

"You must understand, John, that it pleases the Lord
sometimes to try his servant that he be not too puffed up by
his greatness," Farel wrote. Was I so puffed up, thou great
lecturer?—quoting Epiphas to Job for my benefit. "Behold,
happy is the man whom God corrects; despise not the chas-
tening of the Almighty." I despised nothing that the Lord
imposed, and so I told Farel, who wrote back: "If these ignorant people finally expel you, come to my arms."

"How long it will be I do not know," I answered. "But I
keep one foot upraised, and I have estimated exactly how
much time it will take me to get to Cornavin Gate," picturing
myself exiting from this perverse city with my own pack on
my back.

18

WHAT HAD INDUCED ME TO KEEP the letters I do not know, but there they were, a small package underneath some other papers at the bottom of the chest in my study. I pulled them out and laid them before the man who sat across my desk, and with eager, beringed fingers, he untied them and began reading them, pushing his gold spectacles up his nose in growing excitement. "They are all signed Villeneuve," I pointed out. "But in the last one, you will see, Monsieur Trie, he admits what I knew all along, that his real name is Servetus."

These letters I had half-forgotten since dropping them in my chest one day when I decided to put the writer out of my mind for good. Until this moment I had succeeded in forgetting him. I had a dim memory of him, elegantly garbed, standing in a mean little hallway in the rue St-Antoine, where I had gone at Estienne de la Forge's request to save him from his abominable heresy. That was almost twenty years ago.

Monsieur Trie continued to peruse the letters. Guillaume Trie was a merchant who had come to Geneva from Lyon and was a devoted member of my congregation. He had come to me carrying a book that he had picked up at a bookstall in the lower city, where one could sometimes find the lewd writings of Rabelais and such, and had thrust it at me. It was entitled *Christianity Restored,* but bore neither the name of the author nor the publisher. But sentences had leaped out at me. I had recognized immediately what it was and who had written it—a more scandalous version of *The Errors of Christianity,* wherein Servetus had originally propounded his heresies. This one was patched up from the first, with the ravings of all ages, to which were appended arguments against infant baptism, divine election, and other accepted doctrine.

I recognized the thing because Servetus had sent me the manuscript ten years ago, asking for my opinion of it. I sent the manuscript to Viret that he might be forewarned if Servetus communicated with him and recommended that he destroy it. Meanwhile I wrote Servetus that I was too busy to enter into a debate over such notions as he was putting forward and sent him a copy of my *Institutes of Christian Religion,* which, I told him, contained the soundest doctrine I knew of. My letter was courteous, certainly not one to provoke the reaction that it had. He returned my book so written over with insulting comments that parts of it were almost illegible, and had the audacity to suggest, further, that he come to Geneva to discuss our various differences face to face. I did not answer him, and letters began to flow to me forwarded by a publisher in Lyon, until, apparently frustrated by my continued silence, Servetus wrote to Pastor Poupin sneeringly referring to the Trinity as a three-headed Cerberus and accusing our church of closing the kingdom of heaven to men. "Goodbye and do not expect to hear from me again. Woe, woe, woe," he ended. "I will stand above my watch."

I had added Poupin's letter to mine before depositing the whole lot in my chest. I noticed that a number of execrable passages from them were in the book Trie had brought me, added after the manuscript that I had seen.

Trie read on animatedly. "I have a cousin in Lyon," he finally said. "For a long time he has been urging me to return, asking me how I can bear to live in a city so devoid of discipline that it can put up with a notorious apostate like John Calvin. He provokes me. I asked him how he could bear to live in a city like Lyon that burns people for telling the truth. I am thinking of those poor youths from Lausanne. I am going to send him the first folio of this book. I would also like to copy and send him parts of these letters, then ask him how Lyon can put up with having such a heretic as Servetus in its midst."

I told him to go ahead and copy the sentences he wanted. He would certainly be able to hang his cousin, as the saying went, from the end of his nose. "I am only glad Servetus is not in our midst," I told him. "I have enough troubles." I picked up the book, which suddenly seemed to be a living thing, mocking me, and in a rage slammed it back on the desk. "There is no impiety this monster has not raked up. Every single page inspires you with horror. If the man ever comes here it will not be in my power to let him get out alive."

Several weeks went by before Monsieur Trie came to me again. The affair, he told me, had gone a little further than he had expected. It seemed that Ory, the inquisitor, on one of his sojourns out of Paris happened to be in Lyon, and Trie's cousin had shown him the folio and quotations from the letters. Ory had immediately started an investigation. A Villeneuve was easy enough to find in the neighborhood; Dr. Villeneuve was the lieutenant governor's physician and not only that, he was a protégé of the archbishop of nearby Vienne. He enjoyed, according to Trie's cousin, a great reputation for scholarship, which was something the archbishop admired almost to the point of fatuity. Dr. Villeneuve lived near the archbishop's palace.

The inquisitor himself had searched Villeneuve's apartment but had found nothing more incriminating than some works on astrology. From the type face, meanwhile, it was suspected that the book might have been printed by two brothers-in-law, Balthazar Arnoullet and Guillaume Gueroult. Gueroult—I seemed to remember the name.

"They denied ever having seen the thing," Trie said.
"Now, you can imagine my cousin's embarrassment, not to
say the trouble he could find himself in unless he produces
some positive evidence of Dr. Villeneuve's duplicity. He has
begged me to send him the manuscript."

I told him that, so far as I knew, it no longer existed.

"Then let me have the letters. They would be even more
useful. Villeneuve might deny writing the book, but the letters, including his admitting to being Servetus, in his hand-
writing would be conclusive."

I had no doubt the use the inquisitor would make of them.
I told him how distressed I was now, having recovered from
my first rage. "It is our duty to convince heretics with doctrine," I told him, "not the stake."

"But Master Calvin," he pleaded, "think of my poor
cousin. And think how worthily he acted. Servetus's attacks
are against doctrines that we, all of us, Protestants and
Catholics, uphold. And have you thought how we Protestants
are accused of being indifferent to true doctrine? Won't our
refusal to cooperate with the papists in convicting such a
notorious heretic feed the calumny?"

Cooperate with the papists! The idea sickened me. And
yet—did I need Trie to tell me this?—Scripture is not a thing
of indifference for people to content over willfully. There
were reasons why Servetus should be expunged: he was so
obstinate that he could not be brought to the truth by reason,
and his opinions were so vicious that he could no longer be
left to go free. However much it went against my instincts to
do so, I gave him the letters.

I sat, after he had gone, trying to recall the name of
Gueroult, and at length I did. He had dwelt for a time in
Geneva, a man of some literary pretentions, who, having
been discovered in intercourse with several married women,
was thrown out of the city. I remember his having been a
good friend of Ami Perrin.

When several days went by with no word from Trie's

cousin I grew concerned about the letters, which I wanted to get back in the event of Vienne letting Servetus go free. It was Maigret who suggested that he go to Lyon as my agent. He was well acquainted in both Vienne and Lyon, which carried on considerable trade with Geneva in wine and other merchandise. He would keep me informed.

A COMMUNICATION FROM MAIGRET was a long time getting to me. After some characteristic flourishes, he got down to business.

I begin at the beginning when the Inquisitor Ory convened his court in the criminal chamber of the Palace of Vienne adjoining the prison cells where Dr. Villeneuve had been incarcerated. Although he had spent several days there with no one to attend him but his fifteen-year-old valet, the doctor so-called presented an impressive figure, dressed in the height of fashion. I caught a trace of perfume when he brushed by. Lieutenant General Maugiron, a member of the court, gazed on him with undisguised solicitude. Archbishop Palmier, an observer at the proceedings, could hardly take his eyes off him. I do not try to speculate on what emotions were at play here.

Little Ory was his usual bundle of animation. I used to know him in Paris. "You are a doctor of medicine?" he inquired. He said he was, and had written some books on medical matters, including one on syrups. In the case of indigestion, which was what he was treating the lieutenant general for when he was so unjustly seized, he said, his book recommended repose, warm baths, and the eating of citrus fruits.

I was interested in this detail. I myself was taking a syrup Aubert had made up for me—burgundy mixed with absinthe, lemon rind, hyssop, syrup of hart's tongue and alder—which did help relieve my fits of violent coughing. Nothing however, seemed to help my chronic indigestion, except restricting my eating to nothing more solid than an occasional egg.

"Well, will you review your career for the court?" Ory invited. Dr. Villeneuve, patting his lips with a lace handkerchief, would be glad to. He had first launched himself on his career right next door in Lyon, being a young man of literary bent and finding employment with Treschel, the publisher. He had edited, among other items, Pirckheimer's revision of Ptolemy. Ory produced a copy, and at the risk of trying the court's patience, he said, would like to read a few of Dr. Villeneuve's notes. One, more than usually gratuitous, said that Palestine was a barren place whose only promise was that it was promised. Ory waggled his eyebrows significantly while reading this irreverency. "Let us proceed," he said.

Not in the least discomfited, our prodigy now described a book he had written in defense of Dr. Symphorien Champier who was having a debate with Dr. Leonard Fuchs, a Lutheran, over the cause of syphilis, Champier arguing that it was inflicted by God as punishment for immorality, Fuchs maintaining that it came from unsanitary conditions. "Champier thought so highly of my book," our rascal smirked, "that he urged me to study medicine, so I enrolled at the University of Paris."

It was clear that our diligent inquisitor general of the faith had burrowed into every hold in his investigation. He was prepared with reports from the faculty of the School of Medicine. Very original and resourceful student. Supported himself financially. Lectured on geography, astronomy. "You even wrote a book on astrology?" Yes. "The dean asked you not to publish it, but you published it anyhow?" All true, it was a worthy study on the subject, not at all the kind of fakery being put out by mountebanks. "But you were reprimanded by Lizet?" Also true. I indulged myself in the enjoyment of this irony—the chief judge of Parlement censuring Villeneuve for writing on astrology, never knowing that at that very moment he had his hands on the author of the scurrilous *Errors of Christianity*.

I am writing this, incidentally, at the house of a friend. The

Rhone reflects the waning April moon, as our knave's fortune's also began to wane the morning Ory started pressing him further about his activities at the School of Medicine. Had he not produced a certain unusual theory about the circulatory system? Yes, he had—looking very pleased with himself. Now John, it is all a mystery to me; you may be able to understand it. In any case, our clever student and some of his friends had taken to rummaging around in the insides of cadavers. "In the course of this gruesome entertainment did you come to some conclusions?" asked Ory. "I concluded," he said, "that a theory of Galen's that medical science has accepted for thirteen hundred years is wrong." Nothing is beyond the fellow. What was wrong with it? "Galen said the arteries only transmitted nourishment to the lungs. But I observed that the pulmonary artery is too large for this limited function." I copied it down as I heard it, John. "The blood passes through the lungs to be aerated. The vital spirit is generated from a mixture made in the lungs—the inspired air with the elaborate refined blood—then is communicated from the right to the left ventricle." There was more to it that I did not comprehend, and I do not know what is gained by exploring what goes on inside these sorry vehicles that convey us through life. I saw, however, that Ory was building towards something.

I read this several times. I did not understand it fully either, but I marveled at the defendant's recklessness in making this admission: I knew what Ory's motive was.

"What did the faculty of the School of Medicine think of your discovery?" "I did not publish it." We are getting near the end of things, John. Ory now cross-examined so swiftly that Villeneuve looked uneasy, as though he sensed that Ory was about to drop the ax on him. How had Dr. Villeneuve happened to come to Vienne? The archbishop had extended him his patronage, having listened to some of his lectures on astrology (the archbishop's sallow face at this point turned a pretty crimson) and had assured him he would find a profitable medical practice and besides would be close enough to Lyon to pursue his literary interests with the publishers there.

Ory suddenly produced a copy of *Christianity Restored,* and began reading from it a dissertation on the aeration of blood in the lungs. The author used it to make a comparison—just how, escaped me—with the motion of the stars and musical instruments and mathematics, all being a part of the imma-nent force of being in God. You no doubt read it all in the manuscript he sent you. How he made the transition from physiology to metaphysics also escapes me, but that does not matter. "It cannot be otherwise," said Ory, "than the dissector of cadavers is the author of *Christianity Restored.*" And before his victim, half-skewered, could answer, he drove the skewer home. He produced the letters you gave Trie.

What a wiggler-waggler the man is. Skewered, I say, but still breathing, and now breaking into pitiful cries. "You sus-pect me by these letters of being Servetus. There was a Ser-vetus, a Spaniard, I think, who wrote a book I myself read many years ago. I was curious about it and wrote Calvin, knowing little about him except that he was a very learned man. My questions to him were the very ones this Servetus had raised. Calvin accused me of being Servetus. I said I was assuming the role of Servetus for the purposes of our discus-sion, and we wrote each other on that basis until his answers became so heated that I ended the correspondence. There has been nothing between us since." His sighs filled the court-room, while he gave a demonstration of a man maligned beyond all belief and sobbed out, "I never wished to assert anything contrary to the church. This I affirm before God."

The archbishop blustered, "I do not think the evidence is altogether conclusive, Monsieur Ory." Ory did not wish to tread too heavily on these ecclesiastical toes. "Well, let me spend the evening reviewing all the testimony and we will reconvene tomorrow," he said. And, Servetus, still giving voice to his lamentations was remanded to jail.

Well, John, are you still with us? Because Servetus is not. He flew the coop. Being a protégé of the archbishop, he was not locked in a cell. Very early in the morning the jailer heard a knock on his quarters and there stood Servetus dressed in a fur robe and velvet nightcap asking if he could have the key to the garden so that he could go out and relieve himself. The jailer gave him the key and went back to his bed. His wife, I gather, is notorious for the nocturnal demands she puts on him. It was some time before he realized that his prisoner had not returned the key and got up to find out why. All that remained of Dr. Villeneuve was a fur bathrobe and a velvet nightcap beside the garden wall. They have scoured the city for him. Ory is in a state. The archbishop has hurried off to inspect some other part of his diocese. Lieutenant General Maugiron, I expect, is immersed in a hot bath eating an orange. Adieu, dear John, and may God protect you.

Not too many days later, quite fatigued and deploring his old age, my faithful friend appeared to report in person the ending to the affair. They had convened a civil court and declared Michael Servetus, alias Villeneuve, to be guilty of heresy, sedition, and escaping from prison. A portrait of him which the infatuated archbishop had had painted was carried to the market place in Lyon and hanged on a gallows, then put on a pyre and burned along with a copy of *Christianity Restored*. Ory had confiscated the letters. It did not matter; they had served their end. The police determined that Gueroult had printed *Christianity Restored,* burning each page of the manuscript as it was set in type. He had disappeared. Arnoullet protested that he had been hoodwinked by his partner, who took care of the literary side; he was only the business manager. "He has nothing to manage now," Maigret said. "His business is in ruins, Gueroult having absconded with all their money."

Where, I asked Maigret, did anyone suppose Servetus had gone? "No one has any idea," he said. "I know once more they will be looking for him everywhere."

Springtime turned into the heat of August. I had preached a mid-week sermon at the Church of the Madeleine and had gone from there to a meeting of the Little Council to call their attention to the playing of games in churchyards that disturbed our services these summer days, when I saw Maigret hurrying up the street, exerting himself to the utmost. Reaching my side, he whispered, "Servetus is here in Geneva."

19

MAIGRET HAD RECOGNIZED HIM emerging from the Madeleine after the service and had followed him to the Perrins' house where he had knocked but got no answer. "They were away—I happen to know—gone off to the country. He then hurried off to the Inn of the Roses, acting quite furtively. He is thinner than when I saw him in Vienne and has let his beard grow to a great length. He is at the inn now in a corner having something to eat."

Why had he come here? "He hoped Perrin would give him refuge perhaps. Or he is fomenting some mischief against you. I don't know. Why was he at the Madeleine? Curiosity maybe—to have a look at you. All we know is he's a man of reckless and erratic behavior."

I said he must be arrested. I was not eager for it. But here he was, a poisoner of Christianity fallen into my hands. Could I have it said that I was heaven's reluctant hound, letting this man slip away to carry on the devil's work?

I sent my secretary Baudoin off to town hall to inform the authorities. He returned shortly to say that by a lucky stroke he had encountered Jean Darlod, the one syndic whom Perrin did not lead around by the nose, who had dispatched the

police to the inn. Maigret, Darlod said, must make all speed
there in order to point the man out.

I sat at my desk, almost wishing, such a coward I am, that
Servetus would have disappeared, and I would be spared the
ordeal I saw ahead. But in a short while, Darlod arrived to
inform me that he had been seized and none too soon for he
had been negotiating with a boatman to row him up the lake.
Darlod came also to inform me that, as I knew, I would also
have to go to jail to stand trial as a false accuser if there was
not enough evidence of Servetus's criminality. Since I could
send someone in my stead, I had my second secretary,
Nicholas de la Fontaine, deliver himself to the lord lieutenant.

I spent most of the night dictating my presentment to Baudoin. In thirty-eight articles I described the nature of Servetus's heresy and blasphemies, how he had attacked the Trinity as making of God a three-headed Cerberus, how he had
rejected the writing of such doctors of the church as Am-
brose and Augustine and how such worthy men as Melanchthon and Oecolampadius had denounced him. I expounded
on the trouble he had caused in Christendom, and how,
to let him go, would bring dishonor and disgrace on
Geneva. I got out the copy of *Christianity Restored* that Trie
had brought me, and a copy of Ptolemy's geography with the
annotations, and Baudoin tied all this material together to
deliver to Nicholas who would read it to the lieutenant general, Tissot, in the morning.

The night was far advanced. "Shall I blow out the lamp?"
Baudoin asked. I told him to put it beside my bed. Its flame
in the draft from the open window stirred up the shadows of
all those people in the world who would sit in judgment on
me. They are saying, "How often have you inveighed against
the papists for their burnings? Now you have caused this man
to be seized and put in peril of the stake. Do you say, 'But
there is a certain book?' We say, here stands a human being,
whom God created."

Rome slays men merely for abjuring Rome. Servetus ab-
jures the Word of God, and not to himself either. He spreads

his poison abroad. If we spare him, we ourselves become an affront to God. I opened my Bible to Deuteronomy, and by the lamplight read Moses' command to the children of Israel as he received it from God—that they should slay anyone who tried to thrust them away from God, be he brother, son, daughter, or wife. "Thou shalt stone him with stones that he die." God's honor must be put above all else, yea, above every memory of mutual humanity.

The shadows in my room say, "You cause him to die a martyr, suffering."

Suffering does not make a wicked man a martyr.

Sleep would not come to me. I blew out the lamp and lay there thinking of the man in the darkness of a cell not much more than a stone's throw away.

I WAS STILL IN MY BED in the morning, writing, when Nicholas came back from jail. The evidence of Servetus's criminality weighed so heavily in my presentment that Tissot had had no choice but to release my secretary and remand Servetus to his cell to await trial by the Little Council. He had made no effort to deny that he was the author of the writings Nicholas produced but arrogantly asserted their truth and referred to me in scornful, even abusive language. His trial would begin the following day in the Hall of Justice.

I did not attend it. I did not want it to seem that I was thirsting for vengeance. Vengeance was a thing of hateful minds. If he had only gone somewhere else—to Bern, Basel, Zurich. I found myself—could I not be forgiven?—asking God that morning why he had sent the wretched man to Geneva.

The days that followed were a continuous harassment. People crowded around me outside the church demanding, "Are you going to punish this man properly?" Others cursed

me in the streets, shouting that I was doing the pope's work
for him, or inquiring sweetly when it was that God had
anointed me with so much of the truth. The whole population was like a man beset by a furious itch. One would have
thought it was the first trial for heresy in any Reformation
city. How long had they been drowning Anabaptists in
Zurich?

For the first few days of the trial I had young Germain
Colladon who had got his law degree at Orléans, lay out the
charges. He did well, as Nicholas reported to me, but the
pursuer became the pursued. They had appointed as auditor
Philibert Berthelier, whom the consistory had excommunicated and should himself have been before his colleagues
answering for his debaucheries. He dropped any judicial role
and turned on Colladon, demanding: "What is Servetus's real
guilt? Calvin says he brings dishonor on the church, but what
Calvin means is that he brings dishonor on Calvin. Didn't
Calvin bring dishonor on himself by turning this man in to
the papists in Vienne?"

Colladon said to him: "My lord, the auditor, cannot get rid
of the accusations against Servetus by calumniating Master
Calvin."

"So we're having a lesson in law from our young Frenchman," Berthelier sneered. "Rather we should consider how
Calvin is trying to extend over this innocent scholar the
tryanny that he tries to exercise over Geneva."

"We are not here to listen to this kind of ranting," said
Colladon.

"Ranting!" Berthelier shouted, and there was such a commotion then, Nicholas said, that the syndic Darlod, who pre-
sided, ordered an adjournment.

I must step forward.

I had no trouble recognizing the man sitting in the chair of
the accused. He had had the prison barber trim his beard
quite modishly so that he looked pretty much the way he had
looked twenty-four years ago in Paris. His clothes, though
threadbare, still had a mark of elegance. We looked at each

other across the courtroom and the years. I told the Little Council I was taking my place as the accuser. "So you have come out from behind Monsieur Colladon," Berthelier mocked me.

I had Colladon produce for the court copies of letters we had obtained which had been written by Melanchthon and Oecolampadius, who had seen the marks of a fanatical spirit in the author of *The Errors of the Trinity*.

"These are only opinions," Servetus said in a confident voice. "They do not constitute judicial condemnation."

I had Colladon produce a copy of the Pagnini Bible, wherein, in Isaiah 53, that glorious revelation of the coming of a Savior to bear our sorrows, Servetus had appended a note saying Isaiah referred to Cyrus, the king of Persia, who would release the Jews from the Babylonian captivity.

"You all know, my lords," Servetus said lightly, "that there is a twofold sense in the Bible, one literal, applying to contemporaneous events, the other mystical and prophetic. Isaiah 53 can be understood as applying to Jesus Christ, all right. My note only said that the history being reported applied to contemporaneous events. Nothing very wrong in that, is there?"

I cried out: "Nothing abashes him. Everything in Scripture that supports true doctrine he defecates on like a dog, and twitching his muzzle passes on to something else, saying there's nothing wrong here."

"I don't smell anything very wrong," said Berthelier.

Colladon spoke forth: "Then let us inquire, what does Servetus say of Christ? Does he deny that God, the Son, and the Spirit all existed unbegotten before creation?"

Our comic Caesar Perrin interrupted: "In that connection I have often wondered what God was doing all the time before creation."

I told him that Augustine had answered the question: "He was creating a hell for the curious," at which the clown grunted and studied the ceiling. I asked Servetus to address himself to Colladon's question.

"Oh," he said, "he is the Son of God. But mark this, not the eternal Son of God. He did not pre-exist with God. How could he, being a combination of the Word, which is light, and the flesh, which is matter, therefore unable to antedate the union? Not until the nonsense put forth at Nicaea—of God, the Spirit, and the Son being Three-in-One—did Christ officially become God and a man all at once."

I asked the court to note that what he called nonsense was the Holy Trinity. "Holy!" the man exclaimed. "The word Trinity is nowhere in Scripture."

I was not to be trapped into saying that it was. But it served the truth in Scripture, I told the court. It was an acknowledgment of the deity of Christ, which is everywhere affirmed in Scripture. Before his manifestation on earth he was recognized as God by the Old Testament prophets. "Unto us a child is born"—they had only to read Isaiah—"and his name shall be called Wonderful, Counsellor, the mighty God, the everlasting Father." His deity was borne out everywhere in the New Testament—by the apostles, by Christ's own words. "Ye believe in God, believe in me. I am the way, the truth and the life. I am in the Father and the Father is in me." He had the power of the remission of sins, which only belongs to deity. The thing may be beyond human words—this mystery of the Three-in-One. We try to define it; we call it consubstantiation, *homoousios,* in the Nicaean Creed."

The court gawked. "I despise that word," Servetus said.

I asked him, "If Christ is not God, then who is he? Or are there two Gods?"

Servetus began waving his arms as if carrying a banner. "I say he was a spirit walking on the wings of the wind, riding on the air, sitting on the circle of the earth and measuring the heavens with his span and the waters in the hollow of his hands." Arius's heresy unfurling! "But he is God only in the sense that man is God."

I said to the court: "Man is God—also make a note of this."

Colladon put in: "So it is appropriate to inquire what Servetus says of God."

"I say God is that which contains the essence of all things,"

Servetus replied, waving again. "He shows himself to us as fire, as a flower, in wood he is wood, in a stone he is stone, having in himself the being of stone, the form of stone, the substance of stone."

I stamped on the floor. "Am I stamping on God?"

"This floor, this table or anything you point to in this room are all of God's substance—the benches on which my lords sit, the lords themselves."

"The devil," I said, "will he be substantially of God?"

"Can you doubt it? It is my fundamental principle: all things are part and parcel of God and the nature of all things is the substantial spirit of God. That is why I say man himself is God. Do we not feel the divine energy within us? Do we not hear the divine voice?" He made a lofty gesture in my direction. "Why does this man deny it, my lords? Why does he deny the immanence of God in man? Why does he try to separate humanity from divinity? This dog—well, he called me a dog."

"Yes, you called him a dog, Calvin," said Berthelier.

I gazed at the stupidity, ignorance, willfulness, and malice in that room. Divinity in man! "The ultimate degradation of the divine," I said, "is to say that man is of the substance of God—"

"It is true."

"Man is a derivative of God's substance, as if some portion of divinity had flowed into him? Then what is contemptible in man is of the substance of God? So God's nature must be one of passion and wicked desire and vices of all kinds. This is the final blasphemy. It enmeshes God in his own creation. What more do we have to listen to to understand this man's wickedness?"

"We still have to examine him on his rejection of infant baptism," Colladon said.

The councilmen put that off until the afternoon. I went home and lay down. I thought how long Satan had been trying to tear out the roots of our faith by instigating ungodly men to harry orthodox teachers over this matter of Christ's divinity. Today he was kindling new fires with the perverse ravings of these persons.

I returned to the Hall of Justice where the councilmen
were hemming and hawing, pulling on their noses, and passing around a copy of Servetus's *Christianity Restored.*

"You say that infant baptism is an invention of the devil,"
Colladon began. "It is there in your book."

Servetus must have been served a good meal for he looked
quite refreshed. "That is what I say," he agreed. "Children
are born innocent. Until they have acquired knowledge they
can do neither good nor bad. Knowledge comes to them—
oh, sometime after the twentieth year. Not until then should
they be baptized, for baptism is a regeneration, when the
inward man which is God within us is born. Until then the
child cannot hear the voice of the spirit, so unless he is baptized when he is grown, he is denied regeneration."

I said I wanted this point well understood since it came out
of the Anabaptists' bag of poisoned fruit. "He says that until
they are in their twenties they can do neither good nor bad,
which is to say, they can commit no mortal sin."

"Yes, that's the logic of my position."

"Doesn't this give them license to steal, murder, and commit adultery?" Colladon asked. "Isn't our youth corrupt
enough as it is?"

What should happen, I thought, is that Servetus's little
chickens, so sweet and innocent, should dig his eyes out.

"I still don't see how baptizing them as little babies is going
to help us," said Perrin.

I asked the fool: "Don't you understand the sacrament?"

"You will be glad to instruct me?"

I explained that it was a sign, as the mortification of the
flesh by circumcision is a sign to the Jews. It marked the
initiation of the infant into the community of Jesus Christ.

"What does that do for a little baby who has no knowledge
of anything?"

"They are children of Adam and in Adam all die, but
through baptism they become heirs of life. What God gives
them then is beyond our understanding—" I paid no attention to Berthelier inquiring sarcastically, "Do I hear you say
that something is beyond your understanding." I went on:

"Furthermore, infants bear with them the corruption in their mother's womb. They must be cleansed of it before they can be admitted to the company of the elect."

"Oho," said Servetus. "Is what you are saying that baptism only works for those who are of the elect?

I replied: "It is not I who am being questioned in this court. But that is it."

"It's what you have got to say," Servetus crowed as though he had scored a point. "Or else you give up your whole doctrine of predestination, that other invention of the devil. Of Simon Magus. It was Simon Magus who thought it up. And now we see how awful that is. An innocent babe held out to the minister, its eyes closed perhaps in sleep, marked as a reprobate and already assigned to hell. You Simon Magus, barking after me with your terrible formulas!"

I did not answer him. I could not expound the doctrine of election in this court. I was overwhelmed with weariness. Suddenly I could no longer endure the pain of my wretched hemorrhoids, or the ache in my head. I left the proceedings to Colladon and went home and lay down, and began to suffer a mood of unusual depression. I saw men as it were at the bottom of a pit vilifying one another, arguing over uncertainties. What could any of them know for sure; what could any of them attest to as unprovable truths? Some men would explore the walls of the abyss and find a way of logic to climb out. I who was so efficient at logic could only weep, until I thought of Ockham. Nothing can ever be proved; the only salvation is faith.

THEY EXCLUDED ME FROM FURTHER PARTICIPATION in the case. Colladon brought me this news. He had been told at the end of the proceedings that day that the court had decided it had to do with a civil matter and we were no longer needed; the questioning would be pursued by Rigot, the public prosecutor. Certain syndics (I could guess which ones) and members of the Little Council were saying that I was making accusations of a theological nature that were too complicated for them to understand. What mattered was whether Servetus was a threat to the city. I was set aside as an irrelevancy. Beyond this capriciousness I saw the lineaments of conspiracy—to free the man in the end, thus bringing about the disintegration of all my authority.

The hearings were suspended then, for some reason I was not made privy to. I turned my attention to the affairs I had so woefully neglected. I was engrossed in these things when I was suddenly served with an order from the Little Council that showed the vindictiveness of the men ranged against me. If I bowed to the order, no matter what the outcome of Servetus's trial, I would be finished as I would have been finished by the same kind of challenge in the past. It had to do with Berthelier. During the time, almost a year now, that he had been denied communion he had shown no sign of discontinuing his riotous and debauched living. The Little Council instructed me to withdraw the interdiction. I picked my way on my stick up the treacherous cobblestones to the town hall.

I said to their stone faces: "Your order violates the ordinance that makes the consistory the sole arbiter of who may or may not receive the Lord's Supper."

"Actually, that point has never been settled," said Ami Perrin. "Until now. Now we've settled it."

"My lords," I pleaded, "you are trampling on sacred authority."

"Oh, we're just righting a wrong done one of our members. An honorable man—that's been confirmed by the council electing him a syndic. The council supersedes the authority of the consistory. By vote of the majority—that's how we do it, Calvin. Not by having one man, yourself, say do this, don't do that."

"The syndic was excommunicated for good cause." I could no longer restrain my anger. "Does he deny it—sitting there grinning like a gargoyle?"

"All your causes are good ones," Berthelier said.

"He was denied communion because of his whoring and gambling."

"It's how Monsieur Berthelier feels about it, not you," Perrin said pompously. "He feels he's been excluded long enough, and we agree with him."

"I will not receive him at the table."

"He intends to attend St-Pierre tomorrow, and you will see that he is served," Perrin intoned.

"I would rather be slain than subject Christ to such mockery."

He guffawed at me. Sitting beside him Berthelier sniggered, and their sycophants on the council joined in their laughter. Trembling, I left them.

I was trembling when I climbed the steps to my pulpit. I recalled the Easter morning just before Farel and I were expelled, when the Little Council had ordered me not to preach, and I had. People had come to St-Pierre that morning to see what I would do. Because of the mocking in the street I had denied communion to everyone. Now they were jostling one another in the great nave below me. I hurled a sermon at them, using a homily of Chrysostom's: One who serves the Supper to a person he knows is unworthy is as guilty of sacrilege as if he had cast the Lord's Supper to a dog. Then I invited those who had faith and were in good standing to come forward. "But if anyone comes to the table who has been barred from it by the consistory," I told them, "then I will manifest myself. I may be forced into exile, as Chrysostom was when he dared to preach against the immorality of Emperor Arcadius—exiled or even slain, for hatred of me has made some of the leaders of this city insane. But I will not give to anyone who has been condemned the holy things of God." I descended from the pulpit and stood at the table. They pressed forward in some disorder but knelt as I recited, "This is my body, take, eat." I watched for Berthelier, but he had thought better of it and did not appear. I put the cloth back over the plates and the cruets.

That victory was mine.

20

THE DELAY IN THE PROCEEDINGS I learned, was caused by the prosecutor Rigot. I met him one morning hurrying importantly along the street. I believe he had studied some law in Basel. "We must pursue the question of whether this heresy, if such in fact it is, constitutes a danger to the city—hunh?" He was not asking my opinion. He had a habit of ending sentences with an interrogatory grunt or two. "The courts of Europe will have their eyes on me—huhn, hunh?" He had the hearings suspended while he appealed to the authorities in Vienne to send him everything they had in the dossier of Dr. Michael Servetus, alias Villeneuve. August became September while Rigot awaited their replies.

Servetus spent his time writing appeals to the Little Council. Aubert kept me informed of this development. "He says that the lice are eating him alive. His clothes are filthy and worn out, and he has nothing to change to. He wants us to provide him with a lawyer—as though he can't lie fluently enough without a lawyer." The Little Council sent him some clothes but paid no attention to his other requests.

It was evident that Perrin and his friends were only interested in making use of him to achieve their end, which was being served by his continued presence in our midst. The case was disrupting meetings of the council and causing almost daily turmoil in the streets. *Les Enfants* marched around shouting slogans against me and against the French refugees, whose connection with the affair was not made clear, but this made no difference; the French could always be used to incite the populace.

"Ah, the machinations of your comic Caesar," Maigret said. "He foments so much disorder that force will be required to put it down. With the armed men of *Les Enfants,* he then takes control of the Little Council and becomes, in fact, Geneva's Caesar."

The tone of Servetus's appeals abruptly changed. He demanded that the Little Council throw me in prison as a false accuser. I was the spreader of false doctrine, not he, and as such should be condemned and exterminated, he wrote, and my property sold and given to him. I could not doubt that he was now getting encouragement from outside the jail.

My despondency these days, which was not without its cause, weighed so heavily on me that one Sunday morning I turned to Paul's farewell to the Ephesians. And after imploring my congregation to keep Christ in their hearts, as had Paul, said to them, "This may be one of the last sermons I shall preach to you, not because I will take leave of you of my own accord—God forbid that I should wish to abandon the sphere of my rightful authority—but I can only see by what is happening that they who are in power will not be served by me much longer. Dearly beloved, I commend you to God."

I was moved a little by the words of some of them who came to me after the service. "Oh, Master Calvin, don't talk that way."

Rigot finally got his response from Vienne. It was carried by two emissaries, and Servetus was led back into court to answer Rigot's questioning. Had he once been arrested for stabbing a man? Rigot, his little eyes popping in his round cheeks, stared ominously at the papers he had before him. Why yes, in Charlieu, the prisoner admitted. A jealous fellow physician had set some assassins on him, and he had run one of them through, but without serious consequences. Had he once proclaimed that he saw no point in getting married so long as there were so many women in the world? Oh, he might have said it in jest, he laughed. Then why had he never married? He was impotent, having been castrated on one side in an accident when he was five, and later suffering a rupture on the other side. The emissaries from Vienne now came forward, feeling, and rightly, that all this was getting nowhere in respect to Servetus's heresy and requesting that he be released to them to be taken back to Vienne, where he had already been sentenced and only needed to be burned in actuality. His levity disappeared. He fell on his knees and moaned, "No, no, my lords, I would rather be judged by you."

Where else could he have found a body of magistrates so full of mercy and blowing farts at moral law and justice? Oh, such irony I was witnessing; rulers everywhere were executing people who held to God's truth. Lyon slayed the little lambs from Lausanne, Henri sent Huguenots and Waldenses to the stake, and the bloodthirsty Mary in England murdered our disciples (I thought of poor Cranmer, whom I had once chided for dilatoriness, now awaiting death in the Tower of London), while magistrates of Geneva dawdled over this pernicious man.

The emissaries from Vienne went home, Servetus returned to jail, and Rigot, staggering under the weight of his responsibility, came forward with another idea. The court should direct Servetus and me each to write a disquisition in Latin, which, of course, not all of the Little Council would be able to read, but which would be sent around to the magistrates and ministers of Basel, Bern, Zurich, and Schaffhausen for their judgment—hunh, hunh? The court could accept the judgment of our brethren in these Reformation cities, could it not? Basel was full of academic hair-splitters, and Bern's lords would deny that there was light at noon if I had said so!

Nevertheless, I wrote my disquisition, which they showed to Servetus, who disfigured it with scurrilous comments be-

fore returning it. I was permitted to see his work. It was as if
the man stood in my presence screaming at me. "You liar!
You thief! You cheat! You disciple of Simon the Sor-
cerer! . . ." I read his own paper, a reiteration of his ravings
that I found not worthy of my comments. These and other
documents appertaining to the case were put in a packet and
consigned to the messenger of state, Jaquemoz Jernoz, who
departed for the four cities.

Another month went by during which I did not venture
into the lower city or much beyond St-Pierre. Abel Poupin,
who was preaching at the Church of the Madeleine begged
me to transfer him to a parish in the country. I told him I
would take the Madeleine, which was on the edge of the
lower city. No, he would remain, although he was subject to
slurs and threats and on one occasion physical attack by several rowdies. Michael Cop set an example of valor. He
preached at St-Gervais, ostentatiously wearing a sword even
in the pulpit despite the ordinance forbidding the wearing of
swords by Frenchmen.

In the false security of my little walled garden Maigret and
I, at his insistence, sat playing *clef*. "It's twenty years since
they threw out Savoy's bishop," he observed. "Hmm, I remember that our old friend Farel had much to do with that.
One looks at the majesty of the mountains surrounding us
and finds it hard to believe violence exists here, like suppressed insanity."

J AQUEMOZ JERNOZ RETURNED near the end of October. I
took a chair in the back of the Hall of Justice, as the court of
syndics and councilmen assembled to hear him. He had a dry
voice which betrayed no private feelings. "If some of the
replies seem brief," he said, "I can assure you, my lords, they
are the fruit of much discussion. I proceed. Schaffhausen:
'We do not doubt that you in your wisdom will repress

Michael Servetus lest his blasphemies despoil the members of Christ like a cancer.'"

He went on without pausing. "Zurich: 'You should work against him with great diligence, especially as our churches have an ill repute abroad as heretical. God's holy providence has now indeed provided the occasion whereby you may at once purge yourselves from this fearful suspicion of evil.'"

There was no sound in the Hall of Justice.

"Bern," he continued, "is also exceedingly brief, to wit: 'We condemn the errors of Servetus as tending to corrupt and destroy all religions.' But included with this statement was an opinion of the ministers which is quite long and I ask to be excused from reading all of it. It will be here for all of you to peruse. It says in part, 'We see Satan operating through Servetus, who both revives the errors of the ancient heretics and adheres to certain sects of our times by reviling infant baptism. By his arguing the impossibility of mortal sin before the twentieth year he subverts public morality, and at a time when the young are so corrupt. God give you fortitude to avert this pest from our church.' And finally, my lords, Basel."

Jernoz flipped through his papers. "They say they agree with Zurich. I went back and forth among the four cities affording each an opportunity to make revisions, if they liked, after studying the answers of the others. I leave the first part of Basel to your perusal. Let me only read, 'Servetus exceeds all the old heretics since he vomits up their combined errors from one impudent and blasphemous mouth.' They compare him—where is that? Ah, here—to a snake 'hissing curses and contumely against Calvin, that most sincere servant of God—'"

"Calvin!" Perrin roared from his place on the syndics' bench. "Why they are talking about a man who conspired with the papists."

"We are not discussing Master Calvin," said the presiding syndic, Darlod. "Please continue, Monsieur Jernoz."

"Basel suggests that we try to cure Servetus, but in the event of that failing—these are their words—'he should be coerced by the power that the Lord gives us so that he will cause no more trouble to our churches.'"

He sat down. The only sound in the room was his sorting out his papers into piles so that they could be examined separately by the court.

"My lords," Councilman Aubert the apothecary said, "he is no more curable than a leper—"

"They never say in so many words that we should execute him," said Berthelier.

"They leave it for us to say it. I say it because I stand here in fear. If we do not purge the world of this infection God will avenge himself on our city."

"That is fool's talk," Berthelier said.

"It is a fool who would deny it," someone said.

I heard someone else say, "Would my lord want to certify that God is not going to take any notice?"

It was marvelous how quiet the room became then. Darlod rose and announced, "We shall recess until evening to give ourselves time to study these documents."

They came to order after suppertime, and Darlod immediately recognized Aubert, who was standing up waving his hand, and who stated that he thought the case had dragged on long enough; the time had come for the court to take its vote. There were shouts of approval. "We've read the judgments; let us vote," at which Darlod began to call each man's name.

"Guilty; execute him."

"Guilty; execute him."

"Guilty."

"Guilty."

Perrin, when his name was called, cried out: "I say refer the case to the Two Hundred." They shouted him down, whereupon he turned and shook his fist at me. "How much longer are we going to let this preacher have his way with us?"

"That is not what we are voting on, my lord."

He looked around him for support but saw none in their faces which they averted from him.

Suddenly he clapped his hat over his stomach and groaned,

"This terrible pain! Berthelier, help me out of here," and with elaborate gesticulations indicating suffering, he staggered from the hall, accompanied by Berthelier and Vandel, who had sat through the proceedings with a sullen, uncomprehending look.

"The vote," Darlod said, "is to burn Michael Servetus at the stake."

I rose to plead that his execution be carried out more mercifully. "Decapitate him and the world would be rid of him, and God would be satisfied." But they shouted me down as they had Perrin. They would leave the other cities no opportunity to criticize them for leniency. He must suffer at the stake for his blasphemies. Oh, it was extraordinary how the shopkeepers of Geneva stood there now in the fear of God.

Rain fell heavily on the city the next morning when Tissot went to the jail. He had Servetus led in chains around the walls of St-Pierre to the front of the town hall where Darlod had taken a position on a balcony from which he looked down on the poor wretch, who stood in the rain, worn out, I dare say (I did pity him) from their toying with him so long. "For being obstinately employed in infecting the world with heretical poison, in the name of the Father, the Son, and the Holy Ghost, we condemn thee to be bound and led to the place of Champel and burned alive. . . ."

I stood among the little group surrounding him. His eyes started from his face, which seemed to have not a drop of blood left in it. He began to groan then and suddenly shrieked, "*Misericordia!*" and fell to the ground in a faint. When they had revived him by pouring water on his head, they escorted him away to be burned the next morning.

T HE RAIN HAD STOPPED by the time I had finished an egg for supper, which I was just able to swallow. A cold wind blew up the rue des Chanoines, so I wrapped myself tightly in my cloak before going out. I was a little startled to find a man looming in the darkness outside my door. Then I saw it was Hans Hoch. "Antoine had to go to Basel," he said. I knew that (Antoine was buying some type), but I understood Hoch was explaining why he had taken it upon himself to stand guard duty at my house. I saw that the bookbinder was wearing a sword. The wind brought us the sound of yelling in the place du Molard. "Demonstrators," Hoch said. "Do you have to go out, Master Calvin?"

"I'm on my way up to the jail." Servetus had begged the Little Council to let me visit him. I had no wish to go, but I had said I would. Hoch fell in beside me. I confess I was glad to have him. We traversed the tomblike passage beneath the walls of the cathedral, which brought us out to the bishop's palace. The lieutenant general, Tissot, was there and he escorted me past cells filled with shadowy figures to Servetus's cell, and stood in the corridor while a jailer opened the barred door.

It was dank and fetid, and since there was only one chair we both stood. I asked him what he wanted of me.

"To tell you I hold no personal rancor towards you."

I told him I had none for him.

"We are not so different," he said. I recalled the remark he made to me in Paris, that we were both apostates. I did not answer. "I also see the need for logic in all things," he went on. "That's why I reject the doctrine of the Trinity. It is perfectly clear that I believe in God and that I raise Jesus Christ above other men, but the Three-Persons-in-One cannot withstand the assaults of logic."

"Its manifestations demonstrate its logic," I said. Arguing with a condemned man is not much of a game. But I could not refrain from adding, "Entitling your book *Christianity Restored* was the ultimate in profanation."

"I will call the next one *Rationality Restored,*" he crowed. But when I reminded him that there was scarcely time left for him to write another book, and that all of his books that we could lay our hands on would be destroyed, he looked stricken, as though realizing for the first time that his unspeakable dedication was gone up in smoke. "Oh, why did I come here?" he cried. I told him I had also wondered. "I fled from Vienne into the Piedmonts, then Italy. They were hunting me everywhere. Then I thought, I will go to Geneva. Calvin is a man of learning, whatever his views. Men of learning don't act like Turks."

I inquired acidly if he thought he had made an error in his calculations. "I found the same barbarism here as in Vienne," he said. "You will not deny that, looking at the position I am in."

It was not barbarism to defend the name of God Almighty from defamation, I told him.

"You're an erudite man, Calvin, but your learning is narrow." He had regained his arrogance, the dog, barking at me. "What do you know of science, astronomy, mathematics? What have you heard of glorious Copernicus?"

"I know that Luther called him a fool. Did you ask me to come here in order to examine me?"

"No, no—just to ask your pardon." His voice rose almost to a shriek. "Which is the fool? Copernicus showed us that what we think we clearly see can be false; thinking we see the sun moving around the earth when, in truth, the earth moves around the sun, and the moon, and the stars." He shook his finger at me. "We are free; we are freed from a falsehood."

"I know what is said in Job, that God hangeth the earth upon nothing. There may be more to it; let men search further; it will do no harm. All they will find will only further reveal God's wisdom. Has Copernicus improved the lot of man by moving the earth around the sun?"

"Science makes our lot more bearable by banishing lies."

"Science is the greatest lie of all as it exalts men above God."

"Science lifts men up to God," he said insanely. "God constantly beckons us to discover things, explore the workings of our organs, penetrate the heavens, the mystery of

God himself. The lie of the Trinity caused me despair until I discovered the true God and the real Jesus Christ."

"Mankind will not find any comfort in your Christ."

"Will people find comfort in the ratiocination of Nicaea?"

"Yes, because it tells them of the humanity of Christ and that he suffered and died for us as the very Godhead."

He laughed hollowly and grasped my arm. "Two men of learning, each so sure, neither of us knowing. But I am soon to find out; I will know the truth before you do, Master Calvin." But at this, bravado deserted him and the next minute he groaned: "You must persuade them to use the sword. I cannot stand up to the fire."

"I have tried. I could not move them."

He threw himself on his cot. "I may not be strong enough. I may recant."

"Recant now," I said. "Let the Holy Spirit enter into your heart."

He stared at me wildly and whispered, "Get thee behind me," and broke into weeping. "Leave me alone, Calvin, leave me." He rolled off the cot onto his knees. "Listen to me, O Christ," he screamed. "If you are doing this to me, what is left for the devil to do? O, Christ, do you command them to drown men, cut their heads off, burn them? O, Christ, do you go there when you are asked to see such cruelty?"

"There is not a court in all Europe that would not condemn you." It was Tissot in the corridor. "Leave him, Master Calvin. His time is up."

"Leave him, Calvin. Leave him, leave him, . . ." The voices were coming from the other cells.

My throat felt constricted, and I shivered and pulled my cloak more closely around me. I left willingly enough.

Hoch was waiting for me outside. I saw that the sky had been swept clear of clouds, and the moon stood, motionless, over the Juras, and I thought of Habakkuk—"the deep uttered thy voice and the sun and the moon stood still in their habitation."

I must have spoken out loud, because Hoch said, "I don't think I ever read about that one."

We walked down the hill. The shouting from the place du Molard was no longer to be heard. I became aware of Hoch talking: "The jailer told me the prisoner had a gold chain weighing twenty-seven crowns, four gold rings, one with a large turquoise in it, one a white sapphire, one a diamond, and one a ruby and a Peruvian emerald. I was just thinking—one day a man has these possessions. You know how a fellow would turn them over and over in his fingers, watch how the light plays on them, maybe put them to his lips. The next instant—flames—and his rings and stones are gone, and he is choking on fire. It makes you stop and think."

I agreed that it did. We were at the door to my house and I thanked him for his company and went inside, and there to my surprise and great joy found Guillaume Farel no less devouring a supper Marie had fixed for him.

"I thought you would want me here," he said. I told him where I had just been. "Cannot we get this dog to confess his wickedness and save himself?" he demanded. "Wouldn't the city then be willing just to banish him? Wouldn't we forgive him, whether or not we thought he meant what he said? It wouldn't matter; God would be the final judge. His death would not be on our church's head."

"I tried to persuade him. No, he condemns himself to the stake."

"Will you walk with him?"

"I cannot. I would be sick and vomit or faint."

"Then I will. I will pursue him. I will hold God's mercy out to him. As he gets closer to Champel he might yet give up."

F OR SOME TIME PEOPLE HAD BEEN COMING up the rue des Chanoines making their way around the side of the cathedral to the jail. Across the street Hans Hoch appeared from time to time to take a measure of the crowd, obviously not wanting to leave his work any longer than necessary but not wanting to miss anything. He came out finally as the Clemence bell began to ring, and still wearing his apron, locked his shop and broke into a run, tilted forward like a crane. Everyone in the street was running.

The jail was not within my view, but I could picture what was happening—the iron grating swinging open and the bailiffs emerging, dragging Servetus behind them, to proceed thence down the rue de l'Evêché which was the usual way to the execution ground. But wait. They were coming down my street. They had changed the route in order, no doubt, to bring the procession past my house. I saw the bailiffs brandishing their halberds to clear the way, then Servetus in chains, pitifully jerking his head from side to side, and beside him, Farel, alternately pulling at the black robe he had borrowed from me, which was too small for him, and clasping his hands in prayer. The people filled the street, a river of humanity growing in agitation and tumultuousness as it flowed toward me between the banks of stone houses teetering on the hill. Several people looked up and shook their fists at me. Others were shouting at the haggard man in chains, "Recant; save yourself, Servetus," who cried out: "Mercy, mercy; it's unjust!"

Even above this din I could hear Farel's trumpetlike voice. "I came to pray for you, but if you must keep this up I'll leave you alone to God's mercy."

"Don't leave me, Pastor Farel. Save me, Farel."

"Then acknowledge your sin. Witness that Christ is the eternal Son of God."

"I cannot. The Son but not the eternal Son. How can they murder me for this?"

"It is not murder," Farel shouted for everyone to hear. "It's to save the world from heresy."

A woman appeared at the edge of the crowd and shrieked: "You're burning the wrong man," and she pointed up at me. "There's the villain who should go to the stake!" I immediately recognized Madame Perrin. Someone pulled her back, probably her husband; I could not see.

Servetus continued to cry, "God have mercy on me." The sun glinted on the bailiff's helmets. The people pushed and stumbled after one another, until the street was quiet at last, although I could still hear the clamor as the procession turned toward the bridge across the Rhone and the north gate of the town's fortifications. It would proceed along the country road that wound past the vineyards to the Hill of Champel where the pile of wood had been prepared.

THE SUN HAD SET BEHIND MONT BLANC by the time Farel returned, carrying the reek of burning flesh in my robe. "They dragged him to the stake by the chain around his neck," he said. "He could not stand up, so they sat him on a block and put all his writings beside him. The *Errors of Christianity* and *Christianity Restored* both, and his other abominations. They put the straw on his head and sprinkled it with sulfur and the executioner advanced with his torch. He screamed, 'O Jesus, Son of the eternal God, have mercy on me' just as the executioner set fire to the straw. The pyre was wet from last night's rain, and they threw on brush, making a thick smoke. He was already unconscious. Think of his making such an appeal—the last thing he said on earth."

Plunging into hell with the fire all but in his mouth, still denying the divinity of Christ! He had only to say, "Eternal Jesus, Son of God." In the transposition of an adjective had lain acceptance or rejection, everlasting life or death. Perseverance is a mark of grace—so the early martyrs died with grace—but not when perseverance is in evil as it was with Servetus. He died surrounded by his corruptions, his books that mocked the Holy Trinity, and called the Holy Spirit naught but a wind blowing in us, and God not in Christ.

PART SIX

Jeremiah comforts himself:
"The Lord is good to those who wait for him,
to the soul that seeks him.
It is good
that a man should hope
and quietly wait for salvation."

I say,
"A thing is done soon enough
if it is done well enough."

21

As I MADE MY WAY down the hill to the lower city, I recalled preparing a sermon on the day of Servetus's execution in which I quoted that utterance of David when he was surrounded by uncertainties as I was then, two years ago, "My times, O Lord, are in your hands." I could rejoice at how God had upheld me. "Good evening, Master Calvin," people said to me as we passed (it was not always like this). Some of them tipped their hats! I was on my way to Aubert's shop, helped greatly by a cane, to obtain a mixture he hoped would relieve my coughing. He had offered to bring it to me, but I thought the walk on this pleasant May evening, if I took it slowly, would be beneficial.

It is true, I reflected, that power that sides with the devil is ultimately destroyed. One thing leads to another. Fear was in the hearts of the councilmen that day they pronounced the verdict on Servetus, to be followed, I liked to think, by the entrance of the Holy Spirit, which was manifest in the elections that year. Councilmen who had never dared squeak before, informed Perrin they had had enough of him. There were even some who charged his cronies and him with appropriating public funds. Aubert told me it was true, they had, the books disclosed it. Perrin and the others were still

279

on the Little Council, but men of good character, including Aubert, were elected syndics.

I would like to—but I could not yet—tell myself that it was the end of our comic Caesar. I was reminded of all this as I passed by a row of houses in the rue des Chanoines which were occupied largely by refugees, who, Perrin avowed, were crowding Genevans out of their homes, not to say causing a rise in all kinds of prices. That morning a small mob, many of them members of *Les Enfants,* had gathered outside the town hall chanting, "Geneva for the Genevans. Hang the French," and so on. True, there were several thousand of them, including Italians. But had they not improved the properties townspeople had sold them at great profit? I noted the fine condition of their houses. They had also introduced culture and dignity to the city. The majority of the Little Council appreciated them, granting some of them citizenship—those, that is, who could pay the fee. I never could. Thus they hoped to replenish the treasury Perrin had looted.

The young whippersnapper, Charles Conant, who had married my sister, was coming towards me. I actually felt rather well disposed towards him. It was his auditing of the books, Aubert told me, that had disclosed Perrin's manipulations. "There was quite some excitement in the council chamber this morning," he said. "While the mob was outside, Perrin and Berthelier were inside demanding that they withdraw all grants of citizenship to Frenchmen. The Little Council was not being intimidated. They would grant citizenship to whomever they pleased, and they ordered Perrin to take his scoundrels off. Well, he did, but they are still parading around the lower city somewhere. Where are you going, Master Calvin? Had I not better accompany you?" Under the circumstances I did not mind having him see me to Aubert's.

My friend was weighing out flakes of gold on his apothecary's scales for his neighbor, Baudichon, a merchant and one of the wealthier refugees. "I wish to send it to a bank in Strasbourg in order to establish credit there for some of my trading," Baudichon explained. "I don't suppose you have any interest in such matters." He looked at me anxiously. "You may even think it is wicked; Luther did."

"Luther was apt to think of money as sinful because he did not understand the uses of it. Great good can accrue from lending and borrowing. I have preached a number of sermons on wealth that is honestly acquired. You may have missed them—"

He looked embarrassed. "I get to the evening services. The morning services—I have to take inventory and so on. But because I am a very religious man, I sometimes find myself troubled by the story of the rich man, for example, who said that he had obeyed all the laws and now wondered what was left for him to do, and Christ answered, 'Give all your goods to the poor.' I think of what it would do to business if we all followed that command."

Since I had to wait for Aubert, who had gone to mix my medicine, I was quite willing to discuss the matter. "We are not commanded to give all our goods away." I had to admit that it was no great problem for me, who had next to nothing. "People misconstrue Christ's intention. It was to force the man to search his heart, not to state a universal doctrine."

"But he said it is as impossible for a rich man to go to heaven as for a camel to pass through a needle's eye."

"Not as *impossible*—as *possible*. Remember Christ saying, 'By God all things are done'?"

Monsieur Baudichon had an expression of such relief that I was constrained to add a few injunctions. Money, I told him puts men to a singular test. "They walk as it were, on ice. They can so easily slide into pride and come to believe that having money puts them beyond God's reach."

"But you wonder why some have it and some are poor."

"It is part of God's plan. Inequalities exist so that we may strive constantly to correct them and provide for the poor man according to his needs. The rich must not covet wealth for its own sake but be ready to share it. This serves a double purpose. It redistributes wealth and thus increases the flow of goods. And inequality recalls us to God, who places the poor among us so that by charity we can show our love."

"It would be a good society, Master Calvin."

I was now quite wound up, and Aubert in the next room was still shaking up bottles and mixing things that would surely bring me relief from the coughing that often kept me awake all night. I told Baudichon that unfortunately we had to consider men's imperfections. "We see what some will do in avarice, looking for ways to cut their workers' wages and afflicting with all kinds of abuse men trapped in their service. Such employers are content to watch old workers fall into discard, it being all the same to them so long as they make a profit. No wonder workers in desperation will refuse to work."

"Do you approve of strikes?"

"If the demonstrations are not violent. I always deplore violence. That is why I deplore the abuse of workers who feed the rich by their sweat; starving them is a violent act. God's law is being broken when men cannot find employment. I am not talking about loafers—they are cursed—but those who try with all their might to earn a living but are thrown under by society. They stand as an indictment of the society that has destroyed them. I say this, Monsieur Baudichon, such a society will be adjudged by God as wholly without merit and sooner or later will be reckoned by him as worthy of extermination."

I had not meant to deliver an exhortation, but Baudichon had encouraged me by his rapt attention, and I was about to go into the need for the state to control prices which become distorted through monopoly or speculating thus causing the poor to suffer, when we were interrupted by loud noises in the street. Going to the window, we saw that a crowd had gathered in front of Baudichon's store next door. They yelled, "Open up; we know there are armed men inside!"

"What are they talking about?" said Baudichon.

"We know you're going to try to massacre us," came their

voices. "Open your door, you French shit, before we break it down."

"I cannot believe this is happening," said Baudichon.

Aubert appeared beside us carrying his silver-tipped syndic's baton. "Remain here," he ordered, and valiantly strode out while we watched from behind the colored bottles and vials in the window. Aubert waved his baton. "Disperse. In the name of the Little Council I command you to disperse."

There must have been several hundred of them, a conglomeration of *Les Enfants* and roughly attired workmen and boatmen from the poorer quarters of the city.

We saw Ami Perrin riding up on a mule. "Give me the baton, Aubert," he ordered. "You're so short they can't see you," with which he leaned down and wrested it away and waved it on high, proclaiming, "Gentlemen, the syndic's baton is ours." Aubert suddenly bent over from a blow in the stomach, and I saw Philibert Berthelier and his brother Daniel and that lout Vandel ranging themselves around Perrin to lead the mob in chanting, "We're going to hang all the French."

I would go out and lend my authority to Aubert's. Baudichon restrained me. "No, no, it would be imprudent."

At that moment another syndic, Bonna, appeared, waving his baton. He was a man of considerable bearing, but they tried to seize his baton and might have but for the arrival of the police, whereupon Perrin quickly rode off followed by the rest of them.

Aubert came in rubbing his stomach but in possession of his baton, which Perrin had dropped at the sight of the police. "You witnessed it," he said with remarkable calm. "It was an assault on authority, an act of sedition." We sat there, the four of us including Bonna, hearing the mob rampaging past the shops along the rue de Rive, until we heard the firing of arquebuses and then silence.

The captain of the police arrived back at Aubert's. They had dispersed, he said, when he ordered his men to let go a few barrels of shot over their heads. "They were armed with swords, butchers' knives, and a few boathooks, but the ar-quebuses scared them." They had been in and out of the taverns most of the day, including Councilman Perrin and his friends, he reported. "We also learned that Madame Perrin—you know how she is—had been going around to various houses telling people to arm themselves because the French were preparing to massacre the whole populace. First they just paraded around, and then they made for Monsieur Baudi-chon's residence before we realized what they were up to."

"Sedition is punishable by death," Aubert said to us.

I finished my walk, which had started on a pleasant eve-ning, in the darkness of the night, leaning heavily on my cane, the worthy captain of police, who had volunteered to accom-pany me, carrying my bottle of cough medicine.

"I HAVE NOT WRITTEN YOU about the unfortunate events that followed on the riot. . . ." The letter to Farel was long overdue. Out of sheer inertia we let these silences stretch out between us and our dearest friends, trusting that they will know that they have been constantly in our thoughts, and ever heedless of death intervening, perhaps, to make the letter we were going to write unnecessary, leaving us never to be consoled. I will say that in this case it was not so much inertia as fatigue. I wrote: "The Little Council met the follow-ing day to listen to witnesses and to Perrin himself. They spent several days at these proceedings, finally imposing sen-tences. Perrin for one was to have his hand cut off for seizing the baton, then his head. The Bertheliers and Vandel were also sentenced to be decapitated under the city's laws, likewise the boatmen who, the police said, had been instru-mental in gathering up a lot of riffraff from the poorer sec-tions of the city in order to engage in the activities with the intent of fomenting an insurrection.

"Perrin and Philibert Berthelier had not waited to hear the sentence pronounced. In fact, anticipating what it was going to be, they had hurried out of the Little Council on the pretext of having to relieve themselves, and fled from the city. But Daniel Berthelier and the two boatmen were apprehended in time, and they were executed, which I find somewhat grievous in the case of the young Berthelier, who was very much under the influence of his brother. For that matter, the boatmen were also dupes of Perrin. The severed head of one of them was affixed to the top of a post near Cornavin Gate.

"You will find this next hard to believe without being acquainted with the lady, but soon afterwards Madame Perrin put in an appearance at Cornavin Gate riding a horse and seeing the head on the post, screamed, "Murderers, murderers, murderers!" before riding through the gate, lashing at the guards who had no cause to stop her anyhow, and galloping up the road in the direction of Bern. I relate this incident that you may understand how precipitate was the Perrins' withdrawal from the affairs of Geneva. I understand that our Penthesilia's old man, Favre, has also departed, along with others of the Perrin's tribe. It will not astonish you to hear that Bern has taken them all in. . . ."

22

How sweet it was—an end of conflict and no more raging at my door. Now I was able to finish what I had to finish—a fifth edition of my *Institutes*. I marked it *done*, completed, despite attacks of quatran fever which left me for long periods too weak to hold a pen or even dictate. Such delays infuriated me, while Antoine remonstrated that I was lashing myself to death! But I wrote in the preface at last, "A thing is done soon enough if it is done well enough," and had Robert Estienne print it; it was too much for Antoine's little press. He turned out a book so pleasing to the eye that I caressed it like a father his child, albeit a prodigious child it was, six times the size of that first little guide I wrote twenty-five years before—as long, I calculated, as the Old Testament plus a good part of the New.

"Well, now you've said it all," said Antoine. "I hope you've finished with the thing." Could I ever say I was finished with trying to bring the true Word to people? I only gave thanks for the grace of a little time. See, Antoine, how good God is being to me; he rewards me beyond my deserving.

Did he not also reward me with the school I had dreamed about so long? What divine irony—to have money that I needed to get it started, denied me as long as the Perrinists were in power, come from selling the Perrins' and Berth;e-liers' confiscated properties. God provided my faculty, for he instilled with more than their usual foolishness the magistrates of Bern, causing them to depose Pierre Viret in a dispute over his right to excommunicate the unworthy. He came to me, bringing with him most of the faculty of his splendid school in Lausanne. Theodore Beza, such an even-tempered man (not like me in this respect, I fear), so admirably suited to be our rector; Berault to teach Greek; and Tagart to teach Hebrew. Rejoice! Rejoice over a thousand children advancing through the gymnasium modeled after Johann Sturm's, armed for life's challenges by being constantly reminded of God through biblical readings and the singing of psalms every day after lunch, the worthiest of them proceeding into the advanced academy to be trained for the ministry.

There I myself taught. My little seedbed. Tending those precious plants, watering them with truth. Scholars from all over came to me. Did I exhaust myself teaching? In order to feel restored I had only to think of Kasper Olevianus writing my teachings into the Heidelberg Catechism, or of John Knox (oh, Knox, no one understood me better) not Cranmer, certainly, who kept Christ's church hanging somewhere between Rome and Reform. It had not saved him from being beheaded. "In Geneva I found the most perfect school of Christ on earth. . . ." Knox wrote to me. As I told Antoine, "It is what I have tried to make it."

"I despair at what you're doing to yourself," he said.

What was I doing to myself? There was such concern for me.

"I have told you often enough. I come into your house and hear you dragging yourself across the room to your desk. I watch you drag yourself to St-Pierre, then your classes. I suffer at the sound of your footsteps."

"All Europe is listening to my footsteps."

Antoine was concerned about me dragging myself about. Maigret was concerned about me not getting out enough. He must help me down to my little garden to keep me from feeling entombed. Entombed! I remembered telling Louis du Tillet once how God had thrust me onto the stage, an odd figure for me to use, but I had been in an emotional state at the time. I did not approve of the stage, although I was not as strenuously opposed to it as Michael Cop, who once made such objections to a morality play written by Poupin that I had to forbid its going on or lose a good preacher. "It's just a way for people to make a spectacle of themselves," Michael had raged.

What a spectacle *I* was, goutily crawling around. But my room was not a tomb. Figures constantly entered and exited with a myriad of purposes. People bringing me reports— Estienne de la Forge, would you not be astonished to hear?—a congregation worships publicly in Paris! They sought my counsel, which was always the same: the Word must go out not on the wings of violence but of peace.

W HY IS PEACE DENIED ME in my victory? Satan is going to and fro on the earth. I am made to suffer for sins of omission. I weep at the memory of the day I went to the court of the Little Council where my stepdaughter Judith sat beside a man unknown to me, both of them in chains. Oh, this wilful girl I was never able to control. She and the man had been arrested for immoral conduct. He was an utter stranger to me. I tried to close my ears to the night watchman's testimony. "The two of them came out of the tavern, my lords, and stood against a tree, shameless, thinking they could not be seen in the darkness. . . ." When they put her in jail I left the city, unable to face the commiseration in people's faces, which would be as hard to endure as their derision that other time when my brother's wife was banished for fornicating with his valet. Four days I spent in the hills reflecting on the deathbed vow I had made to my wife, whom I loved, that I would take care of her children. I could only give thanks for the blessing of sober Johann, who was in Basel studying for the law and had taken his sister in.

Peace is not the Lord's will; it is so evident. The world must suffer for its sins. Lutherans, Zwinglians, my own followers cannot leave off bickering. Why cannot all be reconciled? Did not Christ's presence at the eucharist transcend the question of the actual eating of his flesh, cannot a divine mystery be accepted and taken into men's hearts?

People in my homeland who profess my doctrine pursue bloody political ambitions. Insane characters cross the stage whispering plots to kidnap the new boy king and hold him as a hostage to the fortunes of Bourbons and Huguenot adventurers, to seize Orléans, to murder the duke of Guise in vengeance for his massacring Protestant worshipers. What do I have to do with armed bands of hot-blooded men? I dispatch Beza to Paris to a colloquy which the regent Catherine de Medici thinks might bring reconciliations. He returns with nothing but a report of papist doctrine drummed into his ears. There are no reconciliations any more anywhere in Christendom. The world is sundered. The pope has succeeded at last in Trent in putting together his forces, the monarchy of Rome is affirmed, anathemas proclaimed. The Antichrist will exterminate those who will not accept all seven sacraments and swallow the fabrications of men, instead of Scripture, as the truth. What can I do, O Lord, but lash myself on? Let it be your will that my death come not just yet.

I am seized by such coughing during a sermon that I cannot finish.

A delegation from the Little Council stands beside my bed telling me they have voted to make me a citizen of Geneva, without fee, on account of various things I have done, and make me a present of a cask of wine. They would also like to pay for all the medicine I have bought. Thank you, my lords, for my citizenship and the cask of wine. The medicine, which I have taken to little avail, I will pay for myself.

"A letter from Master Farel." Baudoin comes into my room with it. I do not want letters any more from Guillaume Farel. I have had enough of his shamelessness. I do not want to hear from him ever again. Couldn't we have been spared the humiliation he has brought on our church?—taking into his house a widow and her daughter from Rouen and announcing he is going to marry one of them—and not the widow, her daughter. Farel was in his seventies! The latest letter? An invitation to the wedding! Neither to hear from him nor see him ever again is my wish, and I tell Baudoin so to inform him.

Antoine and Maigret are both needed to bring me home after the April communion. I lie on my bed, racked by coughing, and I see that the towel Marie gives me is covered with blood.

God forgive my pride. What vanity it is to think of triumphing over anything but oneself, and even that small conquest cannot be made but by God's grace.

"Master Farel writes that he is coming." It is Baudoin with another letter. Is he married? Yes, he is. Why is he coming? "Because I wrote him that you are not well." Baudoin must write him that I do not have very long and that there is nothing to be gained by his wearying himself with the journey.

There come to me at night after Marie blows out the lamp the people I loved. I am grateful for their presence, especially for Olivétan's and Louis du Tillet's—so that I might ask them to forgive me for things I have done. I was so impatient, so often. But Guillaume, Guillaume, I loved you best of all.

He came one night when my room was filled with the fragrance of locust blossoms, and I took his old hand.

Plainpalais

CALVIN DIED ON MAY 27, 1564, two weeks before his fifty-fifth birthday, pulmonary tuberculosis proving to be the end of him. Farel had not long to grieve, or enjoy the company of the young lady from Rouen, for he died the following year.

It is recorded that a few weeks before Calvin's death the whole of the Little Council managed to crowd into his room to pay him their respects, and he found the strength to deliver an exhortation on how the city should be run in the way of God. The consistory also assembled around his bed, and he made a long address, recalling the trials of his ministry, how he had been saluted by gunshots through his door, driven out of the city, and made the object of attacks in the street by people and dogs when he returned. He put bitterness aside then and spoke with utmost humility, presenting himself to the judgment not of men but of God. "All that I have done is of little value," he said.... "I am a miserable creature, but I have meant well. My faults have always displeased me, and the root of the fear of God has always been in my heart." He begged them that if there had been any good in what he had done that they follow that. So far as his doctrine was concerned, he said, "I have taught faithfully, and

God has given me the grace to write. I have done it with the utmost fidelity and have not to my knowledge corrupted or twisted a single passage of the Scriptures; and when I could have drawn out a far-fetched subtlety I have put that under foot for simplicity."

THEY WRAPPED HIS BODY in a shroud, put it in a simple wooden box, and laid it away in the common burial ground of Plainpalais, as he had requested. And since it was also his wish that there be no marker, they merely shovelled a mound of dirt over him, which has long since disappeared so that no one knows for sure today where he rests. But a great crowd gathered at his funeral, and the Little Council declared in part, "God gave him a character of great majesty."

Certainly no one has ever held more firmly to his own principles. He lies somewhere in history's fields in a grave marked *He meant what he said,* buried in his "dreadful" logic (few want to accept the doctrine of predestination), buried in medievalism (he was of his times), buried in piety and in faith in Scripture. He carries some, if not all, of the guilt for Servetus's death. His enemy Sebastian Castellio, whom Calvin dismissed from Geneva, wrote after the execution: "To kill a man is not to defend a doctrine but to kill a man." Both church and state rejected that view in the sixteenth century. Will we contend that governments have not always rejected it?

All these things must stand against Calvin, weighed out however each of us judges. But a soft, ineluctable voice comes from the Plainpalais:

Let us descend into the very bottom of our hearts. Who, even the gentlest, can say he does not harbor envy, pride, selfishness and—in the darkest corners of his heart—lust, vengeance, ha-

treds? The voice rises (does it speak foolishly?): *Ascend to God in order to study and glorify him. This is our chief end and all that justifies our existence. Our hope of salvation lies in him. Faith unrequited may weep and despair, but Hope says, "Wait—in silence."*

Author's Note

Few biographies can be wholly true, while novels may wholly bear their own truth. In the events I have described I have not deviated significantly from history; and except for one or two minor characters and a fanciful Hans Hoch, all the people in this book existed and in their various ways impinged on Calvin's life. How much of John Calvin himself have I imagined? I have "filled in" what was not recorded yet appeared to me to be truthful or at least plausible. He had no contemporary biographer, and in his writings, prodigious as they were, disclosed almost nothing of an intimate nature about himself. But between the lines, especially of *The Institutes of the Christian Religion,* he revealed much.

His writings *were* prodigious, no gainsaying that. To contain his opera of commentaries, sermons, and letters required fifty volumes that were published between 1863 and 1900. His major work was the *Institutio Christianae religionis, in libris quatuor nunc primum digesta, certisque distincta capitibus, ad aptissimam methodum: aucta etiam tam magna accessione ut propemodum opus novum haberi possit*—that is, "now first arranged in four books and divided by definite headings in a very convenient way: also enlarged by so much added matter that it can almost be regarded as a new work"—which was printed in 1559 by the celebrated Robert Estienne.

The Institutes of the Christian Religion stands as the greatest writing in Protestant theology, and has been translated into French, German, Dutch, Spanish, Italian, Hungarian, Japanese, and excerpted in Chinese. The English translation, on which I was given permission to lean when venturing into Calvin's theology, was the book in two volumes published by the Westminster Press (Calvin: *Institutes of the Christian Religion,* I. LCC, Vol. XX, XXI, © 1960, W. L. Jenkins). The editor of the book was the late John T. McNeill, and the translator was Ford Lewis Battles, who rendered Calvin's Latin into modern and singularly poetic idiom. Both men encouraged me. Dr. Battles was particularly helpful in his patient reading of various versions I showed him, as was his colleague then at the Pittsburgh Theological Seminary, John Walchenbach.

The passages in my book on Calvin's doctrine sometimes range back and forth across the *Institutes'* whole structure; the references to Calvin's "two governments," for example, encompass points from three of the *Institutes'* four "books." A poem on predestination, which I recklessly attribute to Calvin, required considerable paraphrasing of Dr. Battles's text.

My other main sources: Roland H. Bainton's study of Michael Servetus, *Hunted Heretic* (1953); *The Social Humanism of Calvin* by André Biéler (1961); *Calvin* by Jules Bonnet (1806); Calvin's *Letters,* edited by Bonnet, translated by David Constable (1860); *The Protestant Reformation* by Henry Daniel-Rops (1958); the seven volumes of Emile Doumergue's biography (1899–1927); Dr. McNeill's *The History and Character of Calvinism* (1954); *Calvin's Geneva* by E. William Monter (1967); *John Calvin* by Williston Walker (1906); *Servetus and Calvin* by R. Willis (1877); and various general histories of the times.